TRUE STORIES
FROM THE
MIGHTY MISSISSIPPI

J.L. FREDRICK

To Donald —
Enjoy!
[signature]
9/16/2023

D1522330

Lovstad Publishing
www.Lovstadpublishing.com

TRUE STORIES FROM THE MIGHTY MISSISSIPPI
First Edition

ISBN: 1540640442
ISBN-13: 978-1540640444

Printed in the United States of America

Cover design by Lovstad Publishing

For Mom and Dad,
who introduced me at an early age to the Mighty Mississippi.
I will always be grateful for that.

CONTENTS

Note: These stories are historically factual. Although some embellishment is present for story line purposes, the events described are historically accurate according to the available information acquired from newspaper articles that reported the actual events. All characters, with some exceptions, were real people.

TRUE STORIES FROM THE MIGHTY MISSISSIPPI

THUNDER
IN THE
NIGHT

Chapter 1
Summer, 1868

He was grubby from the brown dust along the river trail and all around his bright blue eyes there were marks where his dirty fingers had rubbed away the tickling tears. The dust darkened his delicate white skin and matted his strawberry blond curls. But now the chubby little fingers of his hands seemed clean, as he was sitting on a bed of moss near the roadside where spring water came trickling down from the rocky cliff above, and he splashed in the tiny pool till the pearly drops hung in his curls like jewels and dotted the ragged old shirt, many sizes to large, that seemed to make up his only garment. The man-sized jersey hung on the boy of about three with its sleeves cut off at his elbows, and the very bottom torn off and made into a belt tied around the little guy's waist to keep the jersey from slipping off.

Rays of sunlight flashed upon the droplets in his hair and in the ferns, some drooping over the pool and some reaching up as high as the silvery-green foliage of the overhanging birch that fluttered delicately in the soft summer breeze. He laughed merrily when the water flew up into his face, and at the height of his enjoyment he threw back his head. Two rows of pearly white teeth flashed in the sunshine behind his parted lips. As dirty as he was, the water, ferns, moss and wild flowers around him seemed most delightful, and at that very moment he was supremely happy.

After a time he glanced downward; a frown wrinkled his forehead and his lips pursed. Dipping his hands in the clear water he rubbed the little fingers over and between his toes to get rid of the dust and grit. While the breeze whispered and the birch trees gently waved and the wildflowers nodded, from nearby came at regular intervals a low growl, like that of a wild beast.

And then there came the clop, clop, clop of horse's hooves and the rattle of wheels on the dusty road. A sleepy-looking gray mare pulling a green wagon came into sight. Aboard the wagon were a man and a woman, a farmer and his wife on their way into town for supplies. They approached slowly and would have passed by had the woman not caught a glimpse of the little boy and abruptly grabbed hold of her husband's arm and pointed. The man eased back on the reins to stop the horse, and they both stared open-mouthed at the youngster.

"Sakes alive, Isaac! Look at that," the woman said in a whisper, while the little guy continued to wash his toes.

"I'm a lookin' at him. Wonder where he belongs," the man replied. His face twisted into a silent little laugh, and then turned to a frown as his wife began to climb down from the wagon seat. "There... what d'ya think yer gonna do?"

"What a beautiful little boy, Isaac. He must be lost. We should—"

"We shouldn't do nothing," Isaac grumbled.

She was standing only a few feet from the boy. "Oh, Isaac, how I'd love to give him a good bath and dress him in clean clothes."

Isaac sat forward on the seat with his elbows on his knees and continued to grumble. "Bath! He looks perfectly happy where he is. We don't go to market t' find lost children."

She approached the smiling boy slowly and stooped down to caress his golden curls, when a loud roar like that of a vicious beast sounded from a patch of tall grass just beyond the boy. The woman jumped back frightened; the horse jerked to one side; the farmer raised his whip and braced for trouble. They both stared at the grizzly-looking character that rose from the tall grass who had been sleeping, and was now glowering at them with folded arms. He was not a pleasant looking fellow by any means, scraggly beard and uncombed hair; his skin blotched with disease; his clothes soiled and foul.

"Ya leave th' young pup alone!" he growled, half closing his dark eyes.

Astonished more than frightened, the woman flinched. "Oh, Isaac," she gasped.

"Here now," the farmer said fiercely. "Don't you be frightening my wife like that! She was only tryin'—"

"Leave th' youngin alone," the man growled again.

"How did you come by the boy?" the woman asked, somewhat recovering her composure. "Certainly he is not yours."

"Not mine!" the man replied in his harsh voice. "Y' let him be, or I'll show ya 'bout that." He gently clapped his hands together. "Hey! Pup."

The little fellow scrambled to him, threw his tiny arms around the man's thick neck, nestled his head on the man's broad shoulder, and gazed at the farmer and his wife.

"Oh, my," whispered the woman, unable to break her stare at the unusual duo.

"Well? Whatcha lookin' at?" the man growled. "Ya didn't think th' pup was yours, now, did ya?"

It was quite clear to the farmer that the love and affection the boy displayed toward the man seemed genuine, and they must belong together, no matter how absurd it appeared. "Come along, Missus," he said in a stern tone. "We'll be on our way."

She reluctantly climbed aboard the wagon and took her seat beside the farmer. "It just don't seem right," she whispered to Isaac. "That he should have such a child as that."

"Well, it ain't none of our business now," he replied, clicked his tongue and snapped the whip at the horse's hind quarters. The gray mare responded immediately and the green wagon with the farmer and his wife went rattling down the road, but for as long as they were within sight, the farmer's wife stared back; she could not take her eyes off him. "The poor little boy," she thought.

And for as long as they were within sight, the rough-looking tramp glared at her from among the tall grass.

"Must be movin' on," he grumbled to himself several times as he attempted to get to his feet, but his joints seemed so stiff that he could only get to his knees, and he had to set the boy down. After quite a struggle, he managed to get standing upright, holding onto a birch branch to steady himself. He staggered to a large boulder and sat down. "Come here, pup," he growled. His tone of voice should have frightened a child away, but the little guy wasn't the least bit alarmed. He bounded to the tramp with outstretched arms and was grateful for the gnarled hands to pick him up. Then with a mighty swing the man threw the boy over his shoulder and onto his back, nearly losing his balance and barely saving himself from tumbling to the ground. He grumbled a bit, and the little burden uttered a whimpering cry.

"Hold on tight," the old man said, and almost instantly the little white arms were clinging around his neck, the hands hidden under the man's tangled beard. The man got to his feet again and together they ambled along the road.

The day and the miles passed. The sun beat down on the curly little head and the dust rose from the tramp's staggering steps. The cheery songs from the larks, the heat, and the motion finally lulled the boy to sleep. But he did not fall. It was a natural instinct that maintained his hold, so that he clung tightly to the man, who seemed almost oblivious to his existence.

The old tramp continued his deliberate but now faltering journey, often muttering incoherently about things that didn't make sense, even to himself. But even though his alertness was continually fading, more rapidly now than in the past few days, his awareness remained keen enough to know he must reach his destination, for the sake of the little one.

Then came the soft evening light when shadows grew long and the relentless summer heat eased its smothering grip, as the old man struggled along toward houses and the town. Groups of people he passed turned to stare at the coarse-looking creature, some with disgust, some with wonder, and others with grins and less-than-complimentary remarks. The man paid no attention to them and kept on his course, and continued the strange babbling, until he came to a marketplace that seemed familiar, but in his dazed condition he found himself confused and lost. He turned to one idle man standing near and uttered one word: "Mission."

"Beg your pardon?" the bystander replied, in awe that such an abomination of a man could be toting the likes of an innocent, sweet child.

"Th' Mission," the tramp growled again fiercely.

"Oh!" was the response. Now it seemed clear that this derelict was seeking help. He pointed toward the bluffs. "That way... about a half-mile."

The old tramp staggered on his way, but by now his progress had been slowed even more, and by the time he reached the entrance of the familiar stone building, darkness was swallowing everything in sight. His feeble pounding on the wooden door gained no response. Then he remembered the rope hanging beside the doorway, gave a little tug, and heard the bell.

Moments later, the door opened revealing the strange pair to a middle-aged woman, who at first observed nothing more than an unkempt, repulsive harlot. And then from behind the mass of dirty, tangled hair a smiling little face peeked over his right shoulder.

"Me li'l pup... he needs you," the man whispered.

In an instant, the woman's experienced eyes read the urgency, and she took the tramp's arm, steadying him as she ushered him through the doorway.

Chapter 2

The doctor shook his head hopelessly as he looked down at the old tramp lying on a straw tick, mumbling painfully. Mr. Stanley, master of the Mission School, and a couple of his able assistants stood by watching when there was a loud cry from the little boy as the woman who had brought the pair in, took the youngster from where he was seated at the foot of the bed and carried him toward the door. In the next moment, the sick old man sprang up in the bed, glaring wildly and stretching out his arms. He was trying to say something, but the words just wouldn't form.

"Quickly! Take the boy away," said Stanley, but the doctor held up his hand, as if to order silence, all the while watching the sick old man. He whispered to Stanley a few words, who then gave a reluctant consent for the boy to be placed back on the bed within the old man's reach, and when their hands touched, the old man vented a sigh of relief and sank his head into the pillow again. The child nestled to his side, sobbing, but he, too, soon calmed down.

Mr. Stanley approached the doctor. "Seems to be against all the rules," he said in an ill-tempered tone.

"Yes, indeed it is, Mr. Stanley," replied the doctor. "But it will do more good than anything I can do for him." The doctor put his hand on Stanley's shoulder. "Trust me... it won't be for long."

Stanley nodded.

"Mrs. Champlain," the doctor went on. "You can sit with him tonight?"

"Yes, sir," the woman answered. "I can watch him."

"Keep an eye on the boy, in case the old man turns violent," the doctor said. "But I don't think he will."

"And if he does, shall I send for you, Doctor?"

"Yes, by all means. But I don't think he will."

Mr. Stanley turned to her. "You might want to light a fire in the stove if you'd like some tea. And I'll send in some food for you, and milk for the boy."

The doctor and the others left the infirmary, and then Mrs. Champlain settled in for the long night watch. All was very still in the whitewashed room until one of Stanley's assistants brought in a platter of bread, butter, cheese, and a small jar filled with milk. The little boy hungrily ate the bread and butter and cheese that Mrs. Champlain gave him, and sat quietly on the bed, smiling and contented. The only sounds that broke the silence were the occasional mutterings from the sick old man. But that didn't seem to disturb the boy. He finished the bread, drank some of the milk, and then sank into the mattress at the foot of the bed. A short while later he was fast asleep.

The night was comfortably warm, so Mrs. Champlain didn't see the need to cover him. From time to time as the long hours passed, she went to the bed and wiped the sick old man's forehead with a cool, wet cloth, giving him what little comfort she could offer. And then she would stop at the foot of the bed and gently stroke the boy's golden hair with her fingers. Once, the boy gave out a little giggle, still deep in slumber. The woman wiped the corners of her eyes with her apron, and then bent down and kissed his cheek.

The clock in the main hall chimed by the hours, and just past midnight, she slipped into a dream while sitting in her comfortable padded chair. It was a pleasant dream, where she was young again, and her own son who never returned from the war in the south was young again, and they were strolling together through a fragrant meadow with bountiful wildflowers, and scores of beautiful song birds... and a clock's bell that chimed six times. She awoke, startled.

"Oh dear me," she said softly. "I must've dozed off." She gazed at the little boy resting so peacefully. *What a beautiful child* she thought, and then she went to the old man once more with the wet cloth. But as she wiped his forehead this time, she realized that it would be of little use.

Mrs. Champlain quickly swept up the sleeping boy in her arms and hurried out of the room, down the hallway to her own quarters where she laid him on her bed.

About an hour later, he awoke. "Papa!" he cried, wanting to go to the tramp. But there was no tramp for him to go to. During the night, the rough old man had left on a journey where he could not take the boy. As if he had lost his last hope, the boy cried bitterly until the woman returned from the rather unpleasant tasks in the infirmary. Her gentle voice and some more bread and butter and milk seemed to sooth the boy. He liked her, and because of the kindness and warmth she had offered him the night before, she had at once become the next person he would cling to. He offered no objection to be bathed.

"Yes, sir," Mrs. Champlain explained to the doctor. "Went off quiet in his sleep."

"And the boy?" the doctor asked.

"He cried," Mrs. Champlain replied "But I fed him and gave him a good warm bath this morning, which he desperately needed."

"Poor little waif," the doctor mumbled as he left the room with Stanley. "A tramp's child, cast out with nothing but a dirty shirt covering his back."

Mrs. Champlain called to him: "He'll be okay, you can be sure. We'll take good care of him."

"You see, Stanley?" the doctor said. "I was right. It wasn't for long."

Chapter 3
Barron's Island; May 1877

The cabin door opened slowly. A tousled round head of dark hair appeared. The boy's sleepy face turned downward, eyes adjusting to the morning light, then gradually lifted to meet the new day. It seemed to catch the magic of that May morning, brightening like a chalice filling with sunshine. The door swung wider, framing the boy's eager figure, poised as if for flight.

The sun would soon peek over the hills on the other side of the river, but it seemed as though no one else was stirring at this early hour. With motion as light as a dove the boy darted from the step to the footpath that curved toward the beach, his moccasin clad feet scarcely touching the pebbles as he raced past the gardens and the apple trees now laden with fragrant white blossoms. Every muscle in his body strained with the joy of young strength and speed. So swiftly he ran that he almost took wing with the gulls that soared up from his path, and he was gone so quickly that the sleeping dogs barely had time to rise with a quick, savage bark, sniffing the air, not knowing that it was more than a spring wind that had brushed past them.

Finally, Dominic stopped, out of breath. He had run as far as he could without plunging into the river at North Point. He looked back along the shore that curved in a crescent, holding the west edge of the basin where three rivers mingled their waters to become one. Directly across the basin, the La Crosse River flowed from among the hills in the east, and from the north, the Black River opened its mouth wide to accommodate the shipyards and mills, and both contributed to the majesty of the mighty Mississippi that, to Dominic, stretched immeasurably.

His gaze followed the streets of La Crosse on the opposite bank of the river. In the evening sun, the houses there were stained with golden light from the setting sun, but now they were bathed in the grayness of a hazy dawn. His own little village that was known only as Barron's Island would soon feel the warmth of the morning sun, long before the city would creep out from the shadows of the great bluffs behind it. This had all been sacred ground to his mother's people at one time, where tribal gatherings and ceremonies were held, and where games of skill were played on the broad sandy prairie, and where friendship was celebrated among the various tribes regularly. But now it all belonged to the pioneers of the new nation, and Dominic had only the memory of his mother and her stories of how life had once been.

The sun was high above the eastern bluffs when to the northwest, from where the silvery Mississippi meandered down the vast valley it had carved in ancient times, Dominic spotted a familiar sight. Tall twin stacks billowing black-brown smoke appeared just above the treetops, and the baritone hiss of a distant steam whistle echoing between the hills announced the approaching vessel. Perhaps it was just another raft boat bringing a giant raft of logs down from the Chippewa. Or, it could be a packet—the Phil Sheridan, perhaps—on which his father and two older half-brothers would be returning. He raced back to the cabin with wild anticipation. There he would launch his canoe in the lagoon and paddle out to the river, across the basin to the boatyard and the wharfs where all the packet boats docked for passengers and freight. If his father and brothers did not arrive, he could still spend a portion of the day among his boatyard friends. The wharf laborers, mill workers, log rafters, and boat crews all knew him and had become accustomed to his presence there. They had learned to admire his simple-natured qualities, always happy and smiling, but appearing rather unkempt and perhaps neglected, although he never spoke of family to anyone on the docks. His speech indicated French heritage, but his skin was bronze and his hair was dark, suggesting that some native blood ran through his veins. Despite his outward appearances, though, almost everyone on the riverfront adored "Frenchy," as was the only name by which they knew him, and regarded him with a mixture of amusement, affection and respect.

His father and brothers did not arrive that morning, nor did they arrive on any other steamboats that stopped at the La Crosse wharf that day. Near sundown, Dominic put his string of sunfish that he had caught fishing from the pier into his canoe and paddled home. Once again he would eat his supper alone, and go to bed in a lonely house.

It was a fine house, built of logs and chinked with clay, topped with a cedar roof. Facing the river were parlor and dining room. On the island lagoon side were bedroom and kitchen, and a small bedroom had been added for Dominic and his half-brothers. And just to the north, fifty feet away, stood the little log storehouse, mostly empty now, but it would soon contain the wares of which his father made his business.

He lay there that night, unable to fall asleep, gazing out at the stars. A wave of reminiscent love washed over him, followed by a sharp pang of hurt as he envisioned the small headstone in the churchyard bearing the name Felicia Marie Bouton. That name had been given to his mother by Father LeClaire just after Dominic was born. But he knew that she was an Indian woman, and in his heart she would always be Morning Star, the beautiful daughter of a Winnebago chief.

About midnight, Dominic drifted off to asleep.

Chapter 4

Early the next morning he awoke with a start. Three days a week, all spring, summer, and fall, several residents of La Crosse hired him to take their cows to pasture and watch the herd all day while they grazed in the green grassy slopes beneath the bluffs. Today was his day, and by the time the sun was up over the high bluffs, everyone was usually done with the milking chores, and the cows were anxious to get out of the little city barns and out into the open meadow. His pay was forty cents per day, and a quart of chilled milk.

He finished his breakfast of salt pork and bread, and paddled out of the lagoon to the river just as the sun broke through the trees that lined the top of Granddad's Bluff. Learning the skills of paddling and maneuvering a canoe at the age of six from his mother's brother, Gray Wolf, Frenchy was as expert at slicing through the water as any man, and he made quick work of crossing the channel with little effort. He landed below Front Street at Pearl, just across from the Western Enterprise Hotel. Mr. Kellogg, the hotel owner always kept an eye on Frenchy's canoe for him while he tended the cows, one of which was Mr. Kellogg's, and Mr. Kellogg was the one who collected from the other cow owners and paid Frenchy each week. He doled out the quarts of milk, too, but he rarely kept track of how much milk had been dispensed to the boy. He adored Frenchy as much as anyone else in the town.

Frenchy made his usual route across town, leading each cow from its barn, tethering the beasts' halters to a centrally located fence rail until he had gathered all eight animals, and then untied them and drove them a mile or more to the pasture land beyond the reaches of the city.

All day he watched from the higher ground over the rooftops of the town to the sparkling river as the steamboats came and went. He wondered if one of them had deposited his father and brothers at the wharf, and if they would be waiting for him when he got home. And he wondered what present his father would have for him, as he usually did when he returned from a long voyage.

As the sun crept nearer the western horizon, Frenchy heard the church bells in town chiming six o'clock. He rounded up all the cows and headed them down the slope toward the city. Getting them back home was usually quite easy; the cows knew it was almost time for the evening milking, and each one seemed to know its way back to its own little barn without any prodding. When all the cows were safely returned home, Frenchy ran to the back door of the Western Enterprise Hotel where he collected his jar of milk from Mr. Kellogg, and then hurried across the channel to Barron's Island.

But his father's bateau was not tied up in the lagoon, and no one was waiting in the house to greet him.

On his next day in the bluff meadow tending the cows, he thought a lot about his father and brothers. Henri Bouton, his father, the proud French-Canadian had, for many years, been a trader on the island, and even when the town across the river grew to larger proportions, Henri stayed and remained faithful to the few friendly Winnebago Indians who still dwelled among the near hills. That's how he had met his wife, the mother of Dominic, when the untimely death of his first wife left him in a world of grief; she drowned in the river during a raging spring flood, and it wasn't only her death that had troubled Henri: she was with child when she died.

Then Morning Star came into his life. The beautiful Indian maiden agreed to stay after the autumn trading festivities were over, to help Henri care for his two young sons. Exposing her to the more comfortable, luxurious lifestyle of the French trader, she soon fell in love with Henri, and he took her as his wife. A year later, Dominic was born, and Morning Star was christened with her new French name, Felicia Marie.

Eight more years passed. Although he was raised in strong French culture because his father would have it no other way, Dominic secretly admired the Indian side of his heritage, as well. Dominic grew strong, influenced by his mother's family who visited frequently, learning about nature, hunting skills, canoeing and survival from his uncle, Gray Wolf. He savored every moment when his Indian uncles and cousins came to camp on the island during the trading festivals, and he listened intently when his mother told him the stories of her ancestors who had long ago made this wonderful valley their home.

Tragedy knows no mercy. Felicia Marie—Morning Star—fell ill with a fever that no doctor could cure. After a week of torturous misery, she joined her ancestors in the Great Beyond. Her body was laid to rest in the churchyard, next to the grave of Henri's first wife, because that's the way he wanted it.

Now, the memory of her beautiful brown eyes and her flowing black hair haunted Frenchy's dreams. He missed her warm smiles and her motherly touch. He thought about her often, and he found it difficult to understand why his father didn't seem to miss her at all anymore.

And then there were his two older half brothers, Jacques and Louis. They had never felt any close devotion to Morning Star, even though she tried her best to love them as if they were her own. To them she was merely a nanny who prepared their food, washed and mended their clothes, and tucked them into bed at night. But they, too, had suffered a tragic loss when their mother died, so they understood Dominic's painful sorrow, and they had been a great comfort to him at a time when he needed to be close to someone.

Now they were older. Jacques was eighteen, and he was preparing to venture into the western wilderness, to follow in his father's footsteps as a trader. He had been a devoted apprentice, and he was now well acquainted with all his father's business associates in Montreal, as he had accompanied Henri to the Canadian city several times. Soon he would establish his own trade network somewhere in the vast, unsettled west. His diligence promised him a successful future.

Sixteen-year-old Louis had made his choice for the future, as well, and for quite some time, Henri had been determined to ensure his son's acceptance into Montreal College, so that he may enter the Seminary of St. Sulpice to study for the priesthood. He wanted nothing else but to become a missionary for God.

Dominic admired his older brothers, and although he thought he would miss not having them close, he felt a peculiar happiness for them, that they were achieving what they wanted most. But it had not occurred to him, yet, that his lack of enthusiasm to pursue such professional levels was one of the reasons his father did not coddle him, as was the case with his other two sons. But Dominic was about to learn that lesson very soon.

Chapter 5

The church bells in town chimed six o'clock, and it was time to drive his herd back to their little city barns for milking. After he had collected his jar of milk from Mr. Kellogg, Dominic rushed to his canoe. Something in his heart told him that today his father and brothers would be waiting for him.

Joy danced in his big brown eyes when he spotted the bateau loaded with wooden crates tied at the bank of the lagoon. He wasted little time in dragging his canoe aground, and then ran to the house carrying the milk. There, around the plain pine table, polished by daily rubbing by many elbows, sat Henri Bouton and his two sons, Jacques and Louis, each sipping from wine glasses, the bottle at the table's center. When the door flew open and Dominic appeared, they all jumped to their feet. Louis reached the boy first and laid his hands on Dominic's shoulders. "Bless you, my brother," he said. "It is so good to see you again!"

Then Jacques, much taller and stronger, wrapped his arms around Dominic's middle, hoisted him up, and kissed the boy's cheek. "How is mon frère petit? Eh?" Jacques laughed.

Dominic still held the milk in one hand, but he managed to return the hug with sincere affection. "Bien, bien!" he replied. "I am ever so good! And I am ever so happy to see you have returned safely."

Henri grabbed the milk jar from Dominic's grasp, set it on the table, and then took the boy in his arms. "Ahh, *bonjour mon fils,*" he said, squeezing the boy tightly.

"*Bonjour, M'sieur* my Father. Did you have a good voyage? What kept you so long? You are three days late coming home."

"Good voyage? *Oui,*" said Henri. "*Je suis désolé...* I'm sorry for being late. We were delayed visiting mon ami Monsieur Cousteau... in Milwaukee."

"Milwaukee?"

"Oui," Henri replied. "And we just arrived late this afternoon by train." He looked the boy up and down. "You have been tending the cattle today?"

"Oui, M'sieur. I have milk for our supper." He gazed around, puzzled, thinking he had somehow lost the milk. Then he saw the jar on the table and beamed a smile, proud that he could help provide for his family. He looked around again curiously. "Did you bring me a present?"

"Present? Did I not promise you a present?" Henri released the boy to his feet, reached into a carpet bag next to the table, and presented a fancy wooden box with a hinged cover, six inches square, handsomely varnished, and a colorful three-mast sailing ship painted on the top. The brass hinges squeaked just a little as Dominic lifted the cover. Inside were several compartments containing a spool of very thin but strong fish line, and hooks of various sizes. Dominic's small fingers caressed the shiny hooks.

"Do you like?" asked Henri.

Dominic's eyes shone with appreciation. *"Oui! Merveilleux!* Yes, it is wonderful. *Merci!* Thank you! He hugged his father's neck.

"I have a present for you, too, *frère petit,"* said Jacques, retrieving the gift from his bag. He held it out in offering to his "frère petit"—his little brother. It, too, was another attractive wooden box, a foot long and narrow. Birds on the wing decorated the top.

Dominic gently took the box from his brother's hand and carefully removed the cover, not knowing what to expect. On the pillowed lining of red velvet lay an exquisite flute, ornately carved of hard wood and polished to a mirror-like finish, little gold rings inserted around all the finger holes. He didn't touch it; he just stared at it in amazement. Then he glanced up at Jacques with a puzzled look in his eyes.

"I haven't heard you play the flute that your uncle made for you in a long time," Jacques said. "Louis and I thought this might get you started again."

It was true. Dominic hadn't played that flute in nearly a year. Morning Star had taught him to play that simple instrument handmade by Gray Wolf from a willow branch. It was old and dry and cracked, and was unlikely to produce any sound at all now. But at one time, he could out-sing the birds with at least a dozen different melodies.

"Go ahead," Jacques said. "Try it."

Reluctantly, Dominic picked the flute from its velvet bed, positioned his fingers along the tube, and slowly brought the mouthpiece to his lips. He was amazed at the richness of tone the flute emitted as he simply played up and down the scale. He paused and grinned at Jacques, and then he played a soft, happy little lullaby tune—the first one he had ever learned. It wasn't perfect, but it *had* been a long time since he played. As he finished, Jacques, Louis and Henri all applauded his talent.

"Magnifique! Magnifique!" his father shouted. "Now you can serenade the cows out on the hillside."

After they ate their supper of venison and wild rice—and milk—the conversation continued about the voyage just completed to Montreal. Henri told of his experiences bargaining with all the warehouse owners, and all the fine dinner parties he attended as a guest of some of the wealthiest businessmen in Montreal. "And you know, Dominic," he said. "They were quite impressed with Jacques, and they will see to it that he will be very successful as a merchant in the west."

Dominic grinned a congratulatory smile at his oldest brother. Jacques had always been kind to him and treated him well, and he deserved to become successful. Jacques smiled warmly back at him.

"And there is good news about Louis, too," Henri said proudly. "This year he will begin his studies at Montreal College, and then perhaps next year, Louis will enter the Seminary."

Dominic smiled at Louis, but what he saw in return from the future scholar was what he thought to be a sneer.

"What about me, M'sieur?" Dominic asked his father. "When will it be time for me to go on a voyage with you to Montreal?"

Henri gave a hearty laugh. "Listen to *mon petit*... my little one!" he said laughing some more. "Dominic... the lazy one, who only wishes to while away his days watching cattle eat grass on the hillside. If I were to take you to Montreal, I should have to leave you in the bateau, covered with a tarpaulin, so that no one there would see what Henri Bouton fathered in the wilderness. *Bois Brulé*... that's what you are."

"I'm not *Burnt Wood!*" cried Dominic.

"Father," Jacques intervened. "I don't wish to be disrespectful, but *mon frère petit* did not get to choose the color of his skin. And he is but a child. Certainly he has not yet had time to decide on a profession."

"Look at him, Jacques," said his father. "He is a hunter... like his Indian cousins. A merchant he will never be."

"*Mon Pére,*" Dominic addressed his father. "It is true... I do not wish to be a merchant." He moved close to Jacques and leaned heavily against his brother. "I wish to stay here in the sacred valley and grow crops and raise cattle. I want to become a farmer."

"There! You see?" said Jacques. "Mon frère petit *has* chosen a profession." He put his arm around Dominic's shoulders and smiled.

Chapter 6

The next morning Dominic woke early and instead of making his breakfast, he wanted to be on his way to tend the cows before his brothers and father rose from their beds. He carefully and quietly put a chunk of bread and some cheese in his deerskin pouch that already held his new flute, slung the long strap over his shoulder and silently whisked out the door to his waiting canoe.

While he sat on the shady slope watching the cows meander about, sampling the grass here and there until each one finally settled into its choice spot, he nibbled on his bread and cheese. He imagined that on Barron's Island his father, Jacques, and Louis were busy unloading the crates of merchandise from the barge into the storehouse, unpacking them and arranging the wares so that all were displayed on the shelves and tables. He wondered if he had made a mistake by telling his father that he didn't want to be a merchant, and that his interests rather were in farming. Even he realized that he was still too young to understand what his life's ambition should be. "But here is where I will always be," he said. "Let Jacques go off to the far west to become a trader in Father's footsteps. Let Louis travel from mission to far mission as a priest. But *this* is where I belong."

The long sunlit hours passed slowly. Dominic lay back on the green hillside. Behind closed eyelids visions of the valley floated in a hazy warm blur. What a good, peaceful moment this was, and yet, he would like to be roaming the countryside. Not long ago he had seen a loon's nest at the edge of a little inlet. Wild flowers were springing up from the deep dark floors of the forest. Swallows glided and swooped about the rocky bluff's shaded crevices.

Then his thoughts began to fade and the tinkling of the cowbells came only faintly to his senses. On the lap of this glorious valley, he drifted off into a restful nap.

He awoke with hunger. His slight breakfast had not been enough. The sun was still high; it was a long time until supper, and with each passing minute he grew more and more hungry. Finally, in desperation, he knelt at the udder of one of the cows and gently squeezed spurts of milk into his mouth. Not until his fingers were tired and the bossy moved away in search of more grass did he stop. But he felt much better.

Dominic sat down in the grass next to a large boulder that had long ago rolled down from the bluff and leaned against it. He took the flute from the leather bag, admired it for a few moments, and then started practicing some of the songs his mother had taught him. The angelic sounds drifted over the valley, and somewhere there was probably a pair of ears that heard, and recognized the Indian compositions, and perhaps thought Morning Star's spirit had returned to earth.

At six o'clock, the cows were anxious to go home, and Dominic was anxious to collect for his week's work from Mr. Kellogg.

Chapter 7

Henri and Jacques were busy early the next morning preparing for the trading festival. Barron's Island would soon be encamped by Winnebago Indians, tribes from Wisconsin, Minnesota, and Iowa. They came to trade their handcrafted goods and produce and pelts for Henri Bouton's wares—pots and pans, cutlery and utensils, fabrics, thread, needles, buttons, rope, tools, garden seeds, hats —the list went on and on. Henri had always treated them fairly, and they remained loyal to their French trader friend.

Dominic waited at North Point. His uncle and cousin would be among the group coming up the Mississippi from Iowa. He eagerly anticipated their arrival as he had not seen them since last year. True to tradition, his uncle, Gray Wolf, had taught him so many things, and his cousin, Silver Cloud, had always been a wonderful playmate. But they didn't come for visits as often as they once had. Now, it was only during the trading festivals that they camped on Barron's Island, perhaps, Dominic thought, because he was old enough now, and he didn't need as much guidance. Or maybe it was because Morning Star was gone. She had been the real connection to her brother. Dominic didn't let any of that bother him now, and he so looked forward to their visit; four days and nights would offer plenty of time for him and Silver Cloud to do all the things they usually did: target shooting with bow and arrow; fishing; hiking; swimming. And there would be words of wisdom from Gray Wolf in the light of the campfire at night, and stories, and songs, and now Dominic could entertain too, with his new flute. Oh, how he hoped he could play for them!

Then he saw the flash of sunlight reflecting off the canoe paddles as the small fleet rounded the bend in the river, skimming through the silvery ripples, graceful as gulls and brilliant as butterflies, the canoes long and slender like willow leaves. As they drew near, Dominic could see the painted feathers and the colorful blankets and the silver ornaments gleaming in the morning sun.

Now there were others from the little village gathered on the shore watching the arrival of the travelers; it was always a grand event. Dominic peeled off his clothes and plunged into the water as naked as the day he was born. Those watching from the beach saw him swimming rapidly out to meet the approaching canoes, and then he suddenly vanished. The Indians in the canoes laughed and shouted. "He covers himself as with a blanket!" Their wide-eyed glances darted about over the empty surface, but Gray Wolf knew his trick. Silver Cloud had taught the boy to swim under water, like an otter, and he would come up where he was least expected.

Then a clamor of whoops and yells came from the canoes; there was Dominic, spouting water, dodging the paddles, and then turning to race the fleet to the shore. The dogs barked and the Winnebago laughed and cheered, delighted to have such a spectacular welcome.

All of them knew Dominic. They came from his mother's native village, twenty miles downriver, and some were his kin. To them, this journey was a holiday as well as an opportunity for trade. Their canoes were piled with pelts, beautiful woven mats and baskets, moccasins, bags of wild rice and dried corn, clay jars filled with hominy, maple sugar, and wild honey.

Having pulled the boats ashore there was a great flurry as the new arrivals set up their portable tepees and arranged all their possessions. But for the moment, Dominic was only interested in his uncle and cousin. He had pulled on his clothes and they sat talking as Gray Wolf waited for the others to get located. He was representing his father, Chief Red Hawk, so his lodge was to stand a little apart.

"How long will you stay on the island?" Dominic asked.

The Indian's hardened face wrinkled as he looked down at the boy. He suspected that Dominic was looking forward to many days of companionship—hiking and hunting, and absorbing new knowledge and skills from his uncle, and perhaps some recreational time with his cousin. "When three moons have passed," he said, "We must journey back down the river."

Three days wasn't nearly as long as they had stayed in the past, but Dominic didn't feel disappointed; he was glad that he had this time to spend with his Indian relatives.

Gray Wolf gazed around the camp; it appeared that all the others in the party had their tepees located. "Now I must prepare our lodge." He motioned to his son, Silver Cloud.

"May I help you?" Dominic asked eagerly, and his uncle nodded.

The boy was supremely happy as he assisted them to raise and fasten the lodge poles, unpack and stretch the skins over the framework. And when the mats were all spread and a small fire lit with an iron cooking pot hung over it, Dominic surveyed it all with pride. An unidentifiable longing swelled up inside him. "I wish I could share your lodge all the while you are here," he said.

The old Indian laid his hand on Dominic's shoulder. "My lodge is poor and simple, Little Otter. It is not rich with feather beds and glass oil lamps and brass kettles. It is not good enough to honor the son of the French Trader. But later we will hunt, and tomorrow we will feast together. We shall have a good day, you, and I, and Silver Cloud."

That night, after a long afternoon of hunting rabbits on the far side of the island with bow and arrow, Dominic bid his father the customary good-night: "Bon soir, M'sieur," and then turned to go to his bed. Suddenly an arrow of fear pierced his happiness. Framed in the darkness of a far window was a shadowy face—an Indian face, proud and fierce, eyes burning with a secret, menacing stare, unmistakable to Dominic.

Dominic quickly turned his gaze away and forced himself to quietly walk to Jacques. He leaned his head against his brother and whispered: "Fighting Bear! He's outside at the window!"

A slight shiver raced down Jacques' spine, but after a long moment he put a reassuring hand on Dominic's head. His eyes remained perfectly calm as he spoke softly. "Have no fear, mon frère. He will do us no harm... his people would punish him severely. Now, go to your bed, and have good dreams."

Far into the night, Dominic was awakened. In the deep island stillness he heard the quiet, eerie sound of a drum, like the beating of a heart. But it wasn't coming from the distant Indian camp; it was very near, and it kept circling the house, on and on. Dominic knew it was Fighting Bear, attempting to weave some dark spell around the house of Henri Bouton, around the soul that once was *Morning Star.*

Dominic crept silently to his father's bedroom door, where inside, Henri Bouton lay snoring. He had not been aroused by the strange sound of the drum, and he had not been disturbed earlier by the Indian's presence at the window. Perhaps it was just as Jacques had said. There was really nothing to fear. Yet, there it was—a phantom; something savage and secret and haunting.

Chapter 8

Dominic barely recognized Silver Cloud, his cousin and childhood playmate. He was three years older than Dominic, and he had grown tall since Dominic's last visit to their village, over three years ago, just before his mother died.

"My son will soon be a man," said Gray Wolf. "He is a good hunter; he has listened carefully to all that I have taught him. Soon he will be the one who will teach other young ones who follow."

Dominic gazed at tall, lean, muscular Silver Cloud with admiration when they went off together. But his old playmate seemed to be drifting away from him, taking his rightful place in the established ways of Indian adult life and custom. Dominic could understand that lifestyle, but he couldn't enter it; now, more than ever, he was puzzled by the emotions within that were tugging at his soul in opposite directions. His loyalties were divided: he could not abandon his father's French heritage; nor could he be completely Indian.

"I suppose you will no longer want to play with me at so trifling a thing as bow-and-arrow target shooting," Dominic said.

Silver Cloud laid his arm across his cousin's shoulders. "The bow-and-arrow is not trifling," said the Indian boy. "It was the trusted weapon and good friend of the Old Ones, and the Old Ones are very wise.

It still fits the Indian hand as well as the leather glove of the white man. Come... let us play at target shooting right now."

It was a happy afternoon, far away from the island village where all the adults were conducting their trading. Dominic enjoyed running almost naked, covered only by a loin cloth, just like his older cousin. They played at target shooting, and then raced through the woods to the far side of the island where they swam from a sandy beach.

When darkness fell that night after a long, thrilling day and an evening feast, Dominic entertained his Indian relatives with his new flute as they danced around the campfires, drumming and singing the familiar traditional songs.

When the dancing ended and all the others had gone quietly to their tepees, Gray Wolf summoned Dominic to join him. They sat close, cross-legged for a few moments in the firelight. The crackling of the embers and the distant hoot of an owl were the only sounds as Gray Wolf retrieved something from his vest pocket. Ceremoniously he held out a small leather pouch tied tightly at the top with a long lanyard loop. The pouch was decorated with a painted symbol—a bird with outstretched wings. He spread the lanyard loop and slipped it over Dominic's head, placing it around his neck so that the pouch hung at the boy's chest. "Your grandfather, old and unable to come here now, instructed me to give you this, Little Otter."

"What is it?" asked Dominic.

"A medicine bag. It contains a few pebbles and grains of sand from your island...your homeland will now always be close to your heart, and it will protect you from the thunder in the night."

Tired, Dominic—Little Otter—slowly walked back to his house by the lagoon. Although he didn't completely understand all that his uncle had just told him, he cherished the gift hanging around his neck. It was a meaningful symbol of acceptance by his Indian family.

The island had fallen into near silence, with only the murmur of the river current gently washing the rocks along the bank and a soft summer breeze mischievously stirring the forest's branches. He tumbled into his bed.

As he lay there before he fell asleep, he whispered to himself: "Yes, Silver Cloud is different now. All the time, even when we're playing, he's thinking of something secret."

Chapter 9

On their last day together, Dominic was feeling a bit grumpy and out of sorts. He had not rested well because thoughts of things he did not completely understand kept him tossing and turning in a troubled sleep. That morning, neither he nor Silver Cloud was much in the mood for playing, but rather, they stole away to the far beach where they could be alone. They swam for a while, and then lay in silence on the sand watching the gulls swooping about. Finally, Dominic broke the silence. "You seem so far away," he said. "Don't you like me for a playmate anymore?"

Silver Cloud glanced at him in surprise. "Little Otter! Have you not noticed that the childhood of Silver Cloud is nearing the end? Have you forgotten that an Indian boy must perform his vigil before he becomes a man?"

Dominic just stared at him, puzzled.

Silver Cloud continued. "The time has come for me to go into the wilderness to fast and pray. When the moon is next round and bright in the sky, your cousin goes to receive a message from the Great Spirit—a message that will bring me good medicine, and will, perhaps, make me a great leader of my people." He stared deeply into Dominic's eyes as if to intensify the meaning of his words. "If all goes well, the Great Spirit will send me a sign in a dream, to guide me through all my days. This is a most important time for an Indian boy. That is why Silver Cloud seems so strange to you."

All of Dominic's selfish hurt vanished, even though Silver Cloud seemed even more distant now than he ever had. He was filled with awe and strangeness thinking about the hard task his cousin would soon undergo.

"The weather is hot," said Silver Cloud. "Let us go for another swim."

And for the rest of the long, happy afternoon the cousins seemed as once they were, two carefree boys together. Dominic glowed with pride when Silver Cloud praised his swimming. "It was I who taught you to swim under water. Remember? And now you are even more skillful. You well deserve the name of *Little Otter.*"

They laughed and whooped and splashed out of the water, raced each other across the sand, only to plunge into the water again, shouting cries of joy.

On the way back to the island village, they walked together slowly, lingering in the late afternoon sun. Silver Cloud spoke in low, serious tones. "In four days, Cousin, I go to make my vigil. Surely the Great Spirit will send me a vision, and he will give me a guardian spirit of my own. I have kept in my heart the words from the wise Old Ones in the council lodge; I have listened to my parents and have been obedient to them. I know that the Great Spirit gave us life and this earth on which we live. During the last few suns and moons I have tried to prepare myself to be worthy of a message from him."

They walked a little farther in silence. Silver Cloud's expression was bathed in concern. "This is what I have wanted to tell you today, before we say our farewells."

Dominic remained beyond speech. *To be so sure of your destiny, and to have your very own guiding spirit to show you the way,* he thought, *being an* all-*Indian boy must be* magnifique.

"Pray for me, Little Otter, that my dream in the wilderness will bring a sign and that I will not return to my village like Fighting Bear."

Astonished, Dominic stared at his cousin. "Fighting Bear!" he said. "What—?"

"I was told that long ago Fighting Bear's quest for a vision was not successful. Instead, he returned to the village, near death, with wild fire in his eyes. He did not die because the evil spirits initiated him into the dark magic society."

"If he's so evil, why don't your people drive him away?"

"Because many believe he uses his dark magic, and they are afraid if he is exiled, he will cast a spell on the entire village and do great harm. So they don't want to anger him, and they allow him to stay."

Dominic recalled the night he saw Fighting Bear at the window. "So that's why..." He hesitated, and decided not to tell Silver Cloud about his strange experience. "Yes, Cousin, I will pray for your success."

Chapter 10
La Crosse; February 1878

"**W**elcome," said Captain Will Gordon as Frank McIntyre and his sister, the widow Mrs. Wood, entered the den. "I'm so glad you could make it." He rose from his chair, crossed the room and shook hands with his best friend. Then he took Mrs. Wood by the hand, caressed her cheek with a tender little kiss, and guided her to the sofa where she always liked to sit. The captain's daughter, Maria, greeted the two visitors from her place at the writing desk, and then came over to receive her customary hug from handsome Frank McIntyre. Since she was a little girl she had always admired Frank, and now that she was accepted as an adult, she was happy to always be included in the social conversations. Not that she had any romantic interest in Frank—he had always been more like an older brother. She sat beside Mrs. Wood and they immediately dove into conversation about the latest dress and hair styles while the two men engaged in discussion of riverboats over a couple of glasses of brandy. They were both experienced riverboat pilots on the Upper Mississippi.

"The McDonalds are building a new log rafter," Gordon said.

"Yes, I've heard the rumors," Frank replied.

"Oh, it's no rumor. They plan to have 'er on the river towing logs by the spring of 1880."

"And let me guess," Frank said. "You're gonna pilot this new boat."

"Better yet," Gordon said. "They're making me her captain."

"Well, congratulations, Will!" Frank raised his glass in an honorable salute.

"Thank you, my friend." Gordon then raised his glass. "And I sincerely hope that you will consider leaving the Davidson fleet and being my second pilot."

"Well, I don't know…"

"You don't have to answer right now, Frank. But do give it some thought, will you?"

Just then, Helen, the housekeeper entered the den and announced that she was ready to serve their supper in the dining room.

"Come, everyone," said the captain. "Let's see what savory delicacy Helen has prepared for us this evening."

They all filed into the dining room, following the enticing aroma. When they were seated, Helen began serving the roast duck, baked squash, fresh bread still warm from the oven, and all the garnishments to make the perfect meal.

"Would you still ask me to be your second pilot if I were to steal Helen from you?" asked Frank in a joking manner.

"Well," replied the captain. "I should be very lost without her. And I will definitely need her services when I adopt a son."

The statement took Frank and his sister by surprise, but they seemed delighted by the thought. "You're adopting a son?" Frank asked.

"Yes, I have been giving it much thought lately."

"And how do you plan to raise a son when you're on the river from March 'til November?"

"Why, Helen and Maria can care for him and teach him the art of being a gentleman while I'm away... until he's old enough to work aboard a boat. And then I intend to make him a pilot."

"A pilot!" Frank exclaimed.

"I think it's a wonderful idea," Mrs. Wood chimed in. "You know how much I adore my brother...why, I don't know what I'd do if anything ever happened to Frank. It would be such a nice addition to this household for Maria to have a little brother." She glanced across the table to Maria. "Don't you think so, my dear?"

Maria smiled. "Why, yes, it probably would be nice to have someone else here while Papa is away all summer."

Although Frank wasn't opposed to an adoption, he remained a little concerned. "And just where do you think you'll find this boy?"

Captain Gordon gazed into Frank's eyes. "Do you forget?" he said. "I have been on the board of guardians for the Mission School for several years, now. They have plenty of children who need homes."

"But the boys at the orphanage are nothing but a bunch of ruffians... probably illiterate... and certainly not gentlemen."

Gordon grinned. "A boy is a boy. He's made of flesh and blood. I don't care where he comes from. You can make of him whatever you want."

"Flesh and blood, yes," Frank replied. "But if he doesn't have the *right* blood, you can't make him a gentleman."

"Nonsense. It's just a matter of training and education."

"But Will... name one boy who came out of that school who amounted to any more than a common laborer... or a criminal."

"That's because no one ever took any interest in any of them when they were young... or gave them the guidance and opportunity to be anything better."

"I must say, Will... it'll be quite a challenge. Do you think you are up to that challenge?"

"Frank, you and your sister have been our best friends for years. I value your judgment and I respect your opinions. Yes, I think I'm up to the challenge of raising a son... to be a gentleman... and a riverboat pilot. I only ask you for your support."

Chapter 11
Summer: 1878

Captain Gordon stood before the entryway at the Mission School. Never before had he experienced such mixed emotions as he was feeling now. There was the strong compassion; to give a young boy a good life; deliver him from this dismal existence of confinement; to offer him a family and a sense of belonging. But Gordon also was quite aware of the background and origins of most of these children who, perhaps, may have experienced traumatic events that led to their being in this place, who had been abandoned by adults, and therefore had formed a high degree of distrust of adults. Although he had been serving on a board of guardians for the school for several years, and had helped promote its support by the community, he had never become personally involved with its inhabitants, and he had no idea what to expect now.

He was determined, though, to take one of these boys into his home, nurture him to an adult, and transform him into an admirable legacy of which he could be proud. He was certain that with proper training and education, he could condition one of these boys into a gentleman. And after all, his good friend, Frank McIntyre had challenged him to the task.

"Good morning, Mr. Stanley," he greeted as the door opened.

"Good morning to you sir," Stanley replied. "Come to look around?"

"In a manner of speaking. Actually, I'm looking for a boy. Do you have any?"

"Boys, sir? The place swarms with them."

"Well then, show me some."

"Show you some, sir?"

"Yes. I want a boy."

"Certainly, sir. Come right this way. About what age, sir?"

"Not particular," said the captain. "Maybe about fourteen or fifteen."

Mr. Stanley rubbed his chin, as if deep in thought. "Strong young lad for chores around the dock?"

"Oh, no," replied Captain Gordon. "I want to adopt a boy."

"I see," Stanley said, wondering curiously if Captain Gordon was in his right mind. He led the captain through a passageway, and then across a sandy yard to a long, low building that served as the barracks for all the boys of the school, ranging in age from six to sixteen. All orphans, whose parents had become victims of the harshness presented by the frontier, they had somehow found their way here, and the Mission School was now their home until they were able to fend for themselves.

The hum of many voices rolled through the open windows. The boys had just finished their breakfast and were busy tidying up the barracks before they were dispatched to various chores. The noise ceased as if by magic, and 37 faces turned and every eye trained on the accompanying visitor as Headmaster Stanley opened the door.

The captain gazed upon the room, rows of bunks taking up most of the space with little room for anything else. He saw a crowd of heads and dull but curious expressions. All the boys seemed to have been poured from the same mold; all clad in the same gray trousers and faded pale blue shirts. They appeared to be adequately fed, and clean. But somehow, Gordon got the impression that they, perhaps, didn't *enjoy* the food, and were *too* clean, the clothes uncomfortable, and all were well on their way to becoming old men without having been allowed to stop and play, and to be boys.

"As you can see, Captain," Mr. Stanley said quietly, avoiding the boys hearing his words. "We are a bit crowded."

"Yes," agreed Gordon. "But I hope to free up one bed for you today."

Had the boys heard their conversation and known the purpose of the visit, there would have raised a tremendous yell that would have consisted of two words: *"Take me!"*

This was a good orphanage school—one which made the guardians proud; no tyranny or brutality, but there was endless discipline, and of course, the lack of the family-home-sweet-home factor. As hard as Stanley and his staff tried, they could not create that atmosphere for every child, and it must have been the absence of these elements that made the Mission boys look like 37 pale-faced little old men.

"Now, let me see," said the school master. "The matter will have to be put before the board in the usual manner, of course..."

"Usual manner?" Gordon said. "Do you forget that I am *on* that board, sir?"

"Yes. I mean, no, of course not, Captain." Mr. Stanley turned his head toward the boys. "Would you like to make your choice now, Captain?"

Gordon scanned the crowd of heads. "Yes... of course, you will make some suggestions?"

Stanley left the captain's side to stroll among the boys. He stopped occasionally, placed his hand on a shoulder, leaned and whispered something in a boy's ear. When he returned to Captain Gordon, seven boys followed and stood at attention before the master and his guest. Not one smiled, but rather displayed an expression as if he were about to be punished.

Stanley put his hand on the first boy's shoulder, a tall, very thin and pale boy who appeared as though he had been accidently whitewashed. "This is Cogan, a very fine lad; thirteen, and the best marks in his class." Then he moved on to the next boy in line. "This is Duffy, a very good boy..."

Stanley went down the line bragging about each of his selections. But none of them impressed Gordon, as they didn't seem to possess the spirit that he had come to expect in a boy. Once again he scanned the crowded bunk room until his eyes made contact with those of a boy way in the back. His wavy blonde hair glistened in a streak of sunlight coming through a window, and his blue eyes sparkled with... spirit!

"There," said Gordon. "Who is that boy?"

"Which one, sir?"

"The one in the back... the blonde-haired one standing all alone."

Stanley stared at the lone boy, and then with a low, troubled voice said to Gordon, "You mean... I can't recommend... sir... I don't think you want to consider him. He's not a very good boy."

Gordon's face beamed with pleasure, ignoring Stanley's warning.

"Have him come here to me. I want to get a closer look and have a talk with him."

"But... sir... all of *these* boys are of the highest character..."

"*Now*, Mr. Stanley."

Reluctantly, Stanley turned and called out. "Jules Martin. Would you come here, please?"

The boy seemed pleasantly surprised that he would be chosen to join the group that he knew to be the smartest lads in the school. A worried smile squirmed on his face. He hadn't heard the proceedings from his far corner, and weaving his way to the front he wondered what kind of prank he was about to receive.

Stanley pulled Gordon aside and turned him so their backs were to the boys. "Captain Gordon, sir... that boy will not do," he said sternly.

"Why, how do you know that?" Gordon responded.

"Very bad boy, I'm sorry to say," the school master said. "Full of mischief that corrupts the other boys. Can't say a word in his favor... always being punished... and besides... he's younger than you want."

"How old is he?"

"About twelve, sir," Stanley said, and then added, "Yes, sir. Son of a miserable old tramp who died some years ago right here in our infirmary the night he brought the boy to us. The tramp had no identity, so we gave the boy his name."

When Gordon turned back toward the boys, Jules Martin had almost reached the front. The little fellow came full of eagerness and excitement after kicking a bully in the shin who had stuck out his foot trying to trip Jules.

Gordon frowned and gazed sternly at the boy, admirably taking in his handsome features, sparkling blue eyes, and wavy yellow hair that hung down on his forehead. Though it was thin, the boy's face didn't seem quite so pale as the others, nor was it depressed or mournful. His lips were rosy and smiling, and when they parted they revealed his pearly white teeth.

"The school master tells me that you are a bit of a rascal," Gordon said to the boy.

Jules wrinkled his forehead and glanced at Stanley before boldly casting his bright eyes on the Captain. "I d'know," he said, puzzled.

"You don't know, *SIR!*" Stanley said, correcting the boy's lack of respect.

"I'm sorry, sir... you see? I don't mean to, but I'm always findin' trouble..."

"What's your name, lad?"

"Jules Martin."

"*SIR!*" spouted the school master.

"Jules Martin, SIR," the boy said quickly, correcting his error.

"What a name!" said Gordon.

"Yes, ain't it, though? I hate it, sir."

"You do?"

"Yes, sir. All the other boys make fun of it. They call me Julie most of the time, just because..."

Laughter and snickering interrupted him.

"That will do, Mr. Martin," Stanley said. "Don't ramble so."

"Please, sir. He asked me," the boy said in protest. There was a sincere tone in his voice that sat well with Captain Gordon.

"With all due respect, Mr. Stanley," Gordon said. "Please let me talk to the boy."

"Certainly, sir. But he has a very bad record." Stanley was still trying to convince the captain that he had made a wrong choice.

"But he seems truthful. I'll be the judge of his record, Mr. Stanley," Gordon said with a forbidding tone. Then he turned back to the boy and grinned. "Would you like to leave this place?"

The boy's eyes squinted questioningly. He took a step forward, and Stanley moved in as if to force a retreat, but Gordon blocked him with a stiff arm. The boy looked on, intensity multiplying, knowing that the captain was defending him.

"Well?" said Gordon. "Do you want to come and live at my place?"

The boy's face smoothed into a pleasant little smile. Bright light danced in his eyes, and full of confidence he said eagerly, "Yes." He held out his hand.

"And leave all your schoolmates?" Gordon said, taking the boy's hand in his.

Jules' bright face clouded. He turned to gaze at all the scowls of jealousy. Then he looked back to Gordon and nodded.

"He'll be glad to go," Stanley said. "Most ungrateful boy."

The boy swung sharply around toward Mr. Stanley. Now the

sparkles in his eyes were tears. "I didn't want to be bad, sir," he sputtered. "I did try, and... and..." He could say no more, and at last, in shame and agony he covered his face with his hands and dropped to his knees on the puncheon floor, sobbing hysterically.

"Jules! Stand up!" the school master ordered sternly.

"Let him be, Mr. Stanley," Gordon said. He drew in a deep breath and remained silent for a long moment, while the other boys stared in wonder, and he and Stanley exchanged glances.

"Strange boy," said Stanley.

Then Gordon knelt down slowly and caressed the boy's shoulder with a gentle hand. Jules flinched at first, but as soon as he realized who was touching him, he quickly clutched Gordon's hand and rose to his feet. The gaze from Gordon's eyes had a strange influence on him, and he couldn't look away.

"I think you'll come with me now?" Gordon said.

"Yes... but... may I?" Jules' watery eyes pleaded with Mr. Stanley.

Stanley nodded approval to the boy. "Yes, of course, if you wish." Then he turned to Gordon. "I shall have to bring your proposal before the board."

"That is to say, before me and my colleagues," Gordon said smiling. "Well, as one of the Guardians of this school, I think I may venture to take the boy now, and the formal business can be settled later."

"Yes, of course, sir. And I venture to think that it will not be necessary to continue with the formalities."

"And why not, Stanley?"

"Because," the school master said with a peculiar grin. "You will bring him back within a week."

"I will not be bringing him back, Stanley. I have made my decision, and I am certain it is the right one," Gordon said. He laid his hand on the boy's golden head.

"Very well, but if you want to take him now, his clothes must be..."

"He will not be needing his clothes or anything more from the Mission. I will see to that."

"Very well, sir. I hope he will take your kindness to heart." Mr. Stanley leaned closer to the boy. "Did you hear, Jules? Try to be good for Captain Gordon. He seems to like you."

"Yes, yes, yes, Mr. Stanley," Gordon cut him off short. "He will be just fine. Now my little man... are you ready to go?"

"Yes, sir, but..."

"What is it?" Gordon asked.

"May I go say good-bye to my friends and Mother Champlain?"

Captain Gordon gave a curious glance to Stanley. "Mother Champlain?"

"Nurse, sir. The woman who cared for him when he was just a little thing... right after the old tramp died."

"Ah, well certainly. Run along, then, and say your good-byes."

The boy looked up into his eyes with question.

"No," Gordon said, sensing the boy's sudden fear. "I will not run away without you. I will wait for you at the gate."

The boy darted away to the main hall and disappeared into a doorway.

While the boy was seeking the old woman, Stanley led the way to the front gate. "He has no friends, you know," he said to Gordon. "And I must warn you of his character."

"No offense, Stanley," Gordon interrupted. "But I think I would like to discover his true character on my own."

Just then Jules and an elderly woman met them at the gate.

"You are a fortunate man," she said. "He is such an affectionate boy." Jules was clinging to her apron. "Good-bye and good luck," she said, leaned down to kiss the boy in a motherly fashion.

He hugged her affectionately, as if she were the only being he thought he could ever love.

"God bless you, my dear boy," Mrs. Champlain whispered.

As Captain Gordon and Jules passed through the gate and down the walkway toward his waiting carriage, Mrs. Champlain commented, "Very nice man."

"Yes," replied Stanley. "But he'll bring the rascal back."

The captain didn't hear. His attention was focused on Jules who clung tightly to his hand, fighting hard to hold back the tears.

Gordon couldn't help but notice. He gently squeezed the boy's hand.

Chapter 12

On the way to Captain Gordon's house, Jules' heart swelled with sorrow, having to part from Mrs. Champlain, the only person who had been at all kind to him; his recollection of the rough tramp had become quite faint, and he certainly wouldn't miss many of the other boys at the Mission School, who had generally made him their object of teasing and torment. Now it was the captain who offered kindness, but there hadn't been an opportunity, yet, for Jules to evaluate all this that was happening so quickly.

Helen, the captain's housekeeper, met them at the door with an expression of surprise. Captain Gordon had instructed her earlier to prepare an upstairs bedroom, but she wasn't expecting such a young guest.

"Helen, I would like you to meet Jules Martin," Captain Gordon said. He put his arm across the boy's shoulders and pulled him close. "He will be my adopted son. I trust that you have his room ready?"

Helen's eyes opened wide as if shocked by some disturbing news, and her expression turned to a worried one. She recognized the clothing of the Mission School, and she wasn't entirely sure that she was prepared to have a youngster in the house again, much less, an unrefined imp from the orphanage. Helen had been the housekeeper since Mrs. Gordon's passing, and she had cared for Maria, Mr. Gordon's daughter. But that was different—Maria was a girl.

And this was a boy! How could she tolerate a boy?

Jules seemed amused by Helen's facial antics, and he smiled. "Pleased to meet you, Miss Helen," he said. The housekeeper didn't immediately impress him as being the loving, caring, warm person that Mrs. Champlain had been, but he thought he should be polite to her, anyway.

Helen gave a courteous little bow. "If you will excuse me, sir, I will go to finish getting his room ready."

"Very well," said Gordon. "Where's Maria?"

"I believe she's in the study," the maid replied.

"Good. Then that's where we'll be, introducing Maria to her new little brother."

After Helen had disappeared up the staircase, Jules turned to

Captain Gordon. "She doesn't like me much, do she?"

"Oh, give her time, my boy. Give her time. Helen's a very good woman." He guided the boy down the hall to an open doorway that led into a very comfortable-looking den, the walls lined with bookshelves and paintings, the floor covered with carpet, a luxurious sofa and easy chairs, and in one corner flanked by draped windows on either side was a writing desk where sat beautiful Maria. She looked up from the letter she was writing and gazed wonderingly at the boy standing directly in front of her father. "Hello, Papa," she said after turning her quizzical stare to a pleasant smile. "You're back."

"Yes, my dear. Maria, this is Jules Martin. Shake hands with him and make him feel at home."

The captain's sweet, lady-like daughter held out her hand to the boy, who was gazing all around the room with curious delight until his eyes fell upon an elegantly framed, admirably crafted water color portrait of the captain hanging on the wall. It was the work of Maria.

Jules burst into a hearty laugh, ran to Maria and took her hand. He pointed with his left hand to the portrait. "Look at that... it's the cap'n's picture. Ain't it like him, though?"

Maria looked troubled with the boy's roughness, even though he had just paid a compliment to her artistic skill.

A long moment of painful silence was broken by Jules pumping Maria's hand up and down. "How do you do, Miss Maria?" he said solemnly.

A warm smile rippled over Maria's face. The boy's expression brightened, and he, too, smiled in such a way that made him look quite handsome and attractive, despite his forlorn attire. "Oh, but ain't you pretty? Prettier than any gal I ever seen before."

"Ah, yes," the captain interrupted. "Now, Jules... Mr. Stanley, your school master said that you were anything but a good boy."

"Yeah, everybody knows that I'm the worst bad boy in the whole school."

Maria grimaced.

"Oh, you are, are you," Gordon said.

"Yeah. Mr. Stanley told everybody I am."

"But you will start being a good boy from now on?"

"All right, sir."

"And behave yourself like a little gentleman?"

"But... am I gonna stay here?"

"Yes."

"And I ain't goin' back to the school for supper and breakfuss?"

"No, you will eat here with us."

"But will I have to go back and sleep in the dormitory with the other boys?"

"No, you will sleep in your room upstairs."

"Here? In this beautiful house? With you? And this nice lady?"

"Yes, of course."

The boy was almost in tears. "Yyyaahooooo!" he cried in a screeching voice, and then with all the grace of a practiced circus performer he went hands over feet cartwheels in a circle completely around the room, coming to rest perfectly in front of Captain Gordon.

"Here, now! There will be no more of that in this house!" the captain scolded, half angry and half amused.

The boy stood there with such innocent pride. After a few moments of feeling a little annoyed with the boy's behavior, Maria sat back in her chair and laughed, as much at her father's puzzled look as at the boy.

When he saw that Maria seemed amused, he turned to her and said, "That's nothing. Watch this!" And before they could protest against any more acrobatic tricks, Gordon and Maria watched as the boy quickly stepped in front of the fireplace, ducked down with his hands planted firmly on the carpet, and then kicked his heels in the air.

"Get down, my boy! Get down!" begged the captain. "No, I mean... get up!"

"But I'm not done," said Jules. He tipped his legs backward for balance as he walked on his hands in a small circle, lowered his feet to the floor and sprang up as if he had just done a backward flip, directly facing Mr. Gordon. His handsome young face beamed with proud delight.

Gordon caught hold of the boy's strong arms and held him firmly. "Confound you, boy. You certainly are full of the Dickens."

Maria tried to look serious. She held her handkerchief to hide her smiling face, but her eyes twinkled with joy. Her father's plan to raise a gentleman from an orphanage ruffian was certainly off on a rocky start.

"Jules... are you hungry?" she said, hoping to get his mind off any more acrobatic demonstrations.

The boy shook himself loose from the captain and ran to Maria. "Is it dinnertime already?"

"No, but you've had a very busy morning, and perhaps you would like a piece of cake."

Jules stared at Maria, and then at the captain, puzzled. "Is it somebody's birthday?"

"No," Maria said.

"Y' mean... y' have cake here... even when it's *not* somebody's birthday?"

"Oh, yes, my boy," Mr. Gordon replied. "And lots of other good things, too. You'll see."

Maria crossed the room to the hall, summoned Helen, and requested her to bring the cake she had baked that morning, a knife, plate, and a glass of milk. Helen soon returned with a tray that she placed on a table, staring at the boy with anything but favorable eyes.

"You're having milk?" said the boy to Maria.

"Oh, no... it's for you."

"For me?"

"Yes," Maria said. Then she cut a generous wedge of cake, put it on the plate, and slid it and the milk toward Jules. She glanced at her father who sat quietly, brow furrowed, thinking out his plans.

Jules watched her with sparkling eyes, and it pleased Maria the way he examined her, for on the outside he was displaying, at that moment, his school discipline, but on the inside she sensed a little savage, eager and full of curiosity.

"Was that your sister who brought the cake?" Jules asked.

"No, Helen is our servant. She's been our housekeeper since Mama fell ill and passed away many years ago, when I was just a little girl."

"Oh," Jules said. "Kinda like Mother Champlain. She took care of me for as long as I can remember, but they say she's not really my mother." He looked at the piece of cake Maria had given him. "Would y' cut this again? In three? I'd like ever so much to share it with Mother Champlain and Jimmy."

"Who's Jimmy?" Maria asked.

"He's m' best pal at th' school... been sick in bed with th' measles. But he's getting better now, and I know he'd like some cake, too."

"You shall have more cake to send to Mrs. Champlain and Jimmy if you wish. That whole piece is for you. Now, you sit here quietly and eat your cake."

Maria felt her eyes getting a little moist. The boy's genuine unselfish, generous spirit caressed her soul, and she looked at him with a renewed interest. She smiled and laid her hand on his shoulder.

Jules put his hand on hers, like a cat lays a paw in a gesture of affection. As the strange little fellow munched on the cake she didn't take her hand away until her father said sharply, "Maria, come here."

The boy stared, but he went on eating as Maria crossed the room to where Captain Gordon sat.

"Yes, Papa?"

"About this boy..." the captain said.

Maria's heart sank. She didn't know why, but she had suddenly felt a warm closeness to the boy. If she had been asked, she could not have explained her rising compassion for this odd little guy who she feared, now, that her father was about to reject. "You want to raise a boy," she said to her father in a tone that Jules was unable to hear. "But you are taking him back to the school and will select another."

Captain Gordon gazed at his daughter with a questioning expression. "Why would I want to do that?"

"I thought..." Maria hesitated. "I thought you wanted a gentleman son, polished and cultured."

"Oh, nonsense! So he's a little wild and rough; he's a boy—a high-spirited boy, that's all. He's got the right stuff in him."

"But he is so very rough," Maria smiled.

"A *little* rough, maybe," said the captain. "But we can make him a gentleman, and that's why I ask you now to help me with the poor orphan. He seems to like you."

"So... he's an orphan?"

"Yes, the son of some miserable old tramp who just wandered in with the boy and died there in the infirmary."

"Oh, how dreadful. And sad." Maria glanced at the boy. He smiled in a way that made his face light up.

"You see, my dear?" the captain said. "Just look at him. Behind those rough edges is a handsome, charming boy... a gentleman he shall be, with our help, of course."

"Very well, Papa," said Maria. "I will help you all I can."

"Thank you, my dear," the captain said warmly. "I know that someday you will be proud of your efforts, and so shall I. Now, then, where to begin?"

Chapter 13
The Transformation Begins

Noticing the pleased looks on their faces, Jules leaped up from his stool as if preparing to perform another gymnastic feat.

"NO! Sit down!" shouted the captain, and the boy dropped meekly back onto his seat.

"There," said the captain. "You see, Maria? We've already achieved obedience. Now... for the next order of business, the boy needs some good clothes."

Jules spoke up. "Oh, that won't be necessary, sir," he said eagerly. "I have more of these in my trunk at the dormitory."

"Nonsense. You will not be wearing poor orphan child's clothing anymore. Mr. Markos, the haberdasher in town, will come to measure you for all new ones." Then he turned to Maria. "See what you can do to trim his hair, will you?" He stared at the boy's golden locks that were cut uneven and ragged. "I do believe the barber at the school should be flogged."

Mr. Gordon paced across the room and back again, pulled out his pocket watch and glanced at the time. "I have some business down at the boatyard, and I will stop by the haberdasher's. But before I go, there's one more thing." He sat down in his easy chair. "Come here, my boy."

Jules jumped to his feet and went to the captain with bold strides. He stood before Gordon with expectant eyes.

"You told me back at the school that you don't like your name."

"No, sir, I don't."

"Well, then, we'll do away with that right now. What name *do* you like?"

The boy shrugged his shoulders and threw his hands out to the side. His eyes rolled around, searching the ceiling and the walls, and then finally came back to the captain with uncertainty. "I d'know, sir... Jack?"

"No, no, no. Let's see," Mr. Gordon said, rubbing his chin. "How do you like Charles? That's a good gentleman's name."

The boy's lips pursed; his eyes squinted in deep thought. After a long moment his white teeth beamed a broad smile. "Okay," he replied. "Charles Martin sounds good."

"But your official name," said the captain, "will be Charles Martin Gordon from now on. You are to be my son, so it's only fitting and proper that you should have the name as well."

The boy was truly happy with all that had transpired, so far, and he was about to utter his thank you, but he stopped short to first swipe his nose with the cuff of his shirt sleeve.

Captain Gordon immediately turned to Maria. "Tell Helen to monogram a dozen handkerchiefs with CMG for the boy."

Maria nodded.

The boy grinned. "A dozen handkerchiefs all for me?"

"Yes," said the captain. "And don't let me catch you wiping your nose on your sleeve again, okay?"

Charles nodded. He realized that he had been on the receiving end of generosity much to his advantage, and he was quite certain that it all would come at a price. To show the captain that he was willing to accept responsibilities in return, before he was asked, he offered, "What chores will I be doing? Fetch water from the well? Clean the stables? Till the garden? Fill the coal buckets?"

Mr. Gordon laughed. "Aren't you the eager one? You need not worry about any of that for now. Maria will take charge of you for the time being and get you settled in."

"But I will go to my classes at the school?"

"My boy, Charles... I want you to forget that school and everything about it."

"Forget it?" Charles replied with his forehead puckered up.

"In time, Charles, we will send you to a good school. But for now, Maria will teach you all you need to know," Gordon said, and then he got up out of his chair and strolled to the door. He turned to Maria. "Tell Helen that I will be back about six for supper. And Mr. Markos will be by sometime this afternoon to measure Charles for his new clothes, so be watching for him."

"Yes, Papa," Maria said. "I'll take good care of Charles Martin for you till you get back."

After the captain was gone, Charles sat on a hassock. A troubled expression came on his face, and Maria knelt down before him.

"What's the matter?" she asked. "You look worried."

Charles gazed into her eyes for a long moment. "I... I... I never had a father... that I remember, anyway. I... I never had nobody... 'cept Mother Champlain, and she wasn't really my mum."

Maria saw tears beginning to form in his eyes, and she was sure they were tears of joy. She stretched out her arms to him, inviting him to be hugged. He leaned forward, laid his cheek on her shoulder, and soaked up the embrace for at least a minute. Then he pushed himself back onto the hassock and wiped away the tears with the back of his hand.

With a slight crackle still in his voice he said, "But what do I call him?"

Maria smiled. "Oh, I guess you should call him *Father,* or *Papa,* like I do, or you can call him *Sir*... he likes that."

"And you are his daughter. What should I call you?"

"Well, since I am going to be your sister, you should just call me Maria."

He absorbed all that very quickly. "Maria?"

"Yes."

"If I'm not going back to th' school, I won't ever get to see th' boys... or Mother Champlain."

"I'm sure you will make lots of new friends, and perhaps Papa will allow Mrs. Champlain to come visit you here sometime."

"Oh! That would be grand!" Charles grinned. "Could you save her a bit of that cake for when she comes?"

Maria laughed. "I'll have Helen bake another cake... just for Mrs. Champlain." She couldn't help but feel pleased with the boy's concern of others.

In less than an hour, Mr. Markos, the haberdasher arrived at the front door. Helen escorted him to the den where Maria was teaching Charles a few points of protocol and etiquette for the Gordon home, as she knew that her father would expect good manners from Charles very soon.

Mr. Markos gave a little bow to the young lady, and then glanced to the center of the room where the boy still sat obediently on the hassock. "Ah... this must be Charles," he said with a reserved grin, recognizing the orphanage attire. "Mr. Gordon said he was a handsome lad in need of some new clothes." He winked at the boy. "I see he was quite right on both accounts."

Mr. Markos was dressed in a dapper brown suit, white shirt with collar and necktie that matched the suit. His shoes were shined to mirrors, and Charles found him quite pleasant. Even with Charles standing on the hassock, Mr. Markos stood at least a head taller than him, so the tailor still had to lean and stoop to get all the measurements. Charles giggled in amusement as the tailor's hands tickled certain spots. This was a new experience for the boy; he'd never been fussed over like this before... ever. Whenever he had gotten clothes at the school, they were usually well worn hand-me-downs that were always too big, so that he would grow into them by the end of the year when the same process would happen again.

"Sit down, now, and take off your boots so I can measure your feet for some new shoes," Mr. Markos said to Charles.

"New shoes, too!" Charles said.

"Why, yes. Mr. Gordon told me to fit you with anything you need and want. And you certainly could use a new pair of boots."

When Mr. Markos was finished taking the measurements he told Maria the new wardrobe would be ready in a week.

"Oh dear," cried Maria. "A week! And what is the boy to wear until then? He certainly can't go like this!" She nodded to the boy's shabby gray trousers and faded blue shirt, a hole worn in one elbow, making sure the tailor understood her feeling of urgency.

"Well," replied Mr. Markos. "Ready-made, ma'am? I have plenty of new and fashionable garments that would fit the boy perfectly. I could send them over to him yet this afternoon."

"Yes, by all means," said Maria. "Shirts, trousers, jacket, stockings, undergarments... everything... so he will have nice clothes until next week."

"Very well, ma'am. A nice selection will be here this afternoon."

Helen escorted Mr. Markos to the front door.

"A charming little fellow," he said to the housekeeper, and now even

Helen was beginning to soften just a bit.

Back in the den, Charles' bright blue eyes sparkled as he thought about all the new clothes he would soon have, and he commenced a triumphant freestyle dance of spins, shuffles, kicks and flips that would have put an opera house stage performer to shame. Maria caught him by his hand and stopped him. "Okay, Charles Martin! That is quite enough. No more of that in here. Papa wouldn't approve."

"But it was because I was so happy! That's all."

"I understand," said Maria. "But Papa wants you to become a gentleman, and you must start to understand that you will no longer be without."

"Without what?" the boy said curiously.

"Anything a boy... a young gentleman... wants or needs. And if you're a good boy, I know Papa will make sure you have everything you'll need."

"And if I'm not a good boy? Will I get th' switch?"

Maria's expression turned somber. Was this his story of his past at the school? "I don't know. I hope that won't ever be necessary. You just have to learn to be a young gentleman."

"Gentleman? Y' means one of them that wears fancy black suits and turn-down collars and tall hats... and struts down th' street with a silver-handled walkin' stick?"

"Well, maybe not to that degree, yet, but Papa will expect you to have good manners and dress and act nicely... not like some primitive imp."

"Okay, Maria," said Charles. "I'll try real hard."

That reply was all Maria could expect.

After a lunch of ham sandwiches and a rhubarb tart with custard that Helen served them in the dining room, Maria thought there would be enough time to trim Charles' hair, and perhaps a bath. She requested Helen to prepare the bath while she and Charles went to her upstairs dressing room. She sat him in a chair and draped a sheet around him. As she combed and snipped away at his wavy blonde hair, she could only hope that her efforts—to make this boy one of which her father could be proud—would not be in vain. Now that he had won her affection, it would be an unbearably painful day when the boy was sent back to the

Mission School, if he didn't measure up to her father's expectations, and somehow, she feared that was still a possibility.

"What does he do?" the boy asked.

"What do you mean?" Maria returned.

"Your *Papa.* He seems very nice. And he must be rich, to have such a fine house, and to buy me all those wonderful new clothes."

"Well, yes, Papa is quite well-to-do. He's a riverboat pilot... and Mississippi River pilots are some of the best-paid professionals these days."

"Oh, that's grand! D'ya think he'd take me for a ride on his boat someday?"

"I'm sure he will, in due time, Charles. I'd bet that he has plans for your future. But you best not pester him about that just yet."

When she was through cutting, she held up her vanity mirror so he might see what she had done. Not accustomed to often seeing his own image, the reflection in the mirror pleased him.

Just then, Helen knocked at the open door. She held two bundles wrapped in brown paper and tied with string. "These were delivered from Mr. Markos just a few minutes ago," she said, and then she eyed the youngster with his perfectly fashioned new haircut.

He threw back the sheet from around his shoulders and smiled. "Do you like it, Miss Helen?" he said.

Helen felt her reluctance to having a young boy in the house melting away. His charm was busy working its magic on her, too, but she resisted the urge to run into the room and kiss his rosy cheeks. She smiled. "Maria did a very nice job on your haircut... very handsome, indeed." Then Helen turned to leave, but quickly returned. "Maria," she added, "the bath is ready for Master Charles in his room."

"Thank you, Helen," Maria replied, and Helen carried the packages to Charles' room and disappeared down the stairs.

Maria guided the boy down the hallway to another bedroom. She ushered him inside, where Helen had left the new clothing on the bed, and where a bathtub filled with warm water rested in the middle of the room.

Charles gazed around the nicely decorated room. Royal blue drapes half covered a large window; a full-length mirror hung on one wall; on another wall was a painting of mountains and a river; a bird's-eye maple gentleman's dresser stood beside a matching East Lake double bed, a thick soft mattress covered with a plush royal blue quilt. Charles had never seen anything quite like it before. "What room is this?" he questioned.

"Your bedroom," Maria said.

"This is *my* room?"

"Yes," Maria replied. "All yours."

"Y' mean... this is where I'll sleep? All th' time?"

"Yes, Charles. This will always be *your* room. And Helen has prepared a nice warm bath for you. When was the last time you had a bath?"

"Last Saturday," Charles said. "Saturday is always my bath day at the sch..." He hesitated.

"What's wrong?" Maria asked.

"Mr.... I mean... Sir... I mean, *Father*... said I should forget everything about th' old school."

Maria smiled an understanding smile. "That's okay. Now you can have your bath in the privacy of your own room anytime you wish."

"Y' mean... right now?"

"Sure." Maria turned to examine the wrapped bundles on the bed. "Then we can see the new clothes Mr. Markos sent you, and you can try them on." When Maria looked his way again, Charles had disrobed completely, his old Mission clothes in a heap on the floor. The sight of him naked took her breath away. Now she understood why he could perform all those difficult acrobatic stunts so easily—he was quite muscular and well developed for his age. But there was something else that drew her attention: his reflection in the mirror behind him revealed several red scars, like those made by a whip, on his back and buttocks. She turned away quickly.

"What's wrong, Maria?"

"It's... it's not proper for me to see you... like that."

"Why?"

"Because I'm a lady, and you're a bo... a gentleman."

"So what? Mother Champlain saw me like this many times. She even put ointment on the sores after I got wh..." Charles stopped and thought for a moment. "There I go again... rememberin' th' old school."

He climbed into the tub and submersed himself up to his neck into the warm, soothing water. "You can look again. I'm under the water now."

Maria reluctantly turned toward the bathing boy. "The soap is on that little table behind the tub, and your towel is on the bed. I'll be in my room down the hall. Call for me when you're done and I'll help you with your new clothes."

Chapter 14

Captain Gordon returned home just before six o'clock. Helen took his coat and hat to be hung in the hall closet under the staircase. "Supper will be on the dining room table in about twenty minutes," she told him. "And I have your coffee waiting for you in the den."

The captain was glad he had Helen; she always satisfied him with the simplest pleasures... like coffee waiting in the den.

"And where are Maria and Charles?" he asked.

Helen grinned. "Oh, they will be down in time for supper, I'm sure."

"Did Mr. Markos come by to measure the boy?"

"Sure, he did."

"Good. Then I trust we will see the boy clad in descent clothes in a few days."

Helen just grinned some more, knowing the surprised look on Mr. Gordon's face would soon be a priceless treasure. She returned to the kitchen while Gordon went to the den to enjoy his evening coffee before supper.

He was reading the newspaper when Helen announced that supper was ready. Gordon followed her into the dining room where he sat down at the head of the table. He seemed a little irritated that the others were not already there. He should not have to wait for them.

"Oh, be patient, for once," Helen said. "Maria has been busy tutoring your little *gentleman* all afternoon. I think I hear them coming down the stairs now."

In all her radiant beauty Maria entered the room dressed in a lovely pale blue evening gown, appropriate for a formal dinner. She stepped aside to reveal behind her an attractively dressed, handsome young man standing in the doorway. His golden hair, trimmed and perfectly combed, glistened in the lamp light; his dark blue suit fit him precisely over a crisp white shirt with turn-down collar and black batwing tie; his boots shined like a newly-minted Double Eagle.

At first glance, Captain Gordon wondered what stranger his daughter had invited to supper, and then the astonishment overcame him as he realized the stranger was his newly-adopted son, Charles Martin. He looked the boy over from head to toe. The new clothes seemed to define the boy's well-cut features in a different air. The captain was speechless.

Charles offered Maria his arm and escorted her to her chair on her father's right, held the chair for her as she sat. Then he quietly crossed behind the captain, pulled out his chair and sat down, a worried half-smile dimpling his cheeks as he glanced at Maria and then at the captain, and then looked down into the tablecloth.

The captain watched, still unable to make a sound.

"Papa!" cried Maria. "Say something. Anything. Don't you approve?"

Helen stood by, grinning. She hadn't seen anything this amusing in that house for years.

"Yes, yes, my dear," the captain finally spurted out as he continued to stare at the boy. "I just don't know what to say."

That remark was quite unexpected, as the captain usually voiced freely his opinions and comments in any situation. "Well, you could start by telling Charles that he looks nice... that his new clothes are very attractive."

Gordon gave his daughter and indignant stare. Then he turned to Charles. "Are you the same raggedy little boy I left here this morning?" he asked with a warm smile.

"Y-yes, sir, I-I believe so, sir," said Charles nervously.

"Well, it looks as though my daughter has performed some sort of miracle in the span of a few short hours." He turned back to Maria. "But where did these clothes come from. Mr. Markos said he'd be at least a week getting them finished."

"Ready-made, Papa. Mr. Markos had these in his store. Aren't they nice? He sent over enough so Charles would have something to wear until next week."

"Smart," the captain said. "That Markos has a good head on his shoulders. Now, Helen, I believe we're ready to eat."

All the fine China plates, silver, and sparkling glassware captured Charles' attention; for the moment he forgot his hunger until Helen brought in a platter with a dome-shaped cover, and soon the aroma of roasted beef filled the room. She carefully set the platter on the table next to the captain, removed the cover, and eyed Charles with uncertain admiration; she still wasn't completely comfortable with the idea of a boy in the house, especially a little heathen dressed in angel's clothing.

Charles grabbed his knife and fork in fisted hands and tapped their handles on the table at either side of his plate with eager anticipation.

"Put those down, Charles, and be patient," said the captain.

The boy quickly obeyed; his hands dropped to his sides and he watched with big eyes as Mr. Gordon began slicing the roast.

"Would you like a piece of meat now, my dear?" he said to Maria.

She held her plate close to the platter so her father could easily fork a dainty slice of beef onto it. Then he turned to Charles. "How about you, my boy? Would you like some meat now?"

"Oh yes, sir. A big piece... please." His eyes beamed.

The captain frowned just a little, and then gave the boy a generous chunk of meat on his plate.

"We don't get meat like this at th' school... only in stew... if ever," Charles said, and he started cutting and devouring the succulent meat at a furious pace.

"Easy does it!" said the captain. "And what did I say about you speaking of the old school?"

Charles stopped chewing abruptly, glanced at Maria, and then at Gordon. "I'm used to eating fast, 'cuz th' bell will ring and we have to make room at th' table for th' next..." He hesitated a long moment in thought. "Oh... th' bell won't ring here, will it?"

"No, my boy," the captain said sternly. "There are no bells here to make you hurry through your supper. Now, you don't have bread or vegetables yet. And try to behave like Maria and me at the table..."

"Papa," Maria intervened. "Don't be so hard on the boy all at once, or he can't enjoy his supper."

Gordon gazed at his daughter, saying nothing, but his eyes said, *"I see you have become quite fond of the boy."*

Charles accepted a boiled potato and a slice of bread on his plate only because he thought he *had* to, and then went back to the savory beef that was such a treat to him, this time at a painfully slow pace.

Except for the distinct ticking of the clock, for the next few minutes there were no sounds in the dining room but knives and forks scraping on the plates while all three continued their meal. Then the captain broke the silence. "So, tell me, son," he said in a non-threatening tone. "How do you like your new clothes?"

Charles swallowed hard while he thought briefly about his answer. For quite obvious reasons, he was not accustomed to crisp new clothing. He thought the skin might be rubbed off his legs, and one boot pinched just a little, and the starched and buttoned collar might saw his head off. But he didn't dare complain of any of that for fear that something dreadful might result. "Oh, I like 'em just fine," he said. "I'm sure I'll get used to 'em if I may keep 'em."

"Well, of course you may keep them," the captain replied. "But you must promise to take care of them, like a good boy."

"Oh, yes, sir. I will try to be a very good boy." Charles started to reach for the captain's hand, a gesture that he intended to be one of warm appreciation and affection, but his sudden movement knocked a glass off the table. His instant reaction took him off his chair to retrieve it, but when he stooped down, he saw the glass was broken.

"Oh dear!" the captain exclaimed sharply.

The boy misinterpreted Gordon's remark as anger and in one swift movement he was cowered on the floor in a corner with his knees to his chest, sobbing. "I couldn't help it, sir. Don't beat me this time, sir. I promise it won't happen again."

He wanted to dash out of the room or leap out a window, but Helen was there kneeling beside him, preventing him from bolting away. "Bless your soul, you poor child," she said in a pitiful tone. She looked defiantly at the captain, knowing that he respected her position on maintaining good order in the household. "There shall be no beating of a child in this house," she added. Charles' cry for mercy had secured his future with the housekeeper.

Maria was there by him then, too, tears in her eyes. "It was an accident, that's all," she said to the boy softly as she read the agony in his spirit. She urged him to his feet and guided him to his chair at the table, remaining by his side as he clung tightly to her hand.

"I wasn't going to beat you." Gordon reached toward the boy, intending to gently stroke his hair, but Charles flinched away, like a frightened animal anticipating punishment.

"I thought you looked like you was," the boy said, still sobbing. "You sounded angry."

"Perhaps I looked a little cross because you were clumsy and broke the glass," Gordon said. "But I realize, now, that it really was an accident." Then he looked at Maria. "Come sit down again, my dear. Let's finish our supper."

She gently kissed the boy's blond head and returned to her seat.

"Charles," the captain said. "I don't want you to be afraid of me. You and I should become the best of friends... you have my word."

Charles wiped away his tears with a napkin, tried to smile, and then completed the gesture he had intended before the glass fell. He carefully laid his small hand on the captain's for just a moment, and he said not a word.

The meal was resumed, but Charles' appetite was gone. He even had difficulty eating just a little of the baked apple with cinnamon and cream. This most recent incident, along with the entire day's events, lay heavy on his mind. "Would it be all right if I went up to th' room where Maria said I will sleep?" he asked. "I am so very tired."

The captain called Helen into the dining room. "Will you please see Master Charles to his room and help him get ready for bed?"

If someone had told Helen that morning that she would be acting toward the boy as she was now, she would have laughed in utter denial. But in the course of just one day, the boy's charming innocence had captured her adoration. She graciously bowed to the captain and then offered her hand to the boy. "Come along, lad," she said. "You've had a long hard day. Let's get you tucked in."

When he was in his nightshirt and Helen had him settled into the big, comfortable bed, Charles looked up into her eyes. "Will he send me back to the Mission School?" he whispered hoarsely.

Helen smiled and hesitated while she brushed back his golden hair. "Not if *I* have anything to say about it, *Charlie Martin*."

He giggled. "You called me Charlie. I like that."

Helen just smiled. "Good night, Charlie," she whispered, kissed his forehead and then she turned for the door.

Downstairs, Captain Gordon and his daughter had retired to the den where Maria sat reading a book, and the captain sat in his chair pondering the incident with the broken glass and the boy's behavior. "Maria," he said quietly. "Do you think this boy could have been badly mistreated at the school?"

"Why do you ask, Papa?"

"By the way he expected to be beaten, when he broke the glass. I mean, do you suppose that it's just this one boy that is so terribly misbehaved?"

Maria had not yet spoken to anyone about what she had witnessed earlier that day when she saw the boy naked, because that would have been a great embarrassment to her. But now that her father had asked, she would find some way to justify why she, a sophisticated young lady of twenty, had been viewing the naked body of a twelve-year-old boy. "He has scars on his back," she said, looking up from her book.

"What kind of scars?" the captain asked.

"Like... marks made by a whip."

"And just how do you know this?"

"Oh, Papa," cried Maria. "I know it was wrong, but I... I happened to see him without his clothes as he was getting into his bath this afternoon. It was purely an accident that I saw him, Papa... please believe me."

"There, there, Maria. You did nothing wrong. He's just a child needing someone to care for him. It would be no different than if we had reared him from infancy. You would have bathed him many times over."

"Thank you, Papa, for understanding."

"Okay, my dear. Now tell me about the scars."

"He even admitted it. He said this nurse—he called her Mother Champlain, I believe—would put ointment on his back for him after he had been punished."

"And did he mention who had administered the punishment?"

"No, Papa. And I didn't ask. And I don't think you should ask him either."

"Just the same, I believe that I will have a talk with Mr. Stanley about it... just the same."

That night about eleven o'clock when Maria went up to bed she couldn't resist steeling softly into Charles' bedroom, where the moonlight through the window allowed her to notice the sparkle on his cheek. *Poor child,* she thought. *He's been crying.*

She leaned over him and kissed his forehead. Her presence must have influenced his dreams. He moaned a little whimper and smiled.

At that moment Maria became aware that her father was at the door looking on. The next moment she was in his arms.

"Bless you, my dear," he said softly. "I took this on as my challenge, so that I might give you a brother, and that I might have a son. And it seems that this poor little ignorant fellow with his rough ways has roused some strong feelings."

"Yes," Maria whispered. "He needs us. And I think we need him."

Maria had been right—Charles had cried himself to sleep, feeling in his inexperienced fashion that he had failed to please the captain; that he had disgraced himself; that Mr. Stanley was right— he was truly a bad boy; that he would soon be returned to the harsh environment of the orphanage.

Circumstances, however, were influencing his future in ways he could not yet dream of.

Chapter 15

Captain Gordon laid down his pen on the desk when Maria and Charles came into the den. The boy was dressed this morning in more casual-looking clothes—a nicely-pressed white shirt and crisp blue denim trousers—although to him they seemed a bit stiff and scratchy, still not accustomed to the newness. His golden hair was neatly combed and a sheepish smile dimpled his cheeks.

"Ah, good morning, my dear," the captain said to Maria, and then gazed at the boy. "And don't you look just like a little gentleman this morning? Did you sleep well, Charles?"

"Oh, yes sir," Charles beamed. "You should see that bed up in my... er... th' room where I slept. It is *so* big and soft."

Gordon chuckled. "Yes, my boy, I *have* seen that bed."

"We have been filling Charles' dresser drawers with his new things, and hanging his shirts and trousers," Maria said.

Charles put his hand on Maria's arm but kept his eyes on Mr. Gordon. "Yeah, such a lot of things, an' she said that room is to be *my* room... all th' time. Is that so?"

Gordon smiled. "Yes, son, that is very true."

"Papa," Maria said impatiently. "I have some errands to do in town. Is it alright if Charles stays here with you for a while?"

"Why, of course, my dear." He glanced down at Charles. "You can sit here in the den and amuse yourself with a book while I finish my reports." He turned back to the papers on his desk and picked up his pen.

Charles peered around the room at the many books lined up on the shelves that occupied nearly two walls. Then he looked at Maria again. "Can't I just go with you?" he whined.

"Not now, Charles," Maria replied. "I will be very busy with things you would not enjoy at all."

Charles' expression drooped like a wilted flower.

"Later on," Maria said as she knelt by him. "When I come back, we'll go for a long walk by the river, okay?"

"Okay," he said, still sounding quite crestfallen, and he turned and plodded over to the book shelf.

Maria stood and called to her father. "I will see you in about two or three hours."

Mr. Gordon briefly glanced up from his work and gave a little wave as Maria turned and disappeared through the doorway.

Charles stared at the books, just as he had done so many times at the school. There were more books here than at the school, but they certainly didn't appear to be the kind of books he could enjoy. After taking several down from the shelf, he finally found one with many pictures. He sat down on a chair, opened the book on his knees and flipped through the pages, carefully studying the various scenes of landscapes from around the world. Quite some time had passed when he raised his eyes to have a good long look at Mr. Gordon as he sat frowning in deep thought, and scribing a few words on the paper every now and then.

He wondered what the other boys at the school would be doing. Some of them would surely be tending the cows in the pasture, and some would be shoveling the manure out of the barn. Some would be working in the huge vegetable garden, and the older boys would be chopping wood and stacking it in the woodshed for the coming winter. And some would be in the classroom, reading, or learning arithmetic, or practicing writing words and sentences.

Just then the grandfather's clock across the room chimed ten o'clock. Charles looked once again at Mr. Gordon who was still concentrating on his paperwork. "What time will Maria get back," he asked, as impatient boys will do.

"In a couple of hours," Gordon responded without even lifting his eyes from the desktop. "Just keep reading your book." He went on writing with great interest.

But not so with Charles. He had lost most of his interest in the picture book. He yawned and rubbed the back of his neck. Then he reached down to try to relieve some of the pinching of one boot. With legs stretched out, his arms went up over his head waving around in little circles. All that energy wanting to be in motion.

Then he thought he would try to walk around the room with the big book balanced on his head, which he easily did. There was no challenge in that. But when he passed by the open window, his interest was drawn to the hummingbird buzzing and darting about among the flowers just outside.

"Mr. Gordon, Sir?" he called out.

"What is it, my boy? And you shouldn't be addressing me as *Mr. Gordon*... you should be calling me *Father*... or *Papa*, like Maria does."

"Alright, Sir... F-Father, Sir." It was difficult for him to say; there hadn't been quite enough time, yet, for him to fully grasp the family concept, one which he had never really known. "What I really wanted to know... is that your garden out there?"

"Yes, of course, that's my garden."

"May I go out in it?"

"Yes, of course you may," the captain said, still unaware that the boy was balancing a book on his head.

Charles returned the book to its proper place on the shelf and there was the sound of several quick footsteps. With a single bound he was through the open French window and out upon the lawn. The captain didn't notice the boy's method of exit.

And what a wonderful garden it was! All the neighbors said that Captain Gordon's was the best garden for miles around. It was filled with all sorts of flowers—columbine, bluebells, violets, roses and daffodils—growing in great clumps among clusters of white paper birch trees and arbor vitae. There were rhododendron, and cherry and apple trees. Charles wandered past a little rock-lined pond where water lilies and cattails thrived, half-surrounded by weeping willows. Neatly-trimmed elderberry shrubs bordered a stone walkway on one side, and a mass of iris and lilies and geraniums on the other. The walkway meandered to an area of more trees—maples and black walnut, and beyond that were trellises crawling with grape vines that kept hidden the less attractive vegetable garden. Behind another row of apple and plum trees stood a glass-roofed hot house and an eight-foot high stone wall that extended from either end of the hot house past some pine trees and out of Charles' line of sight. He had never seen the likes of such a magnificent, beautiful garden. The simple vegetable garden in which he had often worked at the school was nothing compared to this.

"I wonder what is on the other side of that wall," he mumbled to himself as he gawked at the massive rock structure. His eyes surveyed the top of the wall to where it turned abruptly and tapered downward following the angle of the hot house roof to a height of about four feet. With his strength and agility he could easily scale that wall, and discover what lay beyond.

Chapter 16

"Well, lookee there!" exclaimed James, watching the boy from behind a grape vine trellis. He had been busy pulling some weeds in the cucumber patch and didn't notice the stranger as he passed by on the walkway. Mr. Gordon's gardener, James Wilkins, took much pride in the garden, and because he did most of the work maintaining it, he considered it *his* garden, and Captain Gordon was just someone he allowed to walk through it and admire it whenever he took a notion to do so. But of course, if it weren't for Maria, there wouldn't be so gosh-darn many flowers, some of which grew among the vegetables and fruit trees. He considered them a nuisance when he had to negotiate around them to get to his apples and plums that grew by the bushel and his strawberries and raspberries that were surpassed by no other in the entire county.

James could tolerate Helen's passion for herbs in the vegetable garden, but he still found plenty to grumble about, like blight and birds.

"It's the blightiest garden I ever did see," he'd complain. "And a man might spend all his life keeping the birds down with a gun."

But James did not spend any part of his life keeping the birds down with a gun. The captain caught him shooting one day. "How dare you, James?" he yelled. "I will not have a single bird destroyed on this property!"

"Then you won't get any fruit, 'cause the birds will get it all," James had responded.

"Without the birds, sir, we will be overrun with slugs and snails and harmful insects. No sir, you will not harm the birds. Is that clear, Mr. Wilkins?"

So naturally, Maria was ever so grateful to her father for protecting her beloved creatures, and in season they brightened every day with color and song.

But right now, James was not concerned about the birds. He was agitated by another creature—a strange boy dressed in pretty clothes who climbed to the top of the rock wall as easily as would a cat. Finally, he knew why some of his fruit had disappeared. He was about to catch, red-handed, the culprit that was stealing his apples and plumbs. If only Mr. Gordon had not banned the use of his gun, he'd take the thief down with a single shot.

Charles was unaware that he was being watched, nor was he concerned that his peer would be a potential enemy. He sat on his heels, holding his balance with his hands atop the wall gazing at the quiet, lazy little river some distance on the other side. Across the river he saw tamarack, jack pine, and blueberry bushes.

"Who is that boy?" James mumbled. "Never seen him before. Must be some city kid come out here to steal my apples." He grabbed a bean pole from the garden and began his stealth approach to the wall, concealing himself behind the plum trees. Then he couldn't believe his eyes when the mystery boy got on all fours, scooted down the wall a good distance, turned, and with the grace of a circus performer, kicked his heels up into the air so he was standing on his hands, then *walked* on his hands back toward the hot house.

"He's gonna fall and break his fool neck," James mumbled. But then he saw the boy get back to his feet, and he rushed to the wall to intercept the intruder before he could get away. Poking at the boy with the bean pole, he yelled: "You git down from there, right now, you thievin' little tomcat! D'ya hear? Come down, I say! I should kill ya for stealin' my apples!"

Charles, to say the least, was startled... and frightened. A crazy man with a big stick wanted to kill him! But he felt somewhat trapped there on top of the wall. It was too dangerous to jump off the other side as there were jagged rocks and boulders below. The man didn't look like he was capable of climbing up the wall after him, so the best thing to do was wait. Maybe the lunatic would give up and leave. All the while the man kept poking the stick at him and yelling. But then it appeared as though the man was going to try to climb the wall. Charles looked to his right. He could easily jump to the peak of the hot house, cross over to the wall on the other end, and be gone before the man realized where he had gone. It seemed like a simple solution.

He jumped to the roof peak. He turned to see how far the man had progressed. But the man had seen his move, and was backing down off the wall. Charles knew he had little time to make his way across the roof to the other wall. He started stepping cautiously along the peak. Confidence in his sense of balance would see him through this predicament, he was certain.

Then, suddenly the man shouted at him. "Git down from there, you little rat!" He was still waving the bean pole in the air as if it was a spear and he was a savage warrior, thirsty for blood. This interrupted Charles' concentration of balance. His foot slipped and went crashing through one of the glass roof panels. The next thing he knew, *he* was falling through the window frame, luckily now void of its glass. But he managed to catch himself with his arms wrapped around the rafters on each side, and there he hung, suspended with his bare feet dangling inside the greenhouse.

Chapter 17

Captain Gordon did not realize the lapse of time when Maria opened the door to the den. "I'm back," she announced, proudly showing off her curly new hair style.

"Why, you look absolutely stunning, my dear," her father said.

Maria gazed around the room. "Where's Charles?"

"The boy. Yes... well... I thought he was here."

Just then the tinkling of breaking glass was heard, and immediately following was the gruff shouts of James, the gardener: "Here! You just come down from there!"

The captain leaped to his feet and rushed to the open window, Maria on his heels. "Wilkins," he shouted. "What is going on out there?"

"I've caught me a thief," was the gardener's response. "You'd better come quick!"

"Better stay here, my dear," the captain said. "Could be danger." He quickly headed for the door out to the garden.

But this was one time that Maria decided to disobey her father. She suspected something entirely different from what the gardener was claiming. Following closely behind the captain, they hurried down the pathway to the hot house where the shouts were coming from.

"Ah... glad you're here," said James. "Finally got one of 'em."

"One of what?" said Gordon in a disgusted tone.

"One o' them scoundrels tryin' t' steal our fruit."

"Oh! Papa! Look!" cried Maria, pointing to the roof.

"Why, Charles," the captain called out. He stared wildly at the boy, bare feet and legs kicking, searching blindly for some support. "What on earth are you doing up there?" he snarled.

"It's all right," the boy said calmly. "Only one pane broke."

James scratched his head, confused. The captain seemed to know this boy.

"How did you ever get into such a position?" cried Maria.

"Couldn't help it," Charles answered. "That crazy man there was after me with that big stick, tryin' to kill me."

Gordon glared at James. "Is this so?" he said angrily.

"Well, yes, sir, I s'pose it is," said the gardener. "Y' see, I seen him up on the wall... figured he'd come stealin' apples. Told him t' come down, but he wouldn't... and then he fell through the hot house winder."

"Did ya' think I was gonna come down when you was swingin' at me with that big stick?" Charles called out.

"You had no business up on our wall," James said. "Now look at the damage you've done."

"That will be quite enough, Wilkins," Gordon said sternly.

"But I didn't know it was someone you knew," James said in his defense.

"No, of course you didn't."

"Ah... ain't somebody gonna help me get down," Charles said in desperation.

"Oh, yes," Gordon said. "Keep still so you don't cut yourself."

"I already have cut myself, and it's bleeding," said the boy. "D'ya s'pose somebody could get a ladder?"

"Wilkins!" shouted the captain. "Go to the tool shed and get a fruit ladder! Hurry!"

Maria cried in sympathy. "Are you hurt badly, Charles?"

"I d'know," he replied. "Hurts a little bit. Is that crazy man coming back soon with th' ladder?"

"Yes, Charles, he is," said Maria. "And I'm sure he didn't mean to harm you. You're a good boy."

Charles smiled down at her. "No, I ain't. I try to be. But I ain't a good boy. I broke this here window. S'pose I'll get the switch this time, for sure."

Maria didn't answer. She didn't know what to say.

Charles saw James coming with the ladder long before Maria and the captain knew he was near. "Here he comes, and I'm glad, because my arms are starting to hurt."

"Hang on, Charles," Gordon said. "We'll get you down real soon."

James leaned the ladder against the rafter and held it tight, so as not to let it slip. Charles found a rung with one foot and managed to support his weight well enough to let go with one arm, and then cautiously stepped down the ladder. When he reached the bottom, James stepped away and Gordon was there waiting with a stern frown.

"I'm very sorry, sir," Charles said.

"You rascal," 'Gordon said, seizing the boy's shoulder with a firm grip. "Where is you jacket, and where are your boots?" he asked, staring down at the boy's bare feet.

"I didn't have a jacket, sir, and my boots are under a little cedar by the pond."

"Well then, let's fetch them and go back to the house."

Chapter 18

n the house, Mr. Gordon examined the boy's arms. The cuts were not severe, no more than scratches, and the bleeding had already stopped.

"Now Charles," he said, looking the boy straight in his eyes. "I suppose you know that I am very much displeased."

"Yes, sir. I don't wonder a bit. Do I get the switch now?"

Gordon bit his lip. "No, not now. But I want you to go to your room and get washed up. Put on some clean clothes, and then come back down."

Charles glanced at Maria, but she looked away. He went slowly to his room.

When they were alone, Gordon said: "I'm afraid I shall have to send him back to the school."

Maria fixed her gaze on him.

"I expected him to be a little rough," he continued. "But it seems that he is just too wild. What do you think, my dear? He's too bad to keep?"

After a few moments of silence, Maria spoke softly. "Yes, there are some things about the boy that are distasteful. But on the other hand, I can't help but like him."

"Yes, I know. Sometimes I think he deserves a good thrashing, but I know I could never lay a hand on him. Oh, what should I do? Send him back?"

"No, Papa. If you intend to adopt a boy, this is the one you are meant to have. I think he *is* a good boy inside, and that good boy deserves a chance to show himself."

Just then Helen came in and announced that lunch was ready and waiting in the dining room, and Charles appeared. He was clean and dressed properly.

"May I have some lunch, too?" he asked shyly. "I am so very hungry."

"Yes, of course. But do you have anything else to say?"

"Well, sir, I'm very sorry about breaking that window. I was afraid of the crazy man chasing me with that big stick. I wasn't doing anything wrong when he came after me. Please believe me."

"Yes, I understand. But I have been discussing with Maria about sending you back to the Mission School."

"Sending me back, sir?"

"Yes. I want a good boy; you have been quite a rascal."

"I don't want to be bad," the boy cried. "Honest."

Maria couldn't bear the anguish any longer. She put her hands on the boy's shoulders and steered him toward the dining room. "Come, Charles. Let's go have our lunch."

Charles ate very little of the baked chicken, even though he had been quite hungry. He saw the disappointment in Maria's eyes, but he didn't realize it was her disliking of her father's actions that made her frown. When he had eaten all he could, he asked to be excused so that he might go to his room.

Helen escorted him from the dining room, whispered in his ear, "Everything will be alright," and then immediately returned to the dining table.

"Mr. Gordon, sir, with all due respect, may I give you a bit of motherly advice?"

"Please do."

"I helped you raise your daughter to be a fine young lady."

"That you did, Helen, and I am most grateful."

"I have been watching the proceedings with this young boy. Did you not bring him into your home to show him the value of family? And to make him a gentleman by virtue of good family life?"

"I did, indeed."

"And did you not vow to be a good father to him, and show him love and affection?"

"Y-yes, I did."

"Well, don't you realize that this boy has never known what those values are supposed to be? Fine clothes and a comfortable bed are important, but he needs more than that. He needs something more than scolding. Everything that has happened to make him look bad has been because someone or something pushed him in the wrong directions. The broken water glass happened only because he was nervous and uncomfortable with your lecturing him about how to eat his supper. And today, he was just being a boy. Boys explore new and unfamiliar territory. They go barefoot, and climb, and spend their energy. That's all he did. And then James came along and frightened him into breaking the window. The boy didn't do anything wrong. It's all of us who have been wrong. So far, Mr. Gordon, you haven't shown him what a father really is. And Maria is absolutely right—he is a good boy inside, and he deserves a chance. And one more thing—if you decide that he should stay, try calling him *Charlie*. He likes that. I know."

Reluctantly, Mr. Gordon smiled. He knew Helen was right. He knew Maria had made an accurate evaluation of the boy. *Charlie was here to stay.*

Chapter 19

Captain Gordon spent a great deal of time away from home during the summer months. His employer, the McDonald Brothers, Black River logging magnates, as well as the owners of a riverboat fleet, kept him busy piloting on the Mississippi. Capable pilots were in demand, and therefore were paid quite well—the highest-paid profession of the day.

Charlie Martin settled into his new lifestyle, exercising great effort to avoid activities that might entice a boy into mischief—which included just about everything. He was quite certain that the gardener, James Wilkins, did not like him after the incident involving the wall and the hot house window that he fell through. So the only time he dared venture out into the garden was when Maria would accompany him; they would go for long walks out past the barrier wall where they could access the riverbank. Charlie particularly enjoyed strolling there, for there was a part of him, deep inside, that seemed somewhat familiar with the more natural terrain, and he felt comfortable with it. Not that he disliked the nicely groomed garden—he loved that too. But he never knew when Mr. Wilkins might be lurking about.

Occasionally, while exploring the riverbank, Charlie saw other boys fishing along the opposite side of the little river. They seemed to be enjoying the activity, and Charlie knew he would enjoy it, too... if he were allowed to do it. One of Mr. Stanley's assistants at the Mission School had taken the boys in small groups on fishing excursions several times to a much smaller stream where they caught a few trout. Charlie caught only one, and it was rather small, but at least he had *some* experience. And how much mischief could he possibly get into by fishing?

In time, Maria tired of the walks along the river; she would stay in the garden and admire her beautiful flowers and take in all the fragrances. Every day she would cut a bouquet of fresh blossoms for the house, and meanwhile, she would send Charlie off on his own to enjoy the riverbank.

After several days of noticing the same boy across the river, he decided that this must be a good spot—for the same boy to return every day—and he thought he would ask Maria if she could help him acquire some fishing gear.

"Papa will be home soon," she said. "You'd better ask him."

Later that evening when Captain Gordon arrived, he appeared exhausted and informed Helen that he didn't need any supper, that he had already eaten aboard the boat with his crew. He only wanted a small glass of brandy with his coffee in the den, and then he would go to bed, as he had to rise early the next morning; awaiting his boat was another raft of logs and lumber to be towed down the Mississippi to Dubuque.

While he sipped his coffee, Charlie came into the den and stood at his side.

"Well, there's my boy!" the captain said. "How are you getting along?"

"Very well, sir," Charlie replied with a grin. But then a slight frown of disappointment took away the smile. "Miss Helen says you have to leave again early in the morning."

"Yes, I'm afraid so, Charlie. 'Tis a busy time on the river right now."

"May I come with you on your boat, Sir?"

The captain smiled, proud that his adopted son was showing some desire to spent time with him. After all, it had been his intension to eventually teach Charlie to be a river pilot. "Someday... when you're a little older," he said. "Maybe when you grow a little more, Mr. McDonald will let me bring you on as a deckhand... to start."

"Okay," the boy said. He didn't know what a deckhand was, but he liked the sound of it. "But what I really came to ask you..."

"Yes, Charlie. What is it?"

"Well, I want to go fishing in that little river down behind the wall.

But Maria said I have to wait for you."

"Do you know how to fish?"

"Oh, yes, sir. Otto used to take us boys from the school fishing. He taught me. I caught a dandy trout once."

"Well, then. I don't see any reason that you can't go fishing."

"But I don't have a pole... or line... or hooks."

"Well, I used to do some fishing, and there's a nice cane pole and everything you might need out in the carriage house. I'll set it out for you before I leave. It all belongs to you now."

"Oh, thank you, Sir!" Charlie beamed with joy. He was about to do cartwheels around the room, but then he thought better of it.

"And you know, Charlie," Gordon continued. "Fish don't usually bite after an empty hook."

"No, Sir, they don't," the boy replied. He had been contemplating that as his next obstacle.

"I'm sure if you ask James, he will help you dig up some worms."

"But Mr. James doesn't like me, Sir."

"Oh, nonsense. You ask him in the morning."

The next morning during breakfast Charlie excitedly told Maria about the gift of all the fishing gear from the captain. She seemed quite delighted at first, that Charlie finally had an activity of his own. She had scolded him for throwing stones, when she finally realized that the birds were the targets of his favorite pastime. He had promised not to, but she feared that he still might torment the creatures when he was out of her view. So, with fishing occupying his time, maybe he wouldn't bother the birds anymore.

Then an expression of worry crept onto her face. Fishing, for all practical purposes, should be a harmless activity, but considering Charlie's past record, she wondered if he needed supervision. But her father had given his approval.

After breakfast Charlie darted out to find the cane pole, recalling the instructions and advice he had received from Otto, who had been a fisherman all his life, the river and streams always holding more attraction for him than work. It was a well-known fact that he always knew where to find the fish, but Charlie could not rely on him now for that information. He was on his own.

He discovered the cane pole and all the tackle that Mr. Gordon had promised. It was a splendid bamboo pole, with strong silk line, a cork float glistening with blue and white paint, and at least a dozen extra hooks in a square metal can with a lid. He had everything he needed except bait, and he was not particularly fond of seeking the gardener for help. He thought about finding a spade and digging for worms himself, but the consequences of turning over a bit of soil in James' garden without his permission could be much worse.

James saw the boy coming, but he pretended not to notice and went about his business of cutting dead leaves and branches from the High Bush Cranberry shrubs. "What mischief is he up to now?" he grumbled under his breath, and then he became aware that the boy was searching for him. Avoidance was no longer an option, as Charlie had already spotted him.

"Hi, Mr. James, sir," Charlie said boldly.

The gardener just grunted.

"Would you please help me dig some worms?"

"Ain't got time t' be bothered..." he said gruffly. He hesitated. "Worms?"

"Yes, sir," said Charlie. "I'm goin' fishing, and I want some worms... red ones... please?"

Then James changed his tone, as he, too, had a weakness for the line and hook. "Going fishing?"

"Yes, if I can find some worms."

"Alright. I'll dig you some. Go behind the grape vines, there, by the cucumber patch. Got a pot?"

Charlie shook his head.

"Alright," said James. "I'll get one."

Charlie waited by the cucumbers, and in a few minutes James returned with a five-tined fork and an old flower pot. Because the boy was a fellow angler suddenly seemed to supersede any former ill-feelings. He raked away some dry straw that covered the bare ground and then turned over a few big clumps of the moist soil, displaying plenty of wiggling red worms suitable for baiting a fishhook.

"There you are," James said after they had put a little bit of dirt and an ample supply of worms in the pot. He winked at the boy. "Now you can go fishing. There's a deep hole up near the end of the wall." Right then, James decided that *maybe* the boy wasn't *all* bad.

"Thank you, Mr. James, sir." And right then, Charlie decided that James Wilkins, the gardener, wasn't such a bad fellow after all.

Chapter 20

Charlie hurried down to the riverbank, found the spot that James had suggested, and for the next few minutes, in the shade of a large oak tree, he was busy fitting his tackle. All the while there was that same boy he had seen there many times before, squatting on the opposite bank and staring intensely at his fish line in the water before him, and by the time Charlie had baited his hook, the other boy had pulled in two silvery fish.

The river was only about forty feet wide at that point, and as Charlie prepared his line and hook, he watched the boy across the river, and he knew the boy was watching him, too.

He was dark-haired, dark-skinned, like he had spent his whole life baking in the sun, shabbily-dressed, and instead of a bamboo fishing pole and shiny float he used a rough hickory affair, and his float was just a common piece of wood. Before Charlie was ready to put his line in the water, the shabby-looking boy had caught another fish.

Charlie's heart beat faster with anticipation as at last he threw out his line as far as he could. The float and the baited hook splashed into the water, and the boy on the opposite bank chuckled.

"Why is he laughing at me?" Charlie mumbled to himself. He experimented with trying to watch the other boy with one eye and his float with the other, but that did not work so well, and he found himself gazing from one to the other, always quickly back at the float thinking that it had bobbed.

But the float did nothing but float and its only movement was from the ripples as the boy on the other side jerked his pole, making another strike, and pulled onto the bank yet another fish. In a nonchalant manner, Charlie lifted his line out of the water and swung it toward the bank, only to notice that the worm was gone. Trying to be very casual, conscious of the other boy watching him with critical eyes, he renewed the bait and threw it in again. But there was no bite, and as time went on, it seemed as all the fish had been attracted to the other side of the river where the shabby-looking boy skillfully brought in several more. Granted, they were not huge fish, but they *were* fish.

After another hour, the dark-skinned boy across the river wound the line around his crude wooden pole. He waved and smiled to Charlie as he picked up his basket of fish, briskly making his way along the bank among the jack pines. He stopped to pick a few blueberries, and then he went on. Charlie watched him until he was nearly out of sight, but then the boy thrust a canoe out from the bank, climbed into it, and paddled down the river.

"He's an Indian boy," Charlie said upon seeing the canoe. "No wonder he's such a good fisherman." Then he pondered some more. "If he comes back again, I'll talk to him. I'll find out his secret... how he catches so many fish."

Every morning for the next three days, Charlie hurried to the riverbank with his bamboo pole and flower pot of worms, expecting the Indian boy to return. But the bank on the other side of the river remained void of any fishermen. He had not made acquaintance with that Indian boy, but nonetheless, he felt lonely without him there. He continued to dangle his line in the river with not much more than an occasional nibble, and only once did a sucker take his hook. But he recognized it as a fish not worth taking home—Otto had taught him that —and so he removed it from the hook and threw it back into the river.

Three days of fishing without catching a single keeper can be quite discouraging for any angler, and for Charlie, this was no exception. On Saturday morning, the fourth day, he sat on the steps gazing out at the garden in despair when Maria came out, ready to find a fresh bouquet. She stopped, observed Charlie's gloomy expression, and sat down beside him. "Why, Charlie," she said. "You look quite unhappy today. Are you bored with the fishing already?"

"Well, the fish just aren't biting. I haven't caught a single one worth keeping. I *so* wanted to bring home a good fish dinner for us."

Maria gently caressed his shoulder with her hand. "Maybe the fish weren't hungry for the last few days. Maybe today they are, and today will be your day to catch some."

"D'ya really think so?"

"Sure! I hate to see you so sad. Why don't you go give it another try?"

With a little renewed spirit of encouragement, Charlie found his pole, trudged off to the cucumber patch where James helped him find some fresh worms, and headed toward the end of the wall to the river. After a few minutes of just staring into the water, a reflection caught his eye. It was the reflection of the Indian boy on the opposite bank. Charlie beamed a big smile and waved. The boy returned the greeting.

Charlie went about baiting his hook, and the Indian boy did the same. Within five minutes, the boy across the river struck at a bite and pulled in a fish. Charlie sat and watched his motionless float, working up the courage to call out to the other boy.

When the boy had landed another fish, Charlie finally said: "You sure are lucky!"

The boy smiled, baited his hook, and threw it out again, and just a few minutes later, he was pulling in another fish.

"You sure are lucky!" Charlie called out again.

"Not so much luck," the boy said, his voice easily passing over the water. "You baiting with red worms?"

"Yes, I surely am," Charlie answered.

"Well, I think you're not fishing deep enough," said the Indian boy.

"I ain't?"

"No. Put a little more line below your float… about two more feet."

Charlie thought he had arranged his tackle just the way Otto had taught him, but then he remembered that was when they were fishing for trout in a much smaller, shallower stream. He hauled in his line, attached the float to his line like the boy had told him, and tossed the baited hook back in the water. Sure enough, in about four minutes, Charlie felt a little tug on his line and the float bobbed repeatedly.

"Why don't you strike at it?" the Indian boy shouted.

"I don't think he has the hook yet," Charlie replied, a little excitement in his voice.

"Strike!" the boy yelled again.

Charlie jerked the pole, but up came an empty hook. He swung it back toward him, put on another worm, and tossed it back in the water. Meanwhile, the Indian boy had hooked another one, baited his hook and was patiently waiting for another bite.

Again, there was another sharp tug on Charlie's line.

"There! You've got another bite!" the Indian boy called out. "Look at him… he's trying to run away with it."

Little credit could have been given to Charlie for striking at this one at the right moment, as the unfortunate smallmouth bass had hooked itself. It darted back and forth below the surface, racing as far as the line would allow in one direction, and then the other, trying to escape. More than once Charlie almost lost his grip on the bamboo pole, his eyes widening with astonishment and disbelief as the big fish flew out of the water, momentarily suspended in mid-air, showing its size, and then splashed down again. Finally the creature tired and gave up the battle. Charlie hauled in the line, and this time he had the prize he'd been after.

"Magnifique, mon ami!" cried the boy from across the river. "What a fine fish!"

Charlie had been admiring the five-pound bass that lay at his feet in the grass, and then the boy's words registered. He glanced at the boy on the far bank who he thought to be Indian, but he remembered some of the boys at the Mission School who used those French words in their speech, of which he had learned the English translation by living with them for so long. But this boy didn't look anything like those French boys at the school.

Then the boy across the river called out again. "Au revoir, mon ami! No more fish will we catch today," he said as he waved and headed downriver to his canoe.

"Wait!" yelled Charlie. "Will you be back?"

"Oui, mon ami," the boy replied. "Yes, my friend, I shall return tomorrow afternoon… but on *your* side of the river."

Charlie nearly burst with pride as he displayed the big fish to Maria and Helen back at the house. "May we eat it for supper?" he asked Helen.

"Well, bless your heart, Charlie Martin!" Helen cried. There was no doubt that she was impressed with the catch. She took the fish from Charlie. "You certainly may," she said. "I'll have James clean it and cut it into fillets. It will make a fine supper for you and Maria."

"You see, Charlie?" Maria said. "I knew you would have better luck today."

He said nothing about the French-speaking Indian boy from across the river.

Chapter 21

Sunday morning had always been a time of worship for the Gordon household. But Maria had not attended church services for a while, since her father had to be gone on the river most of the time, and she wasn't comfortable with taking Charlie with her until she felt certain he would not embarrass her. Now that he had gone many weeks without serious incident, mainly because she had devoted most of her time to his conditioning and steering him away from his schoolboy chatter to a more gentlemanly manner of speech, Maria decided to bravely risk public opinion; they should go. Charlie wasn't extremely pleased with the idea, but he took his bath and dressed in his finest—starched white shirt with turned down collar, black tie, and waist coat, even though the weather was still quite hot.

James drove them to the church in the best carriage on that pleasant morning. When they arrived, the widow Mrs. Wood met them in the churchyard. "Well, good morning, Miss Gordon," she greeted. She gazed down at Charlie. "And this must be the captain's protégé."

Maria smiled. "Yes, this is Charles Martin," she said, and then introduced Mrs. Wood. "Charles, Mrs. Wood is a sister of Papa's best friend and colleague, Frank McIntyre. He's a riverboat pilot, too."

Charlie dimpled his cheeks with a boyish smile and bowed his head as a gesture of courtesy, like Maria had taught him, and then gazed around at all the people entering the church while the two women chatted some more.

"What did she mean?" Charlie asked when Mrs. Wood had walked away.

"Who? Mrs. Wood?"

"Why did she look sorry for me and call me a *potato jay?*"

Maria giggled. "Protégé—it's a French word for someone who is adopted or protected... like Papa is protecting you."

"Well, why did she laugh? Is that funny?"

Maria couldn't answer. She only recalled in her mind the conversation that her father had had with Frank about raising a gentleman from a lowly orphan. She tried to put it out of her thoughts as she guided the boy into the church.

She was thankful when the closing hymn had concluded, as Charlie had been quite restless all during the service. He participated nicely by singing the hymns and praying the *Lord's Prayer*, but just as young boys will, he was anxious to be on the move. Outside while the parishioners mingled and chatted in small groups, and while Maria and Charlie waited for James to pick them up again, Preacher Hornsby strolled toward them. "Ah, Miss Gordon... so good to see you here today. And who's this?" he asked, pretending not to recognize the boy. He visited the Mission School weekly, instructed Catechism to the children there, and had been one of the first to know about Captain Gordon's adoption. "Oh, yes," he said, raising his eye glasses to his face. "It's the captain's young protégé. Yes... I remember you now... and I suppose you remember me."

"Yes, I remember you," said Charlie. "You called me a stupid boy because I couldn't remember all of the *Apostle's Creed.*"

"Did I?" the preacher said, a little taken aback. "But you are not stupid now," he said in a guarded, lower tone, hoping that no one else overheard the boy's statement. "I dare say that you now remember every word."

"I don't think so," the boy replied honestly. "It's still hard to remember *every* word."

Maria turned a bright shade of red.

"But I'm not going to ask you to recite it now," said the preacher. "Miss Gordon will help you with it, I'm sure." He shook hands with both of them and nodded as they turned and walked to the gate where they stepped aboard their waiting carriage.

Chapter 22

Charlie was quite anxious to get back to the river. The Indian boy would surely return, and he was the closest thing to a playmate Charlie had seen since he left the Mission School, although he did not miss the other boys there so much. The Indian boy spoke kindly to him and offered him friendship—something he had not seen much of at the school. But his biggest fear was that Maria and the captain would not approve of this friend because he was shabby-looking, so for now, he would keep his new-found friend a secret.

More than an hour passed while Charlie sat on the riverbank

waiting for the mysterious boy to arrive. He thought about baiting his hook and tossing the line in the water, but it was such a pleasant day to just soak up the warm sunshine; there was scarcely a cloud in the sky. Birds sang and the scent of the jack pines drifted on a faint breeze.

"Why aren't you fishing?" a voice asked, and then Charlie realized he had been daydreaming. He hadn't noticed the Indian boy walking along the bank from where he had landed his canoe downstream.

"Oh! Hi," Charlie said. "Um... just got here. Nice day, isn't it?"

And so there they sat, that very mismatched pair, fishing on the bank of the La Crosse River, caring not much about anything else right then. The fish weren't biting, but it didn't seem to matter as they sat in silence, every now and then stealing a glance at each other.

After quite some time, there came a little bob to the Indian boy's wooden float. He gave a tug on the line, but an empty hook came out of the water. He put on another worm and threw it back in.

A couple of minutes later, Charlie's cork float bobbed, and then suddenly glided away beneath the surface. It took him by such surprise; he gave a tremendous jerk with his rod. The fish came sailing out of the water and up among the low, overhanging tree branches. The line caught there, and the fish hung suspended about a foot below a cluster of twigs, frantically flipping about, trying to get itself free.

The Indian boy burst into a roar of laughter, stamped his feet and slapped his knees, while Charlie stood with his pole in hand, tugging at the line.

"You'll break the line," the Indian boy said.

"But I want to get the fish down."

"You shouldn't have struck so hard. You'll have to climb out on that branch to get it."

Charlie stared at the tree for a moment, its branches extending out over the water. Then he stared at the water that looked frightfully deep and dark.

"Who taught you how to fish?" the Indian boy asked.

"Why, it was Otto, at the..." Charlie stopped short. He realized then that he was, perhaps, a little embarrassed to admit that he had lived nearly his entire life at the orphanage, even to this boy who he hardly knew.

"You mean Otto Simonton?" the boy asked.

"Yes, that's him," Charlie said. "D'ya know him?"

"Sure, I know him. We have fished together many times on the Mississippi. But I can't imagine Otto teaching you to chuck a fish up into a tree."

"He didn't. That part was sort of an accident."

"Say," the Indian boy said. "If it was Otto you been fishing with, are you one of them from the Mission School?"

Charlie's stare dropped to his feet. "Yeah... I used to live there."

"Oui... I see you there sometimes when I take the cows from town out to pasture. What's your name?"

"Charles Martin Gordon. But everybody now just calls me Charlie."

The Indian boy stepped closer and held out his right hand. "Pleased to meet you, mon ami, Charlie."

They shook hands and then the boy continued: "My name is Dominic Bouton."

Charlie gave the boy a peculiar stare. "You use so many French words, but you look..."

"Like an Indian?" Dominic finished the statement.

"Well... yeah."

"My father and two half-brothers are French, and living in that house, I learned the French ways. But my mother was Winnebago, and they say I inherited her dark skin and hair. That's why I sound French and look like an Indian."

"And you're so good at fishing. Did Otto teach you?"

"No, no, mon ami. My Winnebago uncle, Gray Wolf taught me how to hunt and fish."

Charlie glanced up to the tree branch where his line was caught and the fish still hung, and then he turned back to Dominic and grinned. "Guess Gray Wolf was a better teacher, huh."

They both laughed.

"I could teach you," Dominic said. "I know all the good places to fish."

"Could you?" Charlie said, awed by such an offer.

"Of course I could, any day... except Wednesday, Thursday, or Friday. Those days I tend the cows and earn my money."

"Earn your money?"

"Oui... to buy food."

"But doesn't your father buy your food?"

"My father is gone," said Dominic. And then, as if he was trying to avoid any further conversation about his father, he nodded toward Charlie's marooned fish line in the tree. "Gonna climb up there and get your line down?"

Charlie examined the tree once more, laid down his pole on the bank, and with determination in his eyes he began the climb. He quickly reached the limb protruding out over the water—the one that had entangled his line.

"That's it," said Dominic, watching from below as Charlie inched his way out along the branch. "Only four more feet and you should be able to reach the line."

Charlie couldn't see the line or the fish for the bushy foliage, so he had to rely on Dominic's guidance.

"It's about a foot in front of you," Dominic called out.

Charlie probed with one hand, hanging onto the branch and maintaining his balance with the other. When he finally found the line, it was too tangled to free with one hand.

"Have a knife?" said Dominic.

"Yes, in my pocket," replied Charlie.

"Maybe you can cut the small branches off... let it all drop down into the water. Then I can haul it in for you."

Charlie thought that was a reasonable solution, but it was not so easy getting the knife from his pocket, or opening the blade, as he was hanging in a very awkward position. All the while he was struggling with the knife, it seemed as though the tree limb was sagging lower under his weight.

Finally the branch with the tangled line was cut completely through. Branch, line, and fish fell to the water, and Dominic hastily reeled it onto the bank. Charlie closed the knife, and with a little difficulty managed to get it into his pocket again.

As Charlie attempted to work his way backward on the limb, he heard an ominous cracking noise. He paused for a moment, and with his next move came another loud, splintering crack. A moment later—PA-LOOSH! Branch and Charlie hit the water with a tremendous splash and both went down out of sight.

Although he knew it was a rather unfortunate situation for Charlie,

Dominic couldn't help but laugh. But then he slowly realized that Charlie wasn't coming up again. He could barely see that Charlie was free from the tree limb, but he seemed to be struggling, as if he might be injured.

Dominic quickly ripped off his shirt and trousers and dove into the dark water, and while still beneath the surface, in one smooth motion grasped Charlie around his chest and brought him to the surface, and then to the shore.

"Are you hurt, mon ami?" he asked Charlie when they were safely on solid ground.

"No, I don't think so," Charlie said, catching his breath.

"Then why—"

"I don't know how to swim."

"Little Otter will teach you."

"Little Otter? Who is Little Otter?"

"My Indian cousins call me Little Otter... because I swim under water... just like an otter."

Charlie examined his wet clothes that were now quite muddy, too, from climbing up the riverbank. "Thanks for saving me," he said. "Now I have to figure a way to save myself from Maria."

Dominic stared curiously. "Who is Maria?"

"She's... er... my sister. She'll be furious with me for ruining my clothes."

"Not if we wash them," suggested Dominic. "And while we're waiting for them to dry in the sun, I can teach you to swim."

It wasn't the worst idea, but then again, climbing out on that branch to retrieve the fish line seemed like a good idea, too, at the time. But at this point, Charlie had nothing to lose. "Okay... but under one condition," he said as he started unbuttoning his mud-stained shirt.

Dominic stared at him questioningly.

"That you promise not to let me drown."

Downstream a short way, they waded out into shallow water and scrubbed away the mud stains from Charlie's clothes, and then hung them in the tree in the afternoon sun. And for the next three hours, Charlie learned the basics of swimming. He was a fast learner when it came to physical activities, and the sport of swimming seemed to come easy. Once again, his strength and agility aided tremendously. He wasn't quite as good or as fast in the water as Dominic, yet, but with a little more training and practice he would get better.

After the strenuous workout, they sat on the bank letting the sun dry them off. When they were getting dressed, Charlie noticed the tiny leather pouch that Dominic hung around his neck. "What's that?" he asked.

Dominic clutched the little pouch in his hand and closed his eyes tightly for a moment. Then he opened his hand and looked at Charlie. "My uncle gave it to me, but it actually came from my grandfather. It is a medicine bag."

"Medicine bag?" It has medicine in it?"

"Oui, mon ami... but not the same kind of medicine you are thinking of. Indian medicine is different. It contains the good spirit of the earth, and if I keep it near me, it will drive away the bad spirits."

"You said your father was gone. Where is he?"

Dominic pointed a far-away stare out to the jack pines across the river. "I don't know," he said, his words soft and solemn. "Last year he took my brother, Louis, to Montreal. Louis was to enter Montreal College. He wanted to become a priest. But my father never came back."

Charlie thought a moment. He remembered from school lessons that Montreal was far away in Canada. "Do you think he stayed there?"

"No... his business is here. He would not stay. I fear something bad has happened to him."

"What about your mother and your other brother?"

"My mother rests in the churchyard. She has been dead four years. And Jacques... he went to the far west to become a trader, like my father, in the wilderness where many people are going now. He has been gone for more than a year."

"So... you're all alone."

"Oui."

Charlie put his arm around Dominic's shoulders. "There must be somebody who can help you."

"Why do I need help? My Indian cousins taught me to hunt and fish; I have a job to earn money for the things I cannot get from the forest; I have my canoe so I can cross the big river whenever I want. So, tell me, mon ami... why do I need help?"

"Why don't you go live with your Indian family?"

"I don't want to live like them, in huts and tepees... and nothing more than a heap of straw and a deer skin for a bed on the ground. *Mon Dieu!* I like my house and my bed."

"But... you're just a kid... like me."

"And we will soon grow, and we will survive. And you must promise one thing, Mon ami."

"What?"

"That you will tell no one who I am."

"Why not?"

"I have many friends in the town. I always speak French when I am around them so they won't think I am Indian, because many people are afraid of the Indians and think of them badly. If they find out I have Indian blood, they might not like me anymore."

Charlie pondered on the request for a few moments. It didn't seem unreasonable, and in just the past few hours, he had become quite fond of his new friend. Dominic had treated him better than anyone had ever treated him at the Mission School; he had given some good fishing advice; he had taught him how to swim. And how could he *not* honor a simple request from someone who had *saved his life?*

"Okay," said Charlie, offering to shake hands on the promise. "I won't tell anybody."

Chapter 23
June 1879

Charlie Martin had spent that entire fall, winter, and spring attending the school in La Crosse, while Dominic laid in a good supply of venison, smoked fish, and firewood, and had hunkered down in his cozy cabin on Barron's Island. They scarcely saw each other once Charlie started school.

Even with Maria's tutoring, Charlie wasn't a star pupil, not much more than average. But when the lessons were done, he listened intensely to Mr. Gordon as he talked about the river and steamboats, and told his stories about experiences with both. Captain Gordon was spending much more time at his home when the river froze, ending the shipping season on the Upper Mississippi; he and Charlie found more and more common ground as the weeks passed, and Charlie even started calling him *Captain.*

Charlie had made a few friends at his new school, but now that summer replaced the classroom, he thought more about his Indian friend from last summer. He hadn't seen Dominic since before Thanksgiving; he didn't know where the boy lived, and because he had promised not to reveal the boy's secret, he dared not ask anyone for fear they might ask too many questions.

Charlie worried about his friend, surviving the winter all alone with no adults to take care of him. He desperately hoped that Dominic had not frozen to death in the frigid cold, or starved, or drowned in the spring flood. Perhaps he had gone to live with his Indian family— wherever that was. Or maybe his father had come back.

Dominic grew further distant from the idea that his father would ever return. His Winnebago friends and relatives from his mother's village in Northeast Iowa had stopped their journeys upriver when they learned that Henri Bouton, their trusted trader friend was not there doing business on Barron's Island. When Gray Wolf offered Dominic a home in their village, he had replied, "Thank you, Uncle, but my home is here, and this is where I will stay." He hadn't seen his Indian family since.

High water of the springtime floods had receded and Barron's Island was once again green and sweet-smelling with wild flowers and apple blossoms, as was the countryside where Dominic tended the small herd of cows, just as he had done for the past three years. Over the long, lonely winter months he had spent endless hours practicing with the flute his brother gave him, and now he could play not only the Indian melodies his mother had taught him, but many of the tunes he had heard in the town and around the riverboats at the docks. So he carried the flute with him when he took the cows to pasture; it helped pass the time, and the cows seemed more contented, too.

Charlie had gained a little more freedom from close supervision by Maria; he knew he was a handful for her, constantly being distracted from his studies by urges to attempt new acrobatic stunts, and sometimes mischievously stealing pastries from Helen's pantry. But for her he had tried harder to become more judicious, and he realized that he would always be indebted to her for taking him so far on his journey to becoming a gentleman. She had sacrificed so much of her time for him, and now the summertime was a time for her, as well as Charlie, to take a break from schoolwork and to enjoy all the great new life that spring had delivered to the garden.

Charlie was ever so grateful to the captain, too, for rescuing him from that dismal life at the orphanage school. Not that he wasn't grateful for that, too, for that place had provided him survival from an uncertain death. But Captain Gordon could offer him so much more, especially the father figure that had always been missing. Now that the captain was away much of the time with the new shipping season, Charlie missed the companionship, of which he had become so fond during the winter months. He longed to go on the boat with Captain, but Gordon had insisted that he wait another year. When he was fifteen—more educated, more refined, more seasoned—he was promised a position aboard the captain's boat, and perhaps, after a couple of years getting familiar with the river and the operation of steamboats, he could begin his training as a cub pilot. For now, though, Charlie was content with fishing and swimming in the La Crosse River, hopeful that the French-speaking Indian boy, Dominic, would return.

James, the gardener had designated particular areas where Charlie could dig for earth worms anytime he wanted to go fishing, so the boy took every opportunity to sit at the river with a line in the water. And as the weather got warmer, and if the fish weren't biting, he spent a good share of the time swimming, practicing and polishing the techniques Dominic had taught him.

And then one Saturday in mid-June while he lay back on the riverbank with one arm covering his eyes a voice yanked him from his drowsiness: "Mon ami... you can't catch fish if you don't watch your line!" He jumped to his feet and let the fish pole drop to the ground. There was Dominic sauntering up the bank toward him, a big grin on his face. Charlie sprinted to meet him and they threw their arms around each other, both glad to be together again.

"I've been worried about you," Charlie said as they pushed each other back at arm's length. "But I didn't know where to find you."

"Been fishing the trout streams... best time in the spring, y' know."

They looked each other up and down; both had grown considerably since they were last together. Unlike Charlie's bright, new, perfect-fitting clothes, Dominic was still dressed in his shabby-looking faded and ill-fitting shirt and trousers that had been handed down from his older brothers. But the appearance of their clothes meant very little, for their friendship had become much stronger than that.

They sat down on the riverbank shoulder to shoulder.

"So, you have been at the big school in town all winter," Dominic said. "Is it better than the Mission School?"

"Oh, yes... I learned ever so much, but I know I won't ever be able to remember it all." Charlie eyed his friend. "Why don't you go to school?" he asked suspiciously.

Dominic frowned and gazed down at his feet. "My father was ashamed of his little Indian boy offspring, so he never sent me to school."

"Ashamed of you!"

"Oui, mom ami. That is why Jacques and Louis were the ones to go with him on voyages to Montreal, but I always stayed at home."

"He didn't come back yet?" Charlie asked.

"No."

"Was he mean to you? Did he beat you?"

"Oh, no! My father was very good to me. And he always brought me presents back from Montreal."

They sat there for the next hour or more exchanging pieces of their personal history, although Charlie remembered nothing of his life before he came to the Mission School. To him, it seemed like his life had started over when Captain Gordon took him in, and his new life had been quite overwhelming at first. Now his best friend was telling him of his family life that had somehow been taken away. It all seemed so unfair.

"I must go now, mom ami," Dominic said. "I must prepare for a journey."

"Journey? "Where are you going?" Charlie asked.

"Down the big river to my uncle's village."

"Are you gonna go live with them? Aren't you coming back?" There was worried concern in Charlie's voice, as if he feared losing his friend.

"No, I am not going to live with them. I will return after three days. I have to tend the cows."

"When are you going?"

"Next Friday evening, when I bring the cows back from pasture."

"Can I go with you?" Charlie asked eagerly.

"It will be a long hard journey," Dominic said, trying to discourage Charlie. But then it occurred to him that maybe a companion on such a voyage would be to his advantage. "Have you ever paddled a canoe?"

"No," Charlie replied. "But I can learn."

Chapter 24

I t wasn't easy convincing Maria that this was to be just a simple fishing excursion that would last three or four days. Charlie was a bit on edge not telling her the entire truth, but he couldn't see that any harm would come of it. "We'll be home again before the captain returns, and I'll be with an expert boatman and fisherman who is going to show me all the good fishing spots. We'll camp in safe places at night and cook the fish we catch during the day and..."

"All right!" Maria finally gave in after hours of pestering from the boy. She thought that perhaps she was making a mistake, but Charlie seemed so enthusiastic about this adventure, and it would be healthy for him to spend some recreational time with someone near his own age. He *had* been quite obedient, and he hadn't been into any mischief lately. And she could use a few days to herself.

"All right," she said again calmly after a brief deliberation. "I'll pack a suitcase for you. You'll need plenty of clean shirts and trousers and—"

"No, Maria," the boy protested. "I'll find the things I need myself. We're camping, and we're traveling light. There won't be any formal dinner parties, so I don't need a suitcase full of clothes."

"Are you sure?"

"Quite."

For the next few days the two boys met on the La Crosse River bank, fished, swam, and occasionally planned their trip down the Mississippi. Since Dominic was the more experienced in such matters, Charlie simply followed his guidance. "We'll take only the things we need: blankets, a hatchet to cut firewood, and our fishing poles and tackle."

"What about food?" Charlie asked.

"We can bring some, but mostly we'll eat the fish we catch."

Charlie was so excited about this new adventure he could hardly fall asleep at night, but finally the day came for their planned departure. So anxious to get started, he carried his bundle of blankets and one change of clothes, the basket of food that Helen had prepared for him, and his fishing pole and tackle to the riverbank more than two hours before Dominic was to arrive. That gave him plenty of time to dig an ample supply of earth worms.

The sun was sinking low in the western sky when Dominic came up the little river. Charlie just gawked at his beautiful canoe; he had never seen such a fine one as this.

"My father gave it to me," Dominic said. "When my uncle taught me how to paddle a canoe alone, my father thought I should have one of my own, and he brought this back from Montreal. He said it would be stronger and safer for me than the Indian canoes."

And it was a fine canoe, made from light-weight but hard and strong wood, precisely hand-crafted by a French-Canadian boatswain, coated with layers of varnish that made it shine like a mirror. Henri Bouton had presented his youngest son with the craft as a gift upon returning from one of his numerous voyages to Montreal. It was one of a kind, and everyone who knew the boy, knew how much he treasured that boat.

They stowed Charlie's things in the canoe, and then Dominic instructed Charlie how to board the canoe, placing one foot carefully in the center when he stepped in, to avoid tipping the boat to one side. Once Charlie was on the front seat, Dominic showed him how to hold the paddle and how to pull strokes through the water. Then he climbed aboard onto the rear seat, and moments later they were gliding down the La Crosse River, headed for the Mississippi.

It didn't take Charlie long to get the feel of it, and by the time they had maneuvered around many bends and reached the Mississippi, the two were paddling in nearly perfect sync.

But by that time, too, the last golden rays of sunshine had given way to the gray curtain of dusk. As they paddled southward by the new Coleman Lumber Mill the shadows grew darker, and soon the lights of the town were left behind them. The farther downstream they drifted, less frequent were the faint glows of cabin lights, visible only moments, sometimes, because of the trees. The river wandered on through what seemed to Charlie a wild territory, especially in the dark, where loomed on either side the silhouettes of hills and bluffs towering over them like giant monsters. But he wasn't frightened by any of this; instead, he was quite intrigued.

"We'll stop to camp soon," Dominic said after they had gone downriver about four miles.

"How will we ever find a place? It's so dark."

"Oh, *mon ami*," replied Dominic. "Don't you remember? I know all the good places on the river... even in the dark."

A short while later they beached the canoe on a sandy strip. Beyond the sand Charlie could barely make out the dark outline of trees.

"This is an island," Dominic explained. "I've been here many times. It's a good place to camp for the night."

"How big is the island?" Charlie asked.

"Oh, big enough to be safe, and small enough so there aren't any wild animals that live here."

"Wild animals?"

"*Oui, mon ami.* None that will bother us or steal our food."

They drug the canoe far out of the water up onto the beach and then went in search of some dry firewood among the trees. Within a short while, Dominic had a crackling campfire that lit up the beach and a small open area in the trees where they unrolled their blankets.

They sat by the fire and ate bread and cheese and pieces of cold chicken from Charlie's basket and drank milk from the jug that Dominic had just received from Mr. Kellogg at the hotel that afternoon. Dominic seemed quiet—more than usual—as if something troubled him.

"Is something wrong?" Charlie asked. "Am I not good enough at paddling the canoe?"

"Oh, *pas du tout*... you do just fine, *mon ami*. I am very tired. We should go to sleep now," Dominic said, changing the subject. "Tomorrow morning we will catch fish for our breakfast."

"When will we get to your uncle's village?"

"Tomorrow afternoon. It's still a long way."

They snuggled into their blankets. Charlie watched the fire until it slowly diminished to a bed of hot red coals. He could hear Dominic's slow, steady breathing in the stillness of the night, and he knew he was asleep. But Charlie wasn't all that sleepy, so he lay there gazing up at the stars and listened to an owl hooting somewhere, and another answering it from somewhere else. Moonlight washed over everything and it made the ripples on the river sparkle.

Chapter 25

Charlie wasn't so accustomed to this type of accommodations, so he drifted in and out of periods of sleep. He didn't know how long he had slept when he awoke and noticed that a tree—a tall poplar—seemed more distinct than any trees had appeared all night, and then more trees revealed their silvery-green leafy details as the soft pearly dawn floated its first light over the river. Then he heard familiar early morning sounds: cher, cher, cher, cher... a blackbird, answered by another farther away.

Charlie sat up, stretched out his arms, yawned, and quickly pulled a blanket up around his shoulders again as it was just a little chilly.

"Bonjour, M'sieur Charlie." His stirring had awakened Dominic.

Charlie giggled at the French greeting. "Good morning to you, too," he replied.

"*Sacre bleu! Merveilleux!*" Dominic said in a loud whisper.

Charlie watched the hills across the water come out of their shadows. "I'm not sure what you just said, but I think it means 'What a wonderful morning.' Is that about right?"

Dominic grinned. "That's close enough."

The glorious morning showered down silver pencils of sunlight through the overhanging tree boughs, and the warm glow gradually spread over the woods and the wild landscape; the river sparkled and danced.

From beyond a bend in the river came the familiar whistle of a steamboat. The sound echoed between the hills, and the boys craned their necks to look upriver. First to appear were the four red-shirted oarsmen at the front of the log raft, pushing on the ends of their long oars or "sweeps" that pivoted on yokes mounted at the very front of the raft, steering the raft around the river bend. Eight hundred feet behind them, the steamboat appeared, pushing the huge mass of logs downstream. Dominic jumped up and waved jubilantly; a few arms aboard the *Nellie Thomas* waved back and the pilot sounded a little toot from the whistle, but the oarsmen at the front of the raft were too busy guiding the raft to even notice him waving on the island.

The two boys watched in awe until the raft and stern-wheeler were out of sight. "Someday," Charlie said, "I'm gonna work on a boat like that."

Dominic jerked his head to look at Charlie, a little surprised. He had never heard Charlie mention any interest in riverboats before. "Me too," he said, after a fleeting thought that it might be better than farming raced through his head. "Maybe we can work together on the same boat."

Just then another steam whistle sounded from downstream, and the *Nellie Thomas'* whistle answered it, just like the owls and blackbirds had done, Charlie thought. A few minutes later, the *Phil Sheridan*, the fastest packet boat on the Mississippi steamed by on its way upriver to La Crosse. Charlie joined in with the waving this time that resulted in another whistle blast and a few hearty waves from the pilot house. And then it was gone around the bend.

"Let's catch some fish for breakfast," Dominic suggested.

After a good meal of sunfish they caught on the other side of the island, they sat on their little beach for a while and watched a couple more raft boats pass by.

"How did you learn to cook fish so good?" Charlie asked.

"I started helping my mother in the kitchen when I was very young. When she got sick and died, I just kept on cooking for our family."

"Well, you sure are good at it."

Dominic shrugged his shoulders. His gaze seemed to be searching for some far-away place, and Charlie thought he might be intruding if he asked any more questions. So he just sat there, shoulder to shoulder with Dominic, watching the river.

It was mid-morning when they packed their gear in the canoe and paddled southward. Charlie watched mile after mile of river valley slide by. They had crossed over to the west shore line, and once they left the little town of Brownsville behind, there was nothing but open prairies, hills and trees. Charlie was so intrigued by all this new and unfamiliar scenery that he didn't realize his hunger until Dominic suggested they should stop and catch some fish for their lunch.

A few trees close to the bank provided a little shade while the boys dropped their lines in the water. They had each caught one small fish and were hoping for something better when an older man rowed past in a shabby-looking canoe. He wore dirty, tattered clothing, a scraggy black beard, and an unpleasant scowl. Charlie waved, trying to be polite and friendly, but the man only nodded and never raised a hand. He kept staring their way until he was well past them, and then he turned the small craft toward the bank and disappeared behind a point.

"I think there's a little stream that comes out there," said Dominic.

"He didn't look too friendly," replied Charlie.

"Prob'ly some old hermit that lives back in the hills."

No sooner than Dominic had spoken, the shabby canoe reappeared and the rough-looking character paddled out into the Mississippi again, headed upriver past the boys, and disappeared around the bend. Gone long enough for the boys to forget about him while they pulled in a few more fish—enough for their meal—the man didn't come by again until Dominic was preparing the fish for cooking and Charlie was tending a small fire.

"That's a mighty fine boat y' got there." The gruff voice startled Dominic. He hadn't noticed the rather stealth approach by the stranger.

"Bonjour, M'sieur," he answered. "Oui, it is a very fine bateau," he said to the man who was still in his canoe nosed up to the bank.

The man stared at the superb craftsmanship with envy in his eyes. "Would ya sell this fine boat?" he asked, never lifting his eyes from it.

"No," Dominic cried. "My bateau is not for sale."

"I'll give ya fair price—"

"No, no, NO!" Dominic repeated. "It is not for sale at any price." His voice growled with anger.

The stranger seemed to understand that his request was not a welcomed one. Now, both boys stood shoulder to shoulder staring at him, suggesting that they no longer had any desire to continue the conversation. He pushed his canoe away from the bank with his paddle and rapidly maneuvered the craft back to the creek outlet where he had disappeared the first time.

Chapter 26

The boys finished their meal and continued on down the river. A couple of hours later, under a hot mid-afternoon sun, Dominic recognized the little inlet that was near the Indian village. His heart raced as they beached the canoe and jumped ashore. This was his mother's homeland, and soon he would see his uncle and cousins, and soon he would seek the answers to questions that had plagued him for so long. But something didn't seem right. The well-worn path from the river inlet to the village in the woods was covered with undisturbed grass and weeds. It looked as though it had not been traveled upon in quite some time. Quiet loneliness drifted on a soft breeze as Dominic led the way up the trail. But when they reached the place that should have been the edge of the village, there was nothing but trees and tall grass and wildflowers. There were no Indian lodges. There were no Indian children playing and running about. There were no steaming pots hanging over cooking fires. There were no Indian women weaving baskets. No fields of corn or squash. No barking dogs. Nothing.

Charlie was quick to figure out that this had been Dominic's destination, even though the Indian boy said nothing. He could see the devastating disappointment in Dominic's eyes, and then waves of something awkward and unspoken passed between them.

Dominic sat down on a fallen tree trunk and gazed about the lost village. "My uncle's lodge was right over there," he said and pointed. "And my grandfather, the chief, lived there." He pointed to another spot.

Charlie sat beside him. "Your grandfather was the chief?"

"Oui."

"Where do you think they went?" Charlie asked.

"I do not know," Dominic replied. With elbows on knees, he buried his face in his hands.

Charlie laid a sympathetic arm across his friend's shoulders. He knew what it felt like to be alone, without family, and he wanted to do anything he could to help Dominic.

After a few long moments, Dominic straightened up again and stared sadly into Charlie's eyes. "I came here to seek advice from my uncle, but now I may never know the answers to my questions."

"What advice? What questions?"

"It all started a long time ago, before I was born," Dominic began to explain. "My mother still lived here in the village, and there was another Winnebago boy—he is a grown man now—who wanted to marry her. But my mother did not like him, did not want him for a husband."

"So... what happened?" Charlie asked.

"My father's first wife was drowned in the river during a spring flood. That next winter, he asked Morning Star—my mother—to stay on Barron's Island to help him care for his two little sons. The chief—my grandfather—gave his permission, because he and his people were grateful to the great French trader who provided so many good things for them. And when my father and Morning Star fell in love, the chief couldn't deny their marriage. That would ensure a strong relationship with the trader.

"Then I was born, and I was raised in French tradition, just as my older half-brothers. But my Indian uncles and cousins taught me how to fish and hunt, and swim and paddle a canoe."

"Well, what does that have to do with you coming here?" asked Charlie.

"Two summers ago, while the people from this village were at Barron's Island for the trading festival, the Winnebago man who wanted to marry my mother put a dark curse on my father."

"What?"

"Fighting Bear came to our house late one night. I saw him at our window looking in. And long after everyone else was asleep, I heard him outside, dancing and drumming and chanting, 'round and 'round the house."

"A dark curse?"

"Oui. You see, mon ami," Dominic explained. "Fighting Bear never saw a vision from the Great Spirit. Instead, he was entered into the circle of dark magic."

Charlie stared at his friend, puzzled.

"I know you do not understand the Indian customs and traditions, and that's why all this seems confusing to you."

"Yes, it *is* a bit confusing," Charlie said.

Dominic tried to clear up the confusion by telling Charlie about the rite of passage from boy to man in the Indian culture. "When and Indian boy reaches the age of manhood, he goes alone out into the wilderness with nothing. He fasts and becomes one with nature, and then in a dream while he sleeps, a vision comes to him from the Great Spirit, and he is given his own guiding spirit that will help protect him through all his days on earth."

"And Fighting Bear didn't see his vision?"

"No. Somehow, the dark spirits gained control of him, and he started performing his dark magic, and all the people of the village became afraid of him."

"So... how could your uncle help?"

"He's the only one who could talk to Fighting Bear... find out about the curse... find out what has happened to my father."

"But maybe nothing has happened to your father," Charlie said. "You were in the house, too, and nothing has happened to you." Then he looked down at the little leather pouch hanging at Dominic's chest and he laid his hand upon it. "Oh, yeah... this is protecting you, right?"

"You learn fast, mon ami."

"Well, it's plain to see that they don't live here anymore," said Charlie, consoling his friend. "Should we go looking for them?"

"Where are you going to look, mon ami? We don't know which direction to start."

Charlie rubbed his chin and stared at the ground, thinking a few moments. "I guess you're right."

"Oui, mon ami. We could spend weeks searching."

Charlie gazed around the site where once had been a village of people. The forest and surrounding hills seemed to hold this spot in a comforting embrace. It was easy to see why they had chosen this location for their village, and he wondered why they would have left such a beautiful place. "So... what should we do now?" he asked.

"There is only one thing to do," replied Dominic. "Start back up the river. We'll find a place to camp for the night."

Charlie soon discovered that paddling the canoe upstream required a little more effort than he had experienced on the trip down with the current. "We must stay close to the banks," said Dominic. "The current isn't so strong there."

They had traveled up the river, waving to the passing steamboats with their rafts of logs and lumber. The crews always returned the greeting, and some called out "Frenchy!" when they recognized the boy and his canoe. Some of the pilots even tooted the steam whistle.

Chapter 27

They were nearly as far as they had come down that afternoon when they spotted a suitable campsite on the west bank where a grove of scrub oak nearly met the water's edge. The bank sloped down from a level plateau that looked as though it had been put there just for them. It seemed quite solitary, and there was a good supply of dry wood for a campfire.

That night, after they had caught fish and eaten their supper, they sat next to the campfire while Dominic told Charlie more about his Indian relatives and how his father was ashamed that he had a son with dark skin. "He was a proud French gentleman," Dominic explained. "He knew a lot of important people in Montreal, and he once said that he would never take me there with him. I would embarrass him."

"So... he didn't love you?"

"Oh, yes, mon ami. He loved me very much. He took good care of me, just like my half-brothers. And he always brought me presents— nice presents—from Montreal." The boy pointed to the canoe that was just barely visible in the light from the fire. "My canoe... he gave me that canoe. He wanted me to have the very best canoe so I would be safe on the water."

Charlie agreed that it was the nicest canoe he had ever seen.

Then Dominic retrieved the polished wooden tackle box and held it for Charlie to see. "This is the last present he gave me," he said as he opened the lid. Charlie felt almost envious because all he had to compare was a rusty tin can.

Then Dominic brought out another wooden box and removed the flute. "My brother Jacques gave me this."

"Can you play it?" Charlie asked.

Dominic just grinned and began playing a lively tune that suggested dancing. And dance he did, around the campfire, and then Charlie joined him, mocking Dominic's steps, clapping and cheering. It was great fun.

The crisp sound of the flute sailed out over the river and echoed among the hills. Charlie was amazed at his friend's musical talent, and he was glad to see Dominic's spirit lifted from his earlier depression.

"Wow!" Charlie said when they sat by the fire again. "How did you learn to play so good?"

"My uncle made me a flute from a willow branch when I was little and my mother taught me a few Indian songs. The rest I have taught myself."

Ever since Charlie had made acquaintance with Dominic he had admired him. But now, he felt even a stronger friendship building between them. He realized what a wonderful person Dominic was, and that it seemed so unfair that he had been left so alone. He was sure, too, that the Indian boy felt more confidence in their friendship, because he seemed more comfortable in talking about himself and his family than he ever had before.

"You're lucky, y' know," Charlie said.

"What do you mean, mon ami?"

"You're lucky that you have a family to remember. I don't have that. I don't remember my real family at all."

Dominic stared questioningly.

"I lived at the Mission School nearly all my life. They told me that I was brought there by a man they thought was my father, but they weren't really sure. He died there that same night. They said I cried, but I don't remember any of it."

"Nothing at all?"

"Nothing."

"But you are not sad about it?"

"It's hard to be sad about something you never had."

They talked for a while longer, and then decided they should try to get some sleep. They had a long day's journey ahead.

Chapter 28

Charlie had slept quite soundly through his second night in the open air, and he awoke startled as Dominic shook his shoulder. "Wake up, mon ami! Wake up! The canoe is gone!"

"Canoe? Gone?" Charlie rubbed his eyes and squinted in the early morning sun.

"Oui. My bateau! *MON DIEU!* It is gone!" Dominic cried.

Charlie sprang to his feet and they both ran down to the riverbank where the canoe had been.

"It couldn't have just floated away," Dominic said. "It was

completely out of the water."

"And you didn't get up during the night and—"

"No, no... I didn't wake up all night. Mon dieu! How can this be?" He fell to his knees and bowed his head in despair.

"Well, someone must've taken it," Charlie said as he gazed up and down the river. He couldn't see very far in either direction because of trees and the river's bends. But a thought suddenly came to him. "That man that we saw yesterday. He sure seemed like he wanted your canoe awful bad," he said.

Dominic lifted his head and opened his eyes wide. "You're right. He probably saw us come here... and then he came to steal it when we were asleep."

"That would be my guess," Charlie added. "That creek we saw him go to isn't far from here, is it?"

"Not far at all. And that's where we'll find my canoe."

"But how will we get it back?" Charlie asked. "He certainly didn't look like the kind of chap that would just give it back."

"Then we will have to just take it... like he took it from us. But first, we must hide our things. We'll come back for them after we get the bateau."

They packed up all their belongings, hid the bundles under some blackberry bushes, and then set out along the riverbank to find the creek. They hadn't gone far when they realized that even paddling upstream against the current was much easier work than getting through the brush, and sometimes wading across swampy inlets and ditches. Their progress was slow and the sun very hot. After more than an hour of fighting their way through the thickets, their further passage was stopped by a muddy inlet partially hidden by reeds, and not more than fifty yards upstream they could see the grassy bank where they had fished the day before.

"This is it," Dominic said quietly as he crouched and gazed around curiously. He seized Charlie's arm and pulled him down, too, to make sure they were both well concealed in the tall weeds.

"The bateau is up there," Dominic whispered, pointing up the stream. He could see a thin column of smoke rising that appeared to be about a hundred yards away. "We need to be very quiet now."

They crept on cautiously, following the creek away from the river until they saw the source of the smoke. Up ahead on the opposite side was a low cabin, just as shabby-looking as the canoe the man had the day before. They had come upon the man's dwelling, but there was no one in sight.

"Where d'ya think he is?" Charlie whispered.

"Perhaps inside the cabin... there is smoke coming from the chimney... he's cooking."

Not far from the cabin, the creek widened to a large pool, a portion of which was occupied by a green new growth of cattails. The old shabby canoe was tied to a post driven into the bank, but the boys could not see Dominic's canoe.

"It must be there somewhere," Dominic whispered.

They continued to sneak closer, watching carefully for the appearance of their enemy.

"Look, there," Charlie said and pointed. Just barely visible he saw what he thought was the shiny wooden hull of Dominic's canoe, mostly concealed by the cattails around it. The man had definitely tried to hide it.

"How are we gonna get it?" Charlie asked. "It's so close to his house."

"I will swim to it," Dominic replied. "You go back downstream. Find a place where you can get close to the water... where we can get into the canoe. I will bring it down and then we can paddle quickly back out to the river."

Dominic took off his clothes and handed them to Charlie. Charlie watched as he slipped silently into the water. When he reached the large pool, Dominic disappeared under the surface.

Charlie watched and worried, but in a short while, Dominic's head popped up near the cattails. He looked around in all directions to see that he had not been detected by the enemy. Then he motioned to Charlie, urging him to go downstream where he would be out of sight.

Charlie didn't want to just leave his friend alone, but he also knew that for the plan to work, he had to be ready to board the canoe quickly, so he turned and hastily backtracked along the creek, confident that the Indian boy would be successful.

Dominic took hold of his canoe and slowly, quietly, inched it out from the cattail bed, raised up high enough to see that both the paddles were still inside, and immediately submerged again, with the canoe between him and the cabin. Without making a single splashing noise, he propelled himself across the pool holding the craft with one hand, and continued downstream until he was out of sight from the cabin.

The creek was much shallower here, forcing Dominic to wade instead of swim, and that made more noise. He hoped Charlie was near.

Charlie *was* near, waiting just around the next bend of the crooked stream. He tossed the clothes into the canoe; they both climbed aboard, and started paddling. But as they got closer to the Mississippi, the creek became too shallow. With two people in the canoe, it drug on the bottom and they could go no farther.

"We'll have to get out... wade the rest of the way," Dominic said.

They both got out and sloshed through the shallow water, pulling the canoe along.

"HEY! You come back here, you thief!" the gruff voice called out from up on the bank. "You stole my canoe!" the man yelled angrily.

The boys turned to look, startled. There was the man stumbling along the bank through the weeds, but keeping pace with them.

"This is not your canoe!" Dominic cried out. "You stole it from us."

But the filthy-clothed stranger kept yelling and cursing. "I'll drown you both in the river when I catch you... you good-for-nothin' thievin' scoundrels!" Then he jumped into the water and came after the boys, splashing through the shallow water, his long legs taking bigger strides than the boys could manage while maneuvering the canoe. He soon caught up to them, grabbed the stern point of the canoe with one hand and Dominic's arm with the other. He stood two heads taller than either of them, and his grip on Dominic's arm was firm and hurtful.

"Let go of me!" yelled the boy, pounding on the man's clenched grip with little effect.

"Let go of my canoe, you little thief!" the mangy character returned.

"It's NOT your canoe!" Dominic repeated.

Out of pure instinct, Charlie scooped up his paddle from inside the craft. The man was so occupied with the struggle from Dominic that he didn't notice Charlie's action, and he didn't see it coming. But Dominic did. He ducked as Charlie swung the paddle with all his might, and— WHAP—the flat end of the paddle struck the side of the man's head, sending him reeling backwards, falling and splashing into the water near the bank. The boys didn't wait to see if he would get up again. When they saw his head wobble a few times and one hand come up to it, they both grabbed the canoe and pushed it as fast as they could muster, splashing their way to the opening with its fringe of reeds, out into the Mississippi and deeper water. When they hopped into the canoe they could hear the nasty oaths the man was yelling at them, promising to kill them if he caught them.

By the time they reached their campsite, the sun had dried off Dominic. He gathered his clothes, hopped ashore, and quickly dressed. "Get our bundles out of the bushes, mon ami," he told Charlie. "Let's get started up the river before that wild man comes after us again."

They were at least thirty yards out into the river when they passed the mouth of the stream where they had had the close encounter. As they paddled by, they saw the man, wild with rage, in his wretched old canoe. "There, you see?" Charlie said. "He's gotten his canoe and he's coming after us again!"

"Paddle fast, mon ami... *à tout vitesse!*"

But they were too far away from the bank, out in the river channel where the current was strong, and making forward progress was difficult and slow. Charlie's arms ached, but he was determined to paddle as long as it took to get away from the crazy man. He glanced over his shoulder, only to see that the man was making faster headway closer to the shore where the current was less. "He's getting closer," Charlie whispered hoarsely.

"Oui, I'm afraid so," replied Dominic.

It was clear to see that the man intended to get ahead of them and then come at them with the current to his advantage. And within a short time, that's exactly what he did.

But there was soon to be another factor that the man did not expect, nor did Charlie. "Turn out and paddle toward the main channel," Dominic said in a loud whisper. "Head right in front of that steamboat coming upstream." Apparently, he was the only one who had noticed it coming.

Charlie looked back. "What? We'll get run over! We'll be killed!"

"No, no, mon ami. Just do it!"

Chapter 29

Charlie followed the instructions and turned the canoe out into the path of the oncoming steamer. He thought he was committing suicide, but when he looked back at the savage man in the other canoe who was about to overtake them, he began to paddle faster. But it was already too late. The man had much more momentum built up coming at them downstream. He managed to get close enough to grab the side of the boys' canoe and held up his paddle in such a way as to ward off the attempts Charlie and Dominic made to beat him away.

Dominic's cries for help were well-received aboard the steamer. She chugged slowly right alongside where the struggle was taking place and then the huge paddlewheel reversed and the big boat stopped. The rafter *Union* was on her way home after delivering a raft of lumber to DuBuque, and the French boy was no stranger to her crew.

Crewmen on the steamer were yelling at the man before he realized that they were not there to aid him. He just kept cursing and snarling. "These varmints stole my canoe! I'll have their hide, I will!"

The close proximity of the steamer turned Charlie's blood cold, especially when the canoe bumped into the hull. He didn't realize the steamer was completely stopped as he had been so occupied with defending himself and Dominic against the onslaught of their vicious pursuer.

"Frenchy!" Charlie heard one of the crewmen call out. "What have you gotten yourself into this time?"

The strange man in the old canoe growled again: "They stole my boat and I want it back."

Just then Captain Anderson appeared at the steamer's gunwale, and Charlie came to realize that the men on the big boat were there to help them. "You'd better back off, old man," said one of the crew, "or I'll poke a hole in your boat and you can swim or drown... I won't much care."

"But that's my boat. They took it, and I want it back."

Captain Anderson stepped forward. "You are a liar, mister. I happen to *know* this boy, and I also happen to know that *this is his canoe*. I should take you aboard and have you arrested for molesting these boys. Now paddle your sorry behind out of here or I'll *personally* sink that tub of yours."

All the time the captain was reprimanding the man, a couple of crewmen pulled Charlie and Dominic on board the big boat, and two more hoisted the beautiful canoe up onto the deck.

"FULL SPEED AHEAD!" shouted the captain. The pilot blasted the whistle a couple of times, and the boiling sound of the paddlewheel churning the water accompanied the hiss of steam escaping from the engine vents. Charlie watched in awe as the boat slowly pulled away from the man in the shabby canoe, sitting there like a whipped pup, knowing he had been defeated.

"Now, Frenchy," the captain said. "What on earth are you doing all the way down here?"

"Fishing, M'sieur Captain Anderson," Dominic replied. "And this is Charlie, *un ami à moi.*"

"A friend of yours, eh?" said the captain. "And why was that nasty old man chasing you?"

"He stole my bateau while we slept last night, and we found where he lived and…"

Dominic told the whole story to the captain while Charlie just stood by and listened. It was clear to him that the captain and all the crew members knew Dominic by the way they greeted each other. And it was clear that Dominic didn't want them to know that the real reason he had come here was to visit an Indian village—his *relative's* village.

"Well, you're safe now," said Captain Anderson. "And we'll have you boys back home in a couple of hours." He put a hand on each of their shoulders and guided them to the stairway to the upper deck. "You boys hungry?"

"Oui, M'sieur. That man kept us from having our breakfast this morning."

"Well I'm sure Cookie can find something for you."

"*Merci, M'sieur.*"

"You are quite welcome, Frenchy."

While they wolfed down stacks of pancakes with maple syrup and butter, Charlie's curiosity got the best of him. "You know all these guys?" he said in a low tone.

"Oui, mon ami. They are all my friends. I know almost everybody at the boat yard."

"They all call you *Frenchy.*"

"Oui. That is the only name they ever call me." Dominic stared seriously into Charlie's eyes. "And you should, too."

From that day forward, *Frenchy* was the only name Charlie ever called his friend.

Chapter 30
Early Spring: 1882

Charlie Martin was starting his second season as a deckhand aboard Captain Gordon's log raft boat. After another year or two of learning the workings of the vessel and understanding the function of every crew member, he would advance to the pilothouse as a cub pilot, and perhaps someday he would wear a captain's hat. That had been Captain Gordon's intensions from the very start—to nurture his legacy—so there would be another Captain Gordon to follow in his footsteps as a Mississippi River pilot.

Now Gordon was Captain of a relatively new boat in the McDonald fleet, the *Bella Mac*, a powerful stern-wheeler that was as good as any rafter on the Upper Mississippi. He had hand-picked his officers to work with him, and he was supremely happy to have his best friend, Frank McIntyre as his second pilot.

Charlie and Frenchy weren't spending so much time together now, as Charlie's life was aboard a steamboat most of the spring, summer, and autumn, and although their friendship had grown stronger, there wasn't much more than a day now and then for fishing and swimming and canoeing. Frenchy spent enough time around the boatyard, though, to know when the big boats would arrive and depart, and he was always there to welcome *Bella Mac's* crew home after a river journey, as he did with many other crews. He wasn't that cute little boy anymore, but instead he was growing into a handsome young man. But he had never lost his charming, boyish personality, and one would be hard-pressed to find anybody who didn't still adore Frenchy. He made the rounds to greet all the crewmen, and for his best friend, Charlie Martin, the customary French hug was secretively a little more meaningful.

Over the years, Charlie had never divulged the secret of Frenchy's Indian heritage, and for that Frenchy was grateful. It was one of the elements that strengthened the bond between them. But sometimes it was difficult to hide their friendship, always sneaking off to some remote rendezvous to fish and swim and explore the unexplored.   And when it became well-known that they were close pals, no one appeared to be concerned for the adopted son of gentleman Captain Gordon. It seemed quite natural that two boys nearly the same age would share so many common interests.

Captain Gordon would have taken a more keen interest in Frenchy, too, had it not been for the boy dressed in peasant's clothing. He didn't realize that the boy was born of aristocratic blood, or that his father was from the upper-class merchants of Montreal. He had never listened to Frenchy talk—other than the usual greetings from time to time—to recognize his speech as being impeccably correct, rarely using slang or inappropriate words. What he did hear was the boy often using French words and phrases; that tended to mask the boy's cultural refinement.

He had been rather displeased with Charlie when he learned that Captain Anderson had rescued the two boys from that madman so far downriver, but he was more upset with Maria for consenting to the departure in the first place. Charlie's punishment had been spending a week helping James with work in the garden and other chores, including putting a fresh coat of paint on the carriage house. No fishing or swimming was allowed the entire week. It proved to be a long week for Charlie.

Now it was early March, and there was always plenty of excitement in the air at this time of year among all the men who made their living on the river. Boats were being readied for when the ice was out and the first log rafts could be taken downriver on the high water. Mills farther south where they didn't have readily available the great pine forests of the north were eagerly awaiting a new supply of logs, so their silent saw blades could once again sing after a long winter.

Captain Gordon was no exception when it came to excitement for the new shipping season, and Charlie, too, had certainly learned to love the river and the life of a river man. He and the captain were spending their days at the boatyard, getting the *Bella Mac* ready for her first trip of the season.

One evening Helen was busy in the kitchen preparing the family supper when she heard a knock at the door. It was a messenger delivering a letter addressed to Captain Gordon, and it was marked *URGENT*. Helen took the letter right to Mr. Gordon in the den where he and Maria and Charlie were relaxing and having coffee. Gordon opened the letter, read, and then handed it to Maria. She studied the paper and frowned.

"What is it?" asked Charlie.

"A letter from Mr. Stanley at the Mission School," said Maria. She stared at her father sadly. "We must..."

"I don't see any harm in it," Gordon said, and he turned to Charlie. "Do you remember Mrs. Champlain at the school?"

"Oh... yes," Charlie replied with a smile. He had fond memories of the old woman who had so kindly cared for him when he was little and helpless. "She was so good to me... and I've never been back to visit her."

"Well, that's mostly my fault, my boy," said Gordon. "It seems that she is in very poor health... maybe dying. Apparently she has requested several times to see you."

Charlie approached the captain's side. "May I go see her?" he asked.

"Of course you may. We'll go and see her right now."

Charlie didn't encounter very many familiar faces at the school—it had been several years since he last saw anyone there. But Mr. Stanley hadn't changed much, although he seemed quite pleased with Charlie, whom he had expected to return to the school a short time after he left. He secretly admitted—if only to himself—that he had underestimated Charlie's qualities, and certainly Mr. Gordon's tolerance and determination. "I'm proud of you, Jules," he said as he shook the boy's hand.

"My name is Charlie Martin, now," the boy replied. He wanted to say *you weren't proud of me five years ago*, but good manners stopped him.

"Well, Mrs. Champlain knew you as her little Jules. She is quite ill, and sadly, the doctor says she is likely to die soon. But lately she has spoken of you often and repeatedly asked to see you again. You were very special to her, and I'm so glad—for her sake—that you're here."

They walked solemnly to the infirmary where the old nurse lay comfortably. Her eyes lit up when Charlie approached; though he had grown and matured since they were last together, she recognized him and she held out a feeble hand, urging him to sit down beside her.

The boy obliged, still holding her hand.

"And you've grown to such a fine lad," she said, but her voice was frail and weak, and it was clear that even speaking was difficult for her.

Charlie gently squeezed her hand, smiled warmly, and leaned down to place a kiss on her cheek. No words were necessary to explain the special place he had for Mrs. Champlain in his heart. She had been like a mother to him —the only mother he could remember. And now, his actions were as if he had answered the most important wish of the old woman's entire life.

She had little more to say other than petitioning Charlie to promise another visit, and as he and Mr. Gordon were about to leave, her gaze shifted from the boy to Mr. Stanley. "The package," she said.

"Oh, yes," Stanley said, as if he had forgotten something. He crossed the room to a table, picked up a small bundle wrapped in brown paper and handed it to Charlie. "She wanted you to have this. She said she found these things in the old man's coat pocket after he died."

Charlie opened the package with Gordon and Stanley looking on. It contained a child's linen undergarment, plainly marked "Reginald Van Hugh III" and a colorful children's picture book, frayed and torn and creased through the center from being folded double to fit in a pocket. It was the familiar old story of *Little Red Riding Hood*, but the hand-written inscription on the cover in a delicate hand read:

"For my darling Reggie on his second birthday,
Rita Van Hugh, Scranton, June 30 1866."

Captain Gordon examined the name on the garment, and then the inscription on the book. "I thought you said the boy's father was a rough old tramp who died here in the infirmary."

"That's what we thought for many years," said Stanley. "Then Mrs. Champlain revealed these things just recently. She had kept them secretly all these years." He pushed Gordon and Charlie out the door and closed it behind him. "My guess is that she didn't want to lose this child, so she hid his real identity."

Gordon stuffed the garment and book in his pocket.

"I have sent several letters," Stanley added. "But so far, there have been no inquiries about the boy."

On the way home, Charlie asked, "Does this mean I'll have to change my name again?"

"I don't know, Charlie. Depends on whether or not any of your kinfolk show up. Do you *want* to change your name?"

"No! I want to be Charlie Martin, and I want you to be my father and Maria to be my sister. And I want to stay here and become a riverboat captain... just like you."

The captain put his arm around the boy. "And we'll try to keep it just that way, Charlie Martin."

Chapter 31

Frenchy wandered among the few stacks of freight on the levee. He gazed at the barges mounded with cordwood and coal that lay in the icy water at the landing. On summer evenings, this is where men sat watching the silent river, telling their river stories. Most of the ice was melted and gone from the Black River, but much of the stuff still floated down on the Mississippi channel, too much, yet, for the big boats to safely navigate. Frenchy knew, though, that there would soon be plenty of activity here. To this port came steamboats up from St. Louis and down from St. Paul. In earlier days, crowds would gather at the first sign of them—a cloud of smoke beyond the bend and the sound of a whistle—and they would remain until the boat came in, hissing and splashing, the pilot's bell clanging signals to the engineer, and the mate calling out orders to the deckhands. Then passengers paraded across the landing stage; freight was carted off and freight was carted on. All this while, the town was linked to far-away, unseen places, and when the boat departed, the world left with it, until the next whistle sounded.

But the excitement of a steamboat arrival drew smaller crowds now, if any at all. Arrivals were commonplace; the novelty had lost most of its brilliance and the railroads had dulled the glamour, stealing much of the passenger and freight business from the river. But one element remained: as soon as the ice was gone, out in the main channel would pass the big log rafts—acres of pine logs from the St. Croix and Chippewa River valleys. For the past decade steamboats had pushed the giant rafts downstream, and for thirty years before that log rafting had been a silent business, the huge slow islands floating on the current without a sound, only the cry of the steersman and the clatter of the cook's kettles. At night, the sounds of singing and frolicking by the red-shirted rafters around a small fire burning on a mound of sand in the middle of the raft could be heard moving slowly down the channel; it was their only entertainment during the long journeys, as the only time the rafts stopped until they reached their destination was when they were tied up at shore or island during storm or heavy fog.

The logs on which they rode came from the greatest pine forest in the world. The northern rivers—the Wisconsin, the Black, the Chippewa, the Red Cedar, the St. Croix—all flowed through the silence of the wilderness to the Mississippi amidst seemingly endless stands of tall pine, spruce and hemlock. And it was of this grand gift of nature that would build cities in the growing West. Everything was wood—barns, houses, shops, churches, fences, plank roads and board sidewalks, wagons, boat docks and steamboats. And it was the lumber industry that so many men's lives depended on. Frenchy realized now that this should his new destiny; that he should follow his heart onto a riverboat and learn the skills of rafting logs and lumber.

Captain Gordon and Charlie gazed around the Boat Store as they waited for Frank McIntyre, Louis, the captain's First Mate, and Bill, the cook, to join them. It was a busy place, buzzing with activity as stock boys emptied crates and filled the shelves and tables with fresh inventory getting ready for the new river season. Charlie had been there quite a few times last summer, when it had been one of his jobs to help "Cookie" carry the grocery boxes hack to the kitchen aboard the *Bella Mac*. He suspected he would be doing plenty of that again this year, too.

Located right on the levee, the Boat Store was operated by the McDonald Brothers. The basement consisted of ship supplies, rope, chain, pike poles, oars, and all the numerous articles used in steamboat operation. The upper or main floor carried a large stock of smoked and salted meats and groceries, usually of better grade than found in the normal grocery store. Packet boats usually wired the store from Lansing on the upstream trip, or from Winona on the trip down, requesting that fresh meat, fresh vegetables, and ice be obtained for them. They would pick up the other groceries from the store's regular stock.

On this day, though, Captain Gordon and his officers were there to make certain that supplies would be available in a few days when the *Bella Mac* would take the first raft of logs of the season down the Mississippi.

Chapter 32
Friday March 17, 1882

Frank McIntyre eased the 115-foot Bella Mac slowly alongside the 600-foot-long log raft that was tied up at the bank just below the McDonald's Black River boom. As the big boat inched along, Louis and his eight crewmen tossed the lines across the raft that would secure it into a manageable mass, and attach it to the tow boat. Charlie was right there helping and learning; Captain watched from the Texas deck. A couple of hours later the massive raft with four oarsmen at its bow coaxing it toward the main channel emerged from the mouth of the Black River. The first raft of the season was headed down the Mississippi.

The first raft to go downriver in the spring was a challenge as new sandbars could have formed changing the channel, and springtime floods were bound to have altered the banks and familiar landmarks that helped guide pilots on the river. But Captain Gordon and his second pilot, Frank McIntyre were up to the challenge. With this smaller raft, maneuvering new, unknown obstacles was less hazardous than with a full raft. Whenever there was nothing else for Charlie to do, he spent as much time as possible in the pilothouse learning from the masters.

So many changes, and yet the river had not changed—the mystery of midnight and the noon glare. Dawn and sunrise was always the same; first the stillness before the daybreak and then the stars blinked away with the approaching light; the black shorelines softened to gray and the river emerged from darkness under puffs of white fog. From the silent forest the first birds called and in the growing light the river reflected the gold and pink sky and the deep green of the tree-lined shores. Then the day suddenly and boldly marched in, and the world was full of sunlight.

And the river had moods: radiant in sunshine, majestic in moonlight, jeweled with the sparkling stars; mysterious in fog, and menacing under stormy skies. It changed with the seasons: frozen and motionless in January; high water in March, carrying fallen trees, fence rails, various pieces of timber, and the occasional skiff or canoe that had been left unsecured, too close to the river; low water in late summer exposing more rocks and sandbars and snags that did nothing but increase the hazards of navigation.

Fifty years earlier, the Upper Mississippi was a wilderness river. For nearly a thousand miles it flowed past forest, bluff and prairie. Then it had been the country of the Sauk, Winnebago, Chippewa and the Sioux, with Indian camps on the hills and Indian canoes and bull boats on the water. Not as frequent was a squatter's hut or a half-breed's shanty on the shore.

Near the mouth of the Wisconsin River the Bella Mac floated her raft past one of the oldest settlements in Wisconsin—Prairie du Chien—spred over a bench of land between the bold bluffs and the shining water. Until the railroad probed its way from Milwaukee to Prairie du Chien's riverbanks, it had been a drowsy place where the Indians brought their peltry to the French fur trading post. But now it had become an important commercial port. Farther south, on the Illinois side, a few miles up the Fever River, what had started as a dozen huts and cabins clustered around a lead smelting furnace, was now the bustling city of Galena. On the west bank in Iowa, high on top of a hill, among the shallow pits of his lead mines, lay the grave of Julian Dubuque, overlooking the city named for him.

And that was as far as the Bella Mac would venture this trip. The logs were delivered and without delay, after all the towing gear was retrieved from the raft and the clerk, David McCannish had finished all the official business with the mill, Captain Gordon gave the order to turn the boat upstream and start the journey back to La Crosse.

Charlie, as well as most of the crew, enjoyed the return trips upriver. Because there was no raft to tend, it allowed a little more leisure time, especially for those manning the oars at the bow of the raft; that was hard work and a break was always welcomed.

The cooks, though, still had a busy schedule; everyone still had to eat. Charlie gave a hand in the galley sometimes so that young George McCannish, the cook's helper, could take a break. He was only twelve years old, and Charlie figured the only reason he had the job was because of his two older brothers, David, the Clerk, and William, one of the deckhands.

And sometimes Charlie would help out the firemen, Maurice and Dick, so they could have a little extra rest, too. Mostly, though, whenever possible, he spent his time in the pilothouse with Captain or Frank, learning navigation skills and how to read the river, and sometimes just to talk.

One evening after supper, while it was Gordon's watch at the wheel, Charlie stood beside him. "Cap'n," he said. "I'm beginning to worry about Frenchy; his clothes seem a bit more shabby and ill-fitting now, and his spirit is drooping just a little."

"Oh?" the captain replied. He was well aware that the two boys were good friends, and although he had never given much consideration to Frenchy, he recognized Charlie's usual manner of caring for other people. He didn't know that Frenchy was wearing the last of the hand-me-down clothing left from his brothers; that the little money he earned during the summer was barely enough to buy food and supplies for the winter.

"I'd like to do something nice for him," Charlie continued. "He *is* my best friend, y' know… and he *did* save my life once. Well, *twice*, if you count the time we were picked up by Captain Anderson on the Union."

"What do you mean? Saved your life. What other time?" The captain tried not to sound alarmed.

"I never told you about it," Charlie said. "But I guess I can now." He hesitated a moment. "I fell in the La Crosse River once trying to get my fish line out of a tree branch. Frenchy pulled me out. And then he taught me how to swim."

"But Charlie," the captain said. "He's just a—"

"A wonderful person, and a real gentleman," the boy interrupted. "He's all alone, parents and brothers gone, has to take care of himself."

Gordon felt a little tickle in his throat. "Where does he live?"

"In a little log cabin on the island. But he can't buy clothes because he only makes enough money herding the cattle to buy food for the winter."

Moved by all this, Captain Gordon's interest grew with Charlie's concern for his friend. "So, what do you want to do?"

"I've talked to some of the guys in the crew; they'd be willing to chip in a little, too. I'd like to bring Frenchy on a trip down the river with us as a guest; treat him to a haircut, and maybe a nice bath, and buy him some new clothes. He really is quite a gentleman, y' know."

The captain rubbed his chin, considering his son's gesture of generosity. "We'll be going to Clinton next trip."

"Could Frenchy come with us?"

"If you really want to do this... I don't see why not."

Charlie hugged the captain. "Thank you, Cap'n. And by the way... I think he'd like to work on a riverboat. He told me once."

When the Bella Mac pulled into her home port a couple of days later, Captain Gordon noticed from the pilothouse an exquisitely-dressed man waiting on the dock, and he appeared to be looking for this particular boat.

Frank McIntyre noticed him, too. "Now that fellow looks out of place as pants on a parakeet," he said to the captain. "Ain't no lumberman, that's for sure."

"I'll go down and see what he wants," Captain Gordon said. He casually ambled down the stairs to the main deck as Louis and his deckhands tied up the boat, and then he stepped across the wide gap between deck and dock as if it weren't even there.

Judging Gordon's attire, the stranger approached the captain. "Are you Captain Will Gordon?" he asked.

"I am."

The stranger offered his hand and they shook.

"My name is Samuel Henderson and I represent the Van Hugh family of New York."

Gordon's smile slowly diminished when he heard mention of the Van Hugh *family*. In a moment he felt as though an anchor chain was wrapped around his heart and the anchor had just been tossed overboard. This could only mean that Charlie *had* a family, and if they had gone to the extent of sending a representative to find him, the chances of Charlie remaining in La Crosse were rather slim.

"We have received word from a Mr. Stanley," Henderson continued, "that you have in your custody a boy adopted from the orphanage."

The captain just listened. He knew what was coming.

"We have confirmed the boy's real name to be Reginald Van Hugh III. Is there someplace we might talk privately?"

Reluctantly, with great sadness in his voice, Gordon invited Mr. Henderson to his private quarters aboard the Bella Mac. When they were behind closed doors, Mr. Henderson presented his ploy.

"Reginald Van Hugh III is the son of Lieutenant Van Hugh II of the Union Army and his wife Rita. Lieutenant Van Hugh was killed during the Civil War. His wife fled to the West with their son. She settled in Winona, Minnesota where she soon fell ill and died."

"So the boy *is* truly an orphan," said Gordon.

Mr. Henderson barely acknowledged Gordon's statement and then went on. "Apparently, the little toddler wandered off while the mother was sick... or dying... and by the time she was found, the boy was gone, miles away, evidently picked up and carried off by some old tramp that happened to be passing by, uncaring of where the boy belonged. A thorough search of the immediate area where the boy disappeared was finally given up weeks later.

"It took some time to piece all this together, but by dates of the mother's death and the boy's arrival to the orphanage, he was with the old tramp for about three months traveling about the countryside where no one questioned the two of them together. It was the ferryboat operator at Read's Landing who remembered taking an old man and a child to Wisconsin, and a farmer and his wife who were on their way to market who had seen them along the river road, and they all said the ragged little boy clung to the old man affectionately. So naturally, it became nobody's business. And when the old man must've realized the condition of his own poor health, he took the boy to the orphanage."

"Charlie was too young," the captain said, "to explain where he came from or what had happened."

Mr. Henderson stared at Gordon questioningly. "Charlie?"

"Charles Martin Gordon. That's his name now."

"Oh, but I must tell you that the boy is heir to great fortune as *Reginald Van Hugh*, and my orders from the family are to return him to New York. He will be well cared for there by his relatives."

Gordon could feel tears forming. It was at that very moment that he came to realize that Charlie meant a great deal more to him than just a legacy to carry on the Gordon name amidst the Mississippi riverboats. He cared deeply for Charlie, and separating would be most difficult... for both of them.

Chapter 33
Friday March 24

I t was a dreamy sort of day as Frenchy watched the cows grazing contentedly. The swallows glided about in the gentle breeze that soothed his skin. The sky was pale blue above, scattered with mounds of shimmering clouds at the horizon. It seemed a day made for dreaming on the quiet slopes of pasture.

High above the city was a silvery cloud shaped like a feather, sleek and slender. Slowly it changed as the edges softened and spread until it had become a great wing. It reminded Frenchy of something that was just beyond the edge of his memory. Then he remembered what Gray Wolf had once said: "There are spirit signs in the clouds."

Could it be, even though he was only half Indian, that the spirits were guiding him? But what were they saying? For many long lazy minutes he watched the cloud as it drifted overhead and past the hills to the east, out of sight.

He leaned back against the big boulder and closed his eyes. He wondered about his future, now that it was quite certain his father and brothers would not return. He thought about his friendship with Charlie Martin: of all the friends he had made at the riverfront, his relationship with Charlie seemed to be the only one meaningful…

As if the very thought of Charlie had brought him up from the river, when he opened his eyes the boy was standing over him, grinning. Frenchy jumped up, catching hold of his friend's hands. Charlie was really there… not a dream.

"The men on the wharf told me I'd find you here."

Frenchy threw his arms around Charlie's shoulders. "Oui, mon ami! I'm so happy to see you again."

They sat in the shade of the big boulder; Frenchy saw the sadness suddenly appear in Charlie's eyes. "What is wrong, mon ami?"

Charlie nearly choked on the words: "A man from New York came to see us," he said.

Frenchy stared questioningly.

"Remember I told you that I lived at the Mission School most of my life?"

Frenchy nodded.

"Well, old Mrs. Chaplain who took care of me when I was little found some things with my real name... and my mother's name. But she kept it hidden until just now. And then Mr. Stanley sent some letters back east, to where my family is, I guess, and then this man showed up."

"Is he your real father?"

"No. According to him my real father was killed in the war."

"And your mother?"

"She brought me here when I was just a baby, but then she got sick and died. I don't remember any of it... I was too young.

"I guess I must've wandered off when my mother was sick. The old man found me and eventually took me to the Mission School by the time anyone realized I was missing. The neighbors searched for me, but they finally gave up, thinking I had either drowned in the river or was carried off by a wolf."

"So, what will happen now, mon ami?"

"The man from New York says I have to go back with him and I have to live with some relatives who don't even know me."

"And so... you are leaving?"

Tears rolled down Charlie's cheeks. "That's just it, Frenchy. I don't want to start over with a new family. I have my family here, and I have you—my very best friend. I love this place and I love the river and the boats... and I love you and all the people in my life now. I'd rather die than leave this place with a stranger."

More tears streaked Charlie's face. He tried to wipe them away with his hand.

Frenchy moved close and put his arm across Charlie's shoulders. "I will miss you if you go away, mon ami. Oh, how I will miss you."

They sat in silence for a while, and then Charlie regained his composure. "Cap'n says I can go on one more trip down the river... and Frenchy, I want you to come with me, too."

Frenchy's eyes lit up. "Me? On the Bella Mac?"

"Yes, my friend. You. On the Bella Mac. And I'll have a surprise for you when we get to Clinton."

"What kind of surprise?"

"If I tell you now, it won't be a surprise."

"When will we go?"

"As soon as our lumber raft is ready... probably Monday or Tuesday, and we'll be gone for about two weeks."

Frenchy didn't have to give it much thought. "Okay. I will ask one of the other boys to tend the cows while I am away."

Chapter 34
Monday March 27

Under any other circumstances, Captain Gordon would not have given that ragged, unkempt little man a second look. But Charlie loved him; and the crew adored him; and now the captain was about to find out why everyone admired this peasant of a boy. He only knew what Charlie had told him and tidbits from the other crewmen. Now he was helping to finance the boy's first trip down the Mississippi, and to fit him with some new clothing, all because he wanted to grant Charlie's wish—perhaps his last wish before he departed for New York to rejoin his family from which he had been lost for so long.

Frenchy had been on the boat with Charlie all night; he didn't want to be late, and Charlie was delighted that he was there. They would have to share a bunk for the entire trip; the Bella Mac was taking a full raft—six strings, 700 feet long and 270 feet wide—requiring a full crew, so all the crew's quarters were occupied.

At dawn, Louis and his men began preparing the raft—half logs and half lumber—while Charlie helped Bill and George tote the last boxes of groceries from the Boat Store. Frenchy insisted on helping with the task, too.

The captain stood in the pilothouse in the early morning light peering out the front windows, watching as the crew lashed the bow of the Bella Mac to the huge raft. She was pointed toward the mouth of the Black River, and soon she would be pushing the huge raft down the Mississippi. The log portion of the raft would be dropped off at Dubuque, and the lumber was destined for Clinton, Iowa, about five or six days away.

Gordon couldn't help but notice the enthusiasm bubbling from the boy he had seen so many times, but to whom he had never paid much attention. His smiling face was warmly received and greeted by every crewman as if they had been best friends for all time. Gordon was still curious to see why everyone liked this shabby-looking boy so much.

As the day wore on, Frenchy never seemed to tire of watching from the boiler deck the miles of river and forest solitude, marked by an occasional Indian mound or a lonely settler's cabin, shadowed by the towering bluffs. He marveled at the far forefront, 700 feet distant, where the oarsmen pulled on the long sweeps, steering the raft, bending it around to match the curves of the river, skillfully guiding it past sandbars and islands, and all the difficult places like Bad Axe Bend and Crooked Slough.

Captain Gordon was making his rounds of the boat late in the afternoon when he poked his head into the galley. Bill was his pride-and-joy cook, as really good cooks were rare, and Bill was one of the best on the river. A good cook with cheerful disposition was a great help to any riverboat captain; he kept the crew contented and happy. Gordon furnished Bill with everything he asked for, because he knew it would be put to good use, and every meal Bill put on the table was nothing but excellent.

Bill was busy preparing chicken for the crew's supper; George was peeling potatoes; and there was an extra person working in the kitchen that day—Frenchy, donned in white apron and hat was mixing batter for the cornbread.

"I see you have an extra helper today," the captain said to Bill.

Bill laughed. "He insisted on helpin', so I put 'im to work. And Cap'n... you should think about keepin' 'im around."

"I'll take it into consideration," the captain smiled, and then went on about his usual daily inspection. But his thoughts that afternoon were more about Charlie Martin. He knew how much the boy had come to love the river, and his life now seemed to be centered on it and the boat and rafting. It pained Gordon to think that Charlie was going to be taken away from all this that he so dearly enjoyed.

By the second day it was perfectly acceptable to everyone that Charlie ate supper with Captain Gordon at the Officers' table that night, and every other night from then on. They all knew by then that this was Charlie's last trip down the river, and that when they returned to La Crosse, that would be the last they would ever see of him.

It was also accepted that his best friend, Frenchy, was on board for the trip, and it was even rumored that he might become a permanent member of the crew. Captain Gordon avoided any comment on the subject when asked, even though he, too, was starting to admire the boy just a little, if for no other reason than his display of enthusiastic energy.

When there was no opportunity to help in the galley, and it was Frank McIntyre's watch at the wheel, Frenchy politely asked the pilot, "Would it be okay, M'sieur Frank, if I stayed here in the pilothouse with you for a while?"

"Well, certainly," Frank replied. "You can stay here for as long as you want."

An hour or more passed while Frenchy asked all sorts of questions about the river and steamboats and rafting, and Frank did his best to supply the answers. Frank McIntyre had known the boy for quite some time, but because of his higher social status as a pilot, only now was their friendship beginning to bud.

"Captain Gordon doesn't like me very much, does he?" the boy asked Frank.

"Why do you say that?"

"Because M'sieur Gordon hardly ever talks to me, and he looks at me as if I am odd."

"Oh, I wouldn't worry 'bout it, Frenchy. Cap'n just takes a little more time getting to know somebody. You'll see. By the time we get to Clinton in a few days, he'll treat you just like the rest of us."

"You really think so, M'sieur Frank?"

Frank put his hand on Frenchy's shoulder and winked. "I know so, *mon ami.*"

The boy looked up at Frank and smiled. Their friendship was sealed.

Chapter 35

The next afternoon the *Bella Mac* was tied up at Dubuque, cooling down the boilers so they could be cleaned. Louis and his crew of eight were busy stowing all the lines and gear after separating the log portion of the raft at the Dubuque mill. David had obtained clear receipts and he was just returning from town after sending a telegram to

La Crosse. The boiler cleaning process would take several hours, so Captain Gordon and Frank McIntyre went into town for a break from the routine as well.

Bill shouted down from the galley door on the boiler deck, "Charlie!"

Charlie looked up from the coil of rope he was securing and waved.

"Will ya go with George in the skiff t' th' Boat Store?" Bill called out.

Charlie looked to Louis for his approval. Louis nodded.

"I'll be right there," Charlie called to Bill, and set out for the stairs. On his way, Frenchy caught up to him.

"May I go too, mon ami? I will help row the skiff."

"Sure, you can go," Charlie replied. "I'd be disappointed if you didn't."

When they got to the galley door, Bill handed George his list; George had already gotten money from the clerk. "Now, yer gonna be bringin' back some ice blocks," Bill told them. "So don't dawdle. I'd like to see some ice left when ya git back, okay?"

Charlie and George smiled and giggled; they knew Bill was just having fun with them about dawdling.

The skiff was still in the water tied to the guard after its use in delivering the logs that afternoon. The boys jumped in, took up the oars and rowed upstream along the shore to the Boat Store. It was similar to the McDonald's store at La Crosse, and just as busy. They waited their turn until a store clerk helped Charlie and Frenchy get the four blocks of ice and the crate of twelve dozen eggs into the skiff. George watched, feeling a little left-out and perhaps a little jealous of Frenchy. Since Frenchy had started helping in the galley, George had developed animosity toward him, worried that Bill wanted to replace him with the new kid. And Frenchy could definitely sense the hostility.

The trip back to the Bella Mac would have been easy and uneventful had it not been for the most vicious wasp that began circling and finally picked George in the middle of the boat as its attack victim. As the bee homed in on him, making several practice dives at the boy, George screamed curses vile enough to strip paint off a church and stood up, flailing his arms in an attempt to fight off the buzzing creature, but only making the bee more angry. Frenchy and Charlie watched this from either end of the skiff, trying to be serious, but they had to laugh. It all seemed quite humorous until George lost his balance and in an instant toppled overboard into the Mississippi. The wasp flew off, having won the battle without firing a single shot.

But George didn't come up out of the dark water.

"Can he swim?" asked Frenchy.

"I don't know," replied Charlie. "Maybe not."

Without any further contemplation, Frenchy quickly slipped off his clothes and dove into the cold, dark water. Charlie could see neither of them in the murky depths until the sudden eruption of their two heads blasted above the surface, about twenty feet downstream from the boat. Frenchy's left arm was wrapped around George's chest; George's arms were still waving, and he was coughing and gasping for air.

"Row the boat this way," yelled Frenchy.

Charlie put his two oars in the water and pulled hard. When he got close to the boys in the water, he back-paddled a couple of times and then leaned over the side to help George into the boat. He flopped onto the skiff's floor like a fish, still coughing and gasping. Once Charlie was certain he was okay, he said, "Can't swim?"

George shook his head and managed a raspy "No."

"Little Otter will teach you," Charlie said with a grin, and then he took Frenchy's hand and pulled him into the boat.

"Who is *Little Otter?*" George wheezed.

"The fellow who just saved you from drowning. Ain't you gonna thank him?"

George stared at naked and dripping-wet, shivering Frenchy. He sat up, and just a little smile came to his lips. "Thanks," he said quietly. "But you better put your clothes back on now."

The skiff had drifted on the current and was now beside the Bella Mac, with at least half the crew staring at them and cheering from the main deck. But Frenchy didn't mind; George was safe and alive.

Chapter 36

At most they were two days away from Clinton, the final destination. Barring any delays or bad weather, Frank calculated the Bella Mac's arrival back in La Crosse after delivering the remaining lumber raft in plenty of time for Easter Sunday. His sister, Mrs. Wood, had a wonderful dinner planned for that day, with Frank and the entire Gordon family as her guests. Frank hoped that Charlie's departure would not occur until after the holiday, so that they might all enjoy one last celebration together.

"LIGHT OFF... WARM UP!" was the call from Captain Gordon when the boiler work was finished. They would run all night, once the steam was up. Double-tripping through the bridges—splitting the raft in half lengthwise and taking each half through the bridge separately, because the whole raft was too wide to fit between the bridge pilings—would not be necessary from there to Clinton. Half of this raft was already gone, so everyone was quite optimistic for an easy trip the rest of the way.

Charlie and Frenchy leaned shoulder to shoulder against the railing on the boiler deck after supper that night, overlooking the bow and the raft of lumber stretching out ahead of the Bella Mac. Twilight was past and darkness had swallowed the river and everything around it. All the birds had left the sky empty and quiet, and now, only the beam of the search light pierced through the misty night air, bouncing from shore to shore as the pilot pointed out landmarks for the oarsmen at the raft's bow.

Some of the off-duty men had gathered on the raft. In keeping with tradition, rafters made their own entertainment, usually in the form of song and dance, and if they were lucky, at least one of the crew was a fiddler or played a banjo.

"So, how do you like the trip so far?" Charlie asked.

"Oh, it is magnifique, mon ami," Frenchy replied. "I have never been such a long way from Barron's Island."

"And it doesn't bother you to be so far away from home?"

"But we will be home again in just a few more days. *Pas du tout*... it does not trouble me at all. And I think I would like to do this always."

"You probably will."

"What do you mean?"

"You can take my place when I'm gone."

"So, it is true, then?" Frenchy said. "You are going away?"

"Like I told you before, Frenchy... I would rather die than leave all this—and you. But I guess I don't have a choice."

Frenchy put his arm firmly around Charlie's shoulders. "I will miss you, more than my brothers."

Down on the raft there seemed to be an argument brewing between two deckhands, and the others were gathered around in anticipation of a fight, as the two were nose to nose, and fingers poking at each other's chests.

"I will be right back," Frenchy said and hurried off.

Charlie wanted to run down there, too, but he remained at the railing watching and listening to hear what the two men were arguing about. It seemed like only seconds had passed when Frenchy returned carrying his shiny flute. He put it to his lips, took a deep breath, and within moments a lively tune that resembled an Irish jig filled the night air. He had heard the song on the wharf one day and learned to play it flawlessly while tending the cows. One by one the men on the raft turned their attention to the melody, not knowing at first where it came from, and then the two arguing men gradually lost their aggressiveness, too, and before long they seemed to have forgotten their differences.

The fiddler soon joined in and the rest of the crew slapped and stomped their feet in time to the music; the nightly get-together was restored to the usual joyous affair. Captain watched from the Texas deck.

Chapter 37

Frenchy had never been to another town other than La Crosse, so naturally, he felt a little intimidated in this strange new place.

Charlie, on the other hand, had walked these streets several times during the previous season when Captain had introduced him to some of the better establishments. And it was to some of these that he would take Frenchy. His best friend deserved the best that this city had to offer.

They had walked a few blocks when Charlie stopped in front of Gunter's Tonsorial Parlor. He thought this was as good a time as any to explain to Frenchy what he had planned. "Now Frenchy... this is where the surprise begins."

Frenchy was still puzzled. He had never been inside a barber shop, much less, a high-class tonsorial parlor. His haircuts, lately, had involved a sharp hunting knife and a self-inflicted compromise to his good looks.

"The rest of the guys and me all chipped in," Charlie explained. "Even the captain contributed some."

"What are you doing?" Frenchy asked.

"We're treating you to the finest, starting with a nice haircut... and then we'll go from there. We're gonna make you look like the fine gentleman that you are."

"You mean, mon ami, I'll get a fancy haircut like yours?"

"Yes, Frenchy. And then we'll get you a nice warm bath, and then we're going next door to the haberdashery for a whole new suit of clothes."

"New clothes? For me?"

"Yes, my friend. New clothes... for you. What d'ya think of that?"

"I have never had new clothes before."

"Well, you will now," Charlie said as he urged his friend through the door.

A little reluctant at first, Frenchy climbed into the barber's chair as he was directed, and then he just listened while Charlie instructed the barber to cut Frenchy's hair the same as his own, and that when the haircut was finished, the boy was to get a deluxe bath in the back room.

When Charlie started to walk away, Frenchy cried out, "Don't leave me here alone, mon ami!"

"I'll be right here," Charlie replied as he sat down in a chair by the front window. He watched as the barber carefully trimmed away the long dark hair, and the beginning of a miraculous transformation.

The first sight of himself in the big mirror was a bit of a shock to Frenchy, but then a little grin slowly crept onto his face and it grew to a smile as wide as Main Street. In a matter of moments he was feeling quite pleased with his new appearance.

The barber directed them through a doorway into another comfortable parlor where a bathtub filled with warm water awaited Frenchy.

"Now, let's get those ragged old clothes off, and you can enjoy a nice hot bath," Charlie said.

Frenchy stared at him, and then at the bathtub, seeming a little hesitant.

"It'll be okay, Frenchy," Charlie assured him. "You'll love it."

Frenchy disrobed as instructed and cautiously stepped into the bath. The warm water was soothing and the soap felt good as it slid over his skin. He hadn't had a bath like this since before his mother died. It was magnificent.

When the bath was finished and Frenchy was dry, Charlie wrapped a robe around him. They went out a back door into an alley, and then into the haberdasher's shop. The clerk there remembered Charlie, as he had been there many times with Captain Gordon getting new shirts and trousers.

"I want to buy a complete suit of clothes for my friend," Charlie told the clerk. "Make him look like a fine gentleman."

The clerk looked Frenchy up and down, covered with nothing but the robe from the bath parlor next door. "Undergarments, as well?" he asked.

"Everything," replied Charlie. "Hat and shoes, too."

The clerk wrapped a tape measure around Frenchy's waist, and then he peeled the robe back from his shoulders to get a better look at the boy's build. Then he disappeared for only a minute, returning with the undergarments. "Put these on," he said, "while I see what I have in your size."

Charlie looked on and reminisced about his own similar experience when he first came to Captain Gordon's home. He was delighted that he could do this for Frenchy. And he hoped it would serve as a long-lasting remembrance of their friendship.

Chapter 38

Frenchy's own mother would not have recognized the dapper young gent who emerged from the haberdasher's front door, his step a little more confident, his smile brighter than Charlie had seen on him since their fishing days on the La Crosse riverbanks. Charlie walked proudly beside him, a wonderful sense of satisfaction pouring over him like a waterfall. It was sad to think that he would soon be leaving his friend behind.

"If I write you letters, will you promise to answer them?" he asked Frenchy.

Frenchy stopped so suddenly that Charlie had taken three strides before he realized his companion was not beside him.

"Mon ami. Do you forget? I cannot read or write," Frenchy said with a frown.

"Oh, yeah." But then as a revelation Charlie said, "Charlie Martin will teach you!"

They both grinned and walked on toward the river. When they arrived at the Bella Mac, none of the crew was there to greet them. Only James Tulley, the Chief Engineer came strolling up the deck from the engine room. "If you're lookin' fer Captain Gordon," he called out, thinking he was talking to strangers, "he's up..." Then he noticed who the pair was. "Well, well, well! Look at you! Ain't you a sight fer sore eyes?" He turned to Charlie. "Your Pop's up talkin' to David."

"Thanks, Jim," said Charlie and they headed up the stairs to the boiler deck. When they reached the clerk's office, Charlie tapped on the open door. "Hi, Cap'n... David. Where's everybody?"

David looked up at the pair standing in the doorway and smiled. Captain Gordon looked up and frowned. "Where's Frenchy?" he inquired.

"Beg your pardon, M'sieur," the boy replied. "I *am* Frenchy."

By association with the distinct voice and upon closer inspection, he finally recognized the boy, and he was truly amazed. It was quite remarkable; in white shirt with collar, fashionable brown suit and vest, Derby hat and shiny new shoes, Frenchy looked every bit the most refined gentleman as anyone the captain had ever laid eyes on.

Charlie noticed a little smile come onto Captain's face. "Well, Cap'n? What d'ya think?"

Captain looked Frenchy up and down, thinking back on the time when he first saw Charlie with his new clothes and fresh haircut. This transformation seemed even more remarkable. "I think you have done nothing short of miraculous," he replied.

"So, where's all the crew?" Charlie asked. "I'm sure they want to see the *new* Frenchy, too."

The clerk offered an explanation. "There was a little disagreement over wages," David said. "I received a wire from La Crosse instructing me how much to pay the mate's crew, and after they discussed it among themselves, they decided the pay was too low, so they all walked off together."

"They quit? Just like that?"

"It happens a lot this early in the season," the clerk went on. "They're a good bunch, though. This is just their way of bargaining. We'll probably see them back again in a couple of weeks."

"Two weeks!" Charlie whined. He was disappointed that he wouldn't get to say good-bye, and he so wanted to show off Frenchy to them.

"They will be here to see us off," Captain said. "You can say your good-byes then. Besides... they have agreed that two of them will be coming with us so we have enough men to cover the watches on the return trip to La Crosse."

Chapter 39

When the *Bella Mac* steamed away from Clinton, six of the mate's crew waved from the riverbank. They had all said their good-byes to Charlie, and they had all admired Frenchy's dazzling appearance. Only Will McCannish and Swift Bell remained on board, as agreed, to fill out the needed number for the return trip to La Crosse.

Monday morning found the *Bella Mac* at the Dubuque levee for coal, some grocery supplies and ice, and there had been a request to pick up a passenger. The Chief Engineer's brother, Henry Tulley, also an engineer, was on his way to La Crosse to join the crew aboard the *Helen Mar*. And while the coal was being loaded, John Nolan, another old river fireman from New Orleans working his way north, approached the First Mate seeking a ride to La Crosse. As this crew was short a few members there was plenty of room, and Louis could see no reason to deny the request.

Any other time, Charlie Martin would have been in high spirits on the return trip upriver. But this was to be his last. Even though his best friend was there with him, he couldn't help feeling a little sad. Frenchy was his real salvation; he encouraged Charlie to view his future as a new beginning, and to hope and expect something even better, although neither of them could imagine anything better than what they had now.

Captain recognized Charlie's depression; he sincerely wished he could alter the coming chain of events that would take Charlie away. But he had already changed that course by convincing Mr. Henderson to allow Charlie one more river trip, and there was little chance of expecting any more.

Charlie tried to make the best of his last trip, savoring every moment of enjoyment. Not all of the crew expected his usual level of enthusiasm, but he refused to let his crewmates down, and fully executed his duties as usual.

"Why don't you spend your time with Frenchy?" asked Swift Bell one afternoon. He leaned on the railing beside Charlie, casually scanning the Iowa hills, never making eye contact with Charlie. "He speaks highly of you, and he will be very sad when you go away."

As much as Charlie was aware, Swift Bell was the one person that knew Frenchy's Winnebago heritage, for he was dark-skinned like the boy, and they seemed to have an unspoken understanding of each other. Perhaps the other crewmen knew, as well, but they never commented about it, and Charlie was quite certain that Frenchy's concern of public knowledge about his Indian family should be nothing to worry about.

"I will," Charlie replied. "But I think he's helping Cookie in the galley now. He really likes to do that. He's a great cook, y' know? He learned it from his mother."

"Yes, I knew Morning Star. She was a fine woman."

"You *knew* Frenchy's mother?"

"Sure, I knew her. And it is too bad that she is gone. Frenchy is a fine boy, and he deserves better than losing his whole family the way he did."

Suddenly Charlie realized that he shared information with Swift Bell that only they knew. "I swore to Frenchy a long time ago that I would take to my grave what he told me about his Indian family. He doesn't want everybody to know, but you do."

"Yes, I know. And for Frenchy's peace of mind, I hope you keep your promise to him.

Chapter 40

They had made good time going upriver; by Thursday night the *Bella Mac* was only a few hours away from homeport, and they would be home in plenty of time to enjoy the Easter holiday.

"Well, Frank... it's officially Good Friday," said Captain Gordon when he relieved the pilot just after midnight.

"Yes," Frank McIntyre replied. "Everything is running smooth. Monahan is your engineer. We should be in La Crosse by two o'clock. Think I'll try to get a couple hours of sleep."

"Okay, Frank. And I'm really looking forward to that Easter Sunday dinner at your sister's house."

Charlie couldn't sleep, so he had stayed up with Frenchy in their stateroom, reminiscing all the good times they had spent together, truly memorable experiences that would stay with them always. Even at their young age, they understood the importance of their friendship. But this was a difficult time for both, as their companionship neared an end. Charlie's future was uncertain, and he was uneasy knowing that all the familiar surroundings and his entire life was about to change. He wished Frenchy could come with him to New York, but he knew that was impossible. And he knew that Frenchy was going to be happy in his new-found career aboard a riverboat, providing that Captain could convince some other boat master in need of a cook to hire him.

About midnight, Frenchy's eyes were beginning to get heavy and his head nodded. *"J'ai besoin de dormir,"* he mumbled.

Charlie stared at his friend questioningly.

"I need to go to sleep," Frenchy explained, realizing that in his tired state, he had spoken words that Charlie didn't understand.

"It's time for me to go to work, anyway," Charlie said. "I'll see you in the morning."

"Bonsoir, mon ami." Frenchy's eyes were already closed.

But Charlie didn't go directly to the main deck; he left the stateroom and made his way forward; he climbed the stairs to the Texas deck to have a chat with Captain in the pilothouse first.

"Hi, Cap'n," he said. Frank McIntyre had just retired to his stateroom to sleep until they reached La Crosse, and Gordon was alone with the river and his searchlight.

"Well, hello, Charlie." He put one arm around the boy's shoulders. He, too, was fighting the urge to cry whenever he thought about Charlie leaving.

Charlie just stood there for a few minutes watching the light beam reflecting off the water and dancing along the riverbanks as Captain expertly maneuvered the craft where the channel crossed to the west shoreline. They were a few miles below Brownsville, and Charlie recognized the little island where he and Frenchy had camped the first night of what Captain had considered their "unauthorized lark" a few years before. But he decided not to mention it, because it might stir up a reason to be scolded once again for something that happened so long ago.

"I was thinking," Charlie said. "D'ya s'pose you could find Frenchy a job on a riverboat?"

"Well, I don't know…" There seemed to be a little skepticism in Captain's voice.

"He's really a good cook, y' know. And he really likes being on a riverboat. He told me."

By this time, Captain had begun to recognize Frenchy's likeability, and he knew the boy had sound, positive character, but he wasn't yet assured of his ability as a faithful and reliable crewman. "I'll take it into consideration," he said, and then, as if avoiding further conversation on that subject he peered at the steam pressure gauge. It showed the normal 135 pounds, but the boat seemed sluggish and slow. He thought, perhaps, that it was his imagination, only because he was anxious to get home.

Charlie saw that he wasn't going to get a better answer than that right then. "I'd better get down to the main deck," he said, "and see what there is for me to do."

As he left the pilothouse, Captain said to him quietly, "We'll talk about it some more at home, okay?"

Charlie smiled, nodded, and sprinted down the stairs.

Chapter 41

"Wake up, you good fer nothin' dog," Charlie heard the fireman, Maurice Leseur calling out. He soon learned that the fireman was trying to arouse the engineer, Charles Monahan. Monahan had taken over the engine room duties from Chief Engineer Jim Tulley a couple of hours earlier. Now he was leaned back in his chair snoozing, apparently blocking the fireman from checking his boiler fires. With all the cursing from Monahan for Maurice disturbing his nap, Charlie left them to their differences, strolled to the bow, and watched the searchlight brighten the very dark night, briefly here, briefly there, like lightning before a storm. After a few minutes he wandered to the stern and listened to the slow rhythm of the paddlewheel churning the dark water. It was a sound that he knew he would not hear again once the boat landed at La Crosse.

Up at the boilers, Monahan and Leseur had discovered trouble. The "doctor" as it was called—the steam driven pump that supplied water to the boilers—had stopped operating. A pipe flange fitting had worked loose, and steam pressure to the pump had dropped, causing the pump to stop, the very reason that was causing Captain Gordon his frustrations with the slowness of the boat. He kept signaling to the engineer, but Monahan was too busy trying to remedy the leaking pipe to respond. Eventually he was successful with the repair, and the doctor resumed its operation, but by that time the water level in the boilers was dangerously low. Cold river water poured into the overheated boilers, and they soon emitted an eerie moan. Monahan recognized the imminent danger; he panicked and ran from the boilers to the far stern, Leseur right on his heels.

Their abrupt actions startled Charlie. The fear in their eyes told him that something dreadful was about to happen. He processed the thought about as quickly as they explained the situation. "Then we have to stop the pump!" He darted toward the boilers before Leseur could catch his arm to hold him back. "It's too late for that," Leseur yelled, still attempting to catch the boy, but young Charlie was too fast for him and kept a few strides ahead. He had learned enough about steamboats to know the consequences; cold water pumped into an overheated boiler could result in an explosion, the force of which could destroy the entire boat, and he intended to save the boat from destruction.

About half-way Charlie found himself on a sandy beach; it was cool and pleasant, and waving to him stood a man dressed in a military uniform, much older than him, but he looked just like Charlie. He was either far in the past or far in the future, and one of them had to be terribly out of place.

Captain Gordon miraculously escaped serious injury as he was catapulted through the front window of the pilothouse, landing on the bow deck, completely disoriented. In his dazed state, he got to his feet and immediately discovered his right foot would not entirely support his weight. He touched his face that stung from cuts, and even in the darkness, without seeing the red on his hand, he knew he was bleeding.

Nothing made sense to him. It was as if he had been launched suddenly into a nightmare. But slowly his senses began to revive, and he realized that he was no longer at the wheel in the pilothouse, and he was not gazing at the river ahead in the beam of the searchlight. As his eyes gradually adjusted to the darkness, he sensed the total destruction all around him, and everything was deathly quiet.

Then he remembered that he had been talking with Charlie in the pilothouse that seemed like just moments ago, but it may have been longer. He didn't know how long he had been unconscious.

Charlie. He had to find Charlie.

Chapter 42
Good Friday April 7, 2:15 a.m.

A thunderous rumble awoke the residents in the little river town of Brownsville, Minnesota, the report so violent that it shook houses and rattled windows and sent sleepy dogs under porches fearful of the unknown cause of the tremor. But some people recognized the horrendous boom; Cy Alexander, an old retired Mississippi pilot had ears like a hawk when it came to river sounds. He had been awake and heard *Bella Mac's* whistle, recognizing the distinct tone. And then, a few minutes later the sickening boom shook his house and rattled the dishes in the cupboard. He knew immediately that *Bella Mac's* boilers had exploded; it was a sound he knew all too well. He bolted out of his chair and rushed to the front door. Outside in the cool April air he discovered that other people had come out of their houses, curious of the noise and what had made their homes tremble.

Out of the darkness they could hear distressed voices calling out for help. "Bring out a skiff!" came shouts from the vicinity of Two Mile Island, just upriver from Brownsville. Alexander understood the urgency, because he knew what had happened. There was bound to be loss of life, and no doubt, there would be injured men on a sinking boat who needed help.

He hurried to his neighbor's house to get some able-bodied help. Frantically he pounded on the door. "John! Wake up! I need your help!"

John Reppy opened the door, sleepy-eyed but alert enough to

recognize Alexander and his urgent request. "What kinda help d'ya need?" he asked, rubbing his eyes.

"I think it's the *Bella Mac*. Her boilers blew. They're calling for help out there."

"Where?"

"Sounds like they're up by Two Mile Island. Get dressed. Hurry! We can row out in a skiff."

In another part of town not far away, Elijah Palmer and his brother George heard the explosion. Elijah had a faint suspicion of its origin. He and George rushed outside where they could hear the mournful cries for help piercing through the dark night from out on the river: *"Bring a skiff. Bring a skiff."*

They responded as quickly as possible and rowed out into the darkness, seeing very little, following only the sounds of distressed voices. By the time they reached the steamer, its wreckage had floated downstream on the current quite some distance from where the disaster had occurred. Without lanterns and no lights remaining operational on the big boat, they could only imagine the destruction by the gruesome silhouette lying in the water. Only a small portion of the upper deck just ahead of the paddlewheel remained intact; the rest of the structure had been reduced to a pile of splintered rubble piled on the hull, or blown out of existence, or scattered about the river's surface from the blast.

When they neared the wreckage, a boy's face appeared, and he seemed to have in tow another man, who Elijah and George helped into the boat. The boy momentarily vanished in the darkness, and then reappeared with another injured man. They helped him and the boy into the skiff. All three looked as though they had been tossed from their beds into the river wearing nothing but their undergarments, speechless from exhaustion and the shock of such a violent awakening.

Rowing vigorously, Elijah and George delivered the three rescued crewmen to shore. By then there were many Brownsville residents waiting at the landing ready to help the victims in any way they could.

Cy Alexander and John Reppy returned to the landing with two more crewmen, one of which they had given up for dead. They had found him afloat, still on a bunk in the wreckage of what remained of a stateroom. The other had been clinging to a large broken beam. He was too incoherent to even say his name.

Alexander caught one bystander by his arm. With authority in his voice he said, "Go to the telegraph office at the railroad depot and have the operator send an *urgent* message to the McDonalds in La Crosse. It's the *Bella Mac* out there. Her boilers exploded. Some dead. Many injured. Hurry!" Then as an afterthought he added, "And be sure to tell the operator to ask for more medical assistance."

Charles Billings and Joseph Williams, another pair of Brownsville residents arrived at the landing with two more survivors; they had rescued the Tulley brothers, Henry and James who they found hanging onto a piece of timber. They had been propelled from their bunks into the water, but neither were injured any worse than they could swim to the safety of the floating beam.

Chapter 43

By then the river was alive with rescue boats manned by Brownsville residents eager to help. When Elijah and George Palmer made it back out to the wrecked steamer they found it marooned on the Wisconsin side of the river against the bank, its hull filled with water. They could hear a frantic voice calling: "Charlie! Charlie! Is that you?"

Another muffled voice answered: "No. It's me, Louis."

Aboard what was left of the *Bella Mac*, Captain Gordon had climbed upon what appeared to be remnants of the upper deck, atop a heap of splintered boards and beams. He could hear the First Mate's voice below his feet. Louis was buried under the wreckage. With blood dripping from his chin and a foot that felt like it was on fire, the Captain started pulling broken boards and timbers from the mound of rubble. "I'll get you out of there," he said to Louis.

"You okay, Cap'n?" another voice said from the darkness. It was Bill Wagner, a fireman, apparently not injured too severely, and Gordon was glad to hear his voice. After much great difficulty and pain, they finally lifted the beam that had Louis pinned down.

As they helped Louis to his feet, they heard a crashing noise. They didn't know then, but they would soon learn that the crash was a falling stove, and its still-burning contents spilled out among the rubble. The kindling-like material quickly ignited, and now they faced another crisis;

the boat would soon be ablaze.

From nearby, Louis could hear a sorrowful moaning. "Cap'n! I hear someone!"

Gordon listened. He, too, heard the moan. "Charlie! Is that you?" he called out, but the only response was another moan.

They followed the sound to the outer edge of the hull. Barely hanging on to the gunwale was the badly injured fireman, Maurice Leseur. Louis and Gordon pulled Maurice up onto the deck but he could not speak more than grunts and groans.

"We'll take him in our skiff," Elijah Palmer offered. His voice startled Captain Gordon, but he was relieved to know that assistance was at hand.

George and Elijah lifted the fireman into their skiff. "Anybody else we can take to shore?"

"Haven't found any more, yet," Bill Wagner replied. "Better take Maurice now... looks like he's hurt pretty bad."

"Charlie!" the Captain called out again, and limped toward the stern of the crippled boat.

"Maybe Charlie is one of them we already took to Brownsville," Elijah called out to him.

"A blond-haired boy? About eighteen?"

"There was a boy," Elijah said, and then started rowing across the channel.

"Help me now, boys," came a cry from under the heap of debris. "Da faar is gettin' close," the voice called out. It was Tommy Rice, the only black deckhand.

"Try to find a bucket," Gordon yelled to the First Mate. "I can see Tommy in the light of the fire."

Gordon and Wagner went frantically to work pulling twisted timbers and splintered wood away from where the deckhand was trapped. The flames were reaching his legs that were caught under several broken beams and tangled in cables. "Thow s'm wata on dat faar!" Tommy said. "M' laigs is burnin' up."

"This is all I could find," said Louis returning with a broken wooden bucket. "But it'll hold water, and it'll hafta do!" He went to the edge of the deck, dipped the bucket full of water and handed it to Wagner, who in turn passed it to Gordon. He dashed the water on the flames, but it did little to subdue the fire. He passed the bucket back, and a few moments later it returned to him full. Again he tried to douse the flames while Wagner attempted to remove some more debris, but the fire raged on.

Now there were more men climbing onto the vessel from skiffs, rushing in to help pass the water bucket. Another wooden bucket was located, and the fire fighting progressed. But when the flames were extinguished, Tommy's legs were badly burned. He had passed out from the pain by the time they extricated him from the rubble and put him in a skiff.

"Charlie!" Captain Gordon called out again, and once more he set out in search of his son. Only a few steps resulted in a fall when he tried to support himself on the injured foot. Bill Wagner came to his aid. "We'll look for Charlie," he said. "You go in a skiff to the landing. You're bleeding, and you need medical attention. We'll take care of things here."

Captain sat there for a moment, weak, discouraged, defeated. His boat was destroyed; his son was missing; and he was losing a lot of blood. He accepted help from one of the rescuers into a rowboat where he sat and watched his wonderful *Bella Mac* slowly receded into the darkness as the skiff moved across the river to Brownsville.

Lights brightened windows in nearly every house in the village, and the residents were eagerly willing to shelter the injured victims that were brought, one by one to the houses. The only physician in the village, Dr. Riley, kept busy, going from house to house administering first aid, and determining which ones needed more attention. Some were beyond his help.

"What's your name, son?" the doctor asked of the young man at Sonja Johnson's house. It was his first test of every patient from the boat to determine if they were coherent.

"Dominic Bouton, M'sieur," he responded. "But everyone calls me Frenchy." He was shivering from spending a considerable length of time in the cold river water, and Mrs. Johnson had wrapped a blanket around him. "My new clothes," Frenchy cried. "I have lost my new clothes." Tears streamed down his cheeks. It wasn't the clothes that concerned him most—it was that Charlie had given them to him, and they held more significance to him than just garments.

"We'll find your clothes," Dr. Riley said. "But right now, let me take a look at you. Do you have any severe pains?"

Frenchy stood and pulled back the blanket to show the doctor bruises and scrapes on his stomach and thighs, but there didn't seem to be any broken bones or bleeding wounds that required immediate attention.

"You're mighty lucky, Frenchy," the doctor said. "You must've been at the stern when the boilers exploded."

"Oui, M'sieur. I was asleep...our room was the very last one at the back of the boat. But how do you know that, M'sieur?"

"Because you're not burned. All the others who were farther toward the bow... above the boilers... were scalded by the steam."

Frenchy clutched the little pendant medicine bag that still hung at his chest, and he recalled what his uncle had told him—that *it would protect him from thunder in the night.* But he said nothing of that to the doctor. He only asked about his friend. "What about Charlie Martin? Have you seen him yet?"

"No one by that name," the doctor replied as he prepared to move on to the next patient. "I'll send over some ointment to put on those scrapes."

Chris Gerhardt was escorting the doctor to the houses where the *Bella Mac* victims had been taken and he was waiting at the door. "Chris," Dr. Riley said. "Send word down to the boys at the landing to try to find some clothes on that boat. All these men need their clothes... that is, if there are any left to find."

Chapter 44

Helen was already in the kitchen baking bread in anticipation of the Captain's and Charlie's arrival. She heard a knock at the door. Certainly *they* wouldn't knock, and it seemed a bit odd for anyone to be visiting at such an early hour. The clock had just chimed five.

"Hi, Helen. Sorry to bother you so early," the messenger said. "But I have an urgent message from the McDonalds."

Helen's smiling face turned solemn. An *urgent message* at this hour could not be good news. "What is it?" she asked. She could sense the young man's troubled feelings. He had been there many times delivering messages to Captain Gordon, but this time she knew something was amiss.

"The *Bella Mac's* boilers exploded early this morning down at Brownsville."

The housekeeper had lived in the midst of a river man long enough to know what that meant. "Oh, dear. Is the Captain...?" She couldn't bring herself to speak the rest of the question.

"We don't know the fate of all those aboard, yet. Alex and Charles McDonald are taking another boat down there. The telegram said '*many injured*' and they've been brought ashore and are being cared for at Brownsville homes."

Tears welled up in Helen's eyes. "I'll wake Maria and have James drive us down to the boatyard."

"Yes, ma'am. That would be a good idea."

News of *Bella Mac's* misfortune spread quickly throughout La Crosse in those early morning hours after the telegraph message from Brownsville arrived. Intense anxiety rose as it was known that many La Crosse men were on that boat. Friends and families of crewmen were already gathered at the boatyard just north of Clinton Street when Alex and Charles McDonald, owners of the *Bella Mac*, arrived at six o'clock accompanied by Dr. McArthur. None of the McDonald's boats were available, but the *Alfred Toll*, a raft boat owned by rival P.S. Davidson, lay in the harbor with steam built up and ready to sail. This was no time to think about rivalry. The *Alfred Toll's* crew didn't hesitate to assist, and not a moment was lost to point the steamer downriver.

Sam Henderson was among the onlookers as they watched the boat pull away. He had been eating his breakfast at the Bellevue Hotel when he overheard a messenger inform the clerk that there would be injured crewmen from a riverboat accident brought there, so the hotel could prepare for their arrival.

"What boat?" the clerk asked.

"The *Bella Mac*... her boilers exploded near Brownsville."

Henderson recognized the name and a cold chill raced down his spine. Although he hadn't lived his life in a river town, he had read plenty of news reports of steamboat boiler explosions, and he was well aware of the destruction and injury—and death—they could cause. Reginald Van Hugh III was aboard that boat, and suddenly he was angry with himself for allowing Captain Gordon to take the boy on one last trip.

By nine o'clock there had been no word from Brownsville. Newspaper reporters, among many other curious citizens and anxious families, wanted to go to the scene. But the southbound train to Dubuque had suffered engine problems and was running quite late, so getting to Brownsville by rail was out of the question. No other means of conveyance presented itself. One reporter for the *Republican Leader* grew more impatient as the minutes ticked by; he needed his story for the afternoon edition. Recruiting the help of a couple of old experienced river men he knew, they set out in a skiff. After an hour of vigorous rowing they could see the *Alfred Toll* and another freight boat, the *Vigor,* at the Brownsville landing, but they pointed their skiff to the site of the forlorn remains of the *Bella Mac* beached on the Wisconsin shore nearly opposite the village. Hardly anything remained to suggest that this pile of rubble was once a riverboat—only the paddlewheel and a small portion of the rear cabin. The rest looked like a disorderly stack of kindling on the sunken hull, a demoralizing sight.

A number of men from Brownsville were busy searching through the rubble on the main deck for the missing crew members thought to be buried under the debris. So far, they had only found one body that now lay on the forward deck covered with a quilt.

"Who's the dead body?" the reporter asked one of the men.

"Don't know for sure. We sent Fred over to give his description to the Captain. He'll prob'ly know."

"So, Captain Gordon is alive?"

"Sure is. He's cut up and limpin' and pretty discouraged, but he seems to be okay."

"All the others over in Brownsville?"

"Them that survived. Some are still missing. We only found the one. The rest prob'ly drowned."

The reporter quickly jotted everything down in his notepad, made a mental sketch of the wreck, and then he and his two assistants rowed across to Brownsville.

Chapter 45

All of the *Bella Mac's* surviving crew had been carried or helped aboard the *Alfred Toll*. And now, with the report of the one body found aboard the wreck, eleven of the seventeen were accounted for; six were still missing.

The newspaper reporter approached the *Alfred Toll's* captain on the levee. Reluctantly, permission was granted him to ride back to La Crosse. But before the pilot pointed the steamer upriver, he steered toward the Wisconsin shore to the wreck site. They had a body to retrieve.

As the steamer crossed the channel, a telegraph message was being transmitted to La Crosse: *One dead. Ten injured. Returning to La Crosse now aboard the Alfred Toll.*

The water was deep enough for the boat to pull alongside the sunken hull. Captain Gordon hobbled with a crutch to where three members of the search party were lifting a body wrapped in a quilt onto the deck of the *Alfred Toll*. Two others were transferring stacks of clothing and a few personal belongings they had found in the wreckage.

Whoever was under that quilt, Captain Gordon knew his emotions would overwhelm him, and he tried to prepare for the worst. When the cover was pulled back from the cut and burned face of the victim lying on the deck, Gordon stared a few moments, covered his eyes with one hand and turned away so the others wouldn't see his tears.

Frenchy sat next to the bunk where Maurice Leseur laid, his entire body scalded and his face and arms bandaged to stop cuts from bleeding. It was comforting to him to know Frenchy was there. "I tried to stop him," Leseur could barely speak.

The boy leaned closer to hear.

"That brave young fellow was gonna shut down the pump... save us all," Maurice continued. "I tried to stop him... knew it was too late... but he ran too fast for me."

"Who?" Frenchy asked.

"Charlie, mon ami. Charlie." The horribly burned fireman's pain was too intense, and he could say no more.

Bill Wagner came into the room carrying a bundle of clothing.

"They found your clothes, Frenchy. Well, most of them anyway." He handed the bundle to the boy, still draped with Mrs. Johnson's blanket. Tears of joy trickled down his cheeks. With the exception of the derby hat and one shoe, his new clothes had been recovered. And equally important, in the bundle was a tattered wooden box, and inside, his cherished flute seemed unharmed.

"Merci, mon ami," Frenchy beamed.

The reporter snuck from room to room where the injured crewmen awaited their arrival at La Crosse. Those who were able gave him their accounts of what had happened to them, but most had been sleeping at the time of the explosion. Their only recollections were of being rescued.

Only the on duty engineer, Charles Monahan, was able to tell him anything about before the boilers exploded. "Everything was running normal," he lied. "Steam pressure was at 135 and a full gauge of water in the boilers. Why they blew is a mystery to me."

But the reporter wondered, if Monahan had been in the midst of the machinery at the time of the explosion, why he wasn't scalded or injured as severely as the others. *That* was a mystery to the reporter.

An enormous crowd had gathered at the La Crosse levee by noon when the *Alfred Toll* landed. Hundreds of voices hushed and only murmurs floated about in speculation as the quilt-wrapped body was carried off the boat and placed in the waiting undertaker's wagon.

One by one the victims of the *Bella Mac* disaster were carried or assisted of the boat, Dr. McArthur directing the assistants to take the badly injured to the Bellevue house where they would all be under one roof for further medical attention. Sadly, he knew he would see some die there.

Captain Gordon was the last to leave the boat. He had stayed behind to see that everyone of his crew was safely on shore. As he approached, Dr. McArthur was instructing the blanket-clad Frenchy to follow the men who were taking the badly injured to the hotel.

"No," Captain intervened. "He will come with me. I need his help to get to my carriage."

Frenchy, cradling the bundle of clothes, gazed curiously at the captain.

"I guess that will be okay," said the physician. "His injuries aren't so severe. But I will be to your house later to look after you."

Maria spotted Captain and the boy as they walked toward the carriage. She lifted the hem of her skirt and ran to meet them.

"Oh! Papa!" she cried. "I've been so worried." She threw her arms around him and hugged him tightly as tears streamed down her face. Then she released her embrace and gazed briefly at Frenchy, on whose shoulder Captain leaned. "Where is Charlie? Is he okay?" Her eyes stared a worrisome look into her father's.

Captain only shook his head, and then nodded toward the hearse that was slowly making its way through the crowd.

"Oh, Papa. No!" Maria bawled uncontrollably. Helen arrived to help her back to the carriage.

"Help young Frenchy into the carriage," Gordon said to his gardener, James. "He will be coming home with us."

Chapter 46
June 3, 1882

Helen was pleased that another boy was there to fill a void in Charlie's absence, especially for Captain's sake. She knew Frenchy had been the one who lured Charlie on that excursion down the river in his canoe, and that he had remained a sore subject with Captain for quite some time after that incident. But that was long ago, and in time, the story had become one of those endeared and humorous memories of the past.

And what a gentleman he was! So appreciative of the bedroom that had been Charlie's, and of all the fine clothes that fit him as if they were custom-made just for him. His manners at the supper table astounded even Maria, until she learned of his upbringing in a home of distinguished French culture. He was eager to learn to read, and Maria enjoyed tutoring him; she would gladly direct her efforts to prepare him for school. It all made missing Charlie less painful.

No longer did he have to tend the cattle on the hillside meadow, and now his beautiful canoe rested out of the weather in the carriage house instead of on the bank of that algae-covered lagoon behind a deteriorating log house on Barron's Island. No longer did he have to hunt rabbits, or prepare venison, or chop firewood to survive through the winter. Being a kind-hearted, caring friend had paid its rewards. But he still missed his best friend.

A knock came at the door. Helen was not surprised to see Andy, the messenger from the McDonald boatyard, as there had been considerable communication with Captain Gordon during his time of convalescence. He no longer needed the crutch, but he still limped noticeably, and the cuts on his face were still healing.

Helen escorted Andy to the den where Captain was having his morning coffee and reading the newspaper.

"Hi, Cap'n," the messenger said. "How are you feeling today?"

"Like an old man with a broken foot and cut lip. What brings you here, Andy?"

"Well, there's been a body found in the river down below Brownsville."

Captain jerked his attention away from the paper and stared at the messenger, waiting for further explanation.

"They think it's one of your lost crewmen from the *Bella Mac*. The McDonalds want you to go down there and identify the body 'cause you knew those men better than anyone. The *Mollie Mohler* packet boat will stop at the Brownsville landing for you and the body on her way upriver this afternoon." He reached in his breast pocket. "Here is your rail ticket to Brownsville. Louis will be at the depot, too. He'll go with you."

Gordon took the ticket and bid Andy a farewell as Helen escorted him back to the door.

This had been a trying time for Gordon: he'd sat through excruciating examinations as government officials investigated the accident. He'd attended more funerals than he cared to think about. And then there was the formal hearing when his Second Engineer, Charles Monahan was charged with carelessness and neglect by sleeping while on duty, and was stripped of his engineer's license. Losing Charlie and his best friend, Frank McIntyre had been the most devastating blow to his morale, and apparently, the nightmare hadn't ended yet.

The body that he and Louis viewed on the levee at Brownsville that day was that of an average sized man, but it was so badly decomposed there was nothing left to identify.

"It's Frank McIntyre," declared Captain Gordon.

Louis, however, wasn't in total agreement. Judging by the plaid flannel shirt and jeans, he thought the remains were Will McCannish, whose two brothers, George and David had been buried nearly two months earlier.

The captain thought for a moment how he would justify his decision. Frank had always been his best friend, and he owed to Frank's sister the end of her grieving, wishing for Frank's decent burial. "Those are the clothes I saw Frank wearing when I relieved him in the pilothouse the last time I saw him alive."

The captain's decision was final, for it was he who had been given the responsibility. When they returned to La Crosse, they visited Mrs. Woods, Frank McIntyre's sister and informed her that they had found her brother.

After the funeral two days later, Captain Gordon limped out to a bench in the garden that was in full bloom. Birds were singing; butterflies flitted about. He hoped it was all over.

On the other side of the wall next to the La Crosse River, Dominic Bouton sat on the bank thinking about a friend.

Postscript

Although it is a work of fiction, this story is based on true historic events. The two main characters, Charlie Martin and Frenchy were real people, as were most of the characters depicted in the story. The *Bella Mac* was an actual riverboat owned by the McDonald Brothers of La Crosse, Wisconsin. Its demise described in this book is factual, according to newspaper accounts that were published by the *La Crosse Republican Leader*, written by surviving crew members, and reporters who saw, first-hand, the wrecked boat and interviewed surviving crew shortly after the catastrophe occurred.

A government investigation of this accident followed and attributed the cause of the boiler explosion to carelessness and neglect by Charles Monahan, second engineer, who was on duty at the time of the blast. His engineer's license was revoked as a result. A total of nine lives were lost.

They were:

Swift Bell, deckhand, body never found.

Maurice Leseur, fireman, died Apr. 9, 1882.

Charles Martin, deckhand, adopted son of Captain Gordon, died instantly.

David McCannish, Chief Clerk, died Apr. 10, 1882.

George McCannish, assist. cook, body recovered Apr. 9, 1882.

William McCannish, deckhand, body never found.

Frank McIntyre, Second Pilot, body recovered June 3, 1882.*

John Nolan, fireman, (Not employed on *Bella Mac* but was working his passage upriver) body never found.

Tom Rice, deckhand, died Apr 8, 1882.

*Many years after the *Bella Mac* explosion near Brownsville, Minnesota, and long after the death of Captain Gordon, the last surviving crew member, his First Mate, Louis Suelflohn submitted his story of the incident to the *La Crosse Tribune*. In comparison, his account was consistent with news reports filed at the time of the accident, but he revealed one fact that had been kept a secret for fifty years.

Mrs. Woods (Frank McIntyre's widowed sister) cared for the grave of a total stranger. She never learned the truth about the deed committed by close friend, Captain W.W. Gordon, intended as a gesture of compassion. Many years later, the Captain confidentially acknowledged to Louis Suelflohn that, at the time, he was aware the body he identified on June 3, 1882 at Brownsville was not that of Frank McIntyre. In answer to the question, "Why, then, did you insist that it was?" he replied, "To satisfy his sister that her brother would have a decent burial."

Only the two of them—Gordon and Suelflohn—were ever aware of the substitution until 1932 when Louis' story was published in the newspaper.

Cursed
by the
Wind

Chapter 1

"**W**hat's that you just stuffed in your pocket?" Dorothy Duncan stepped out onto the back porch from the kitchen, her razor-sharp voice cutting through thirteen-year-old Bobby's concentration.

"It's nothin', Ma," Bobby Duncan responded to his mother's stern voice. "It's just a piece of paper. It's nothin'."

The boy knew he couldn't reveal to his mother the true identity of the letter he had received from his older brother. Ever since Nicholas had announced to the family that he was joining the Minnesota National Guard, she had all but disowned her oldest son. Bobby recognized his mother's bitterness as an extension of her grief, after her husband of eleven years had left her a widow with three children to care for in a pioneer environment. She viewed Nick's decision to join the military as just another disappointing gesture of abandonment, and she hadn't gotten over it yet.

Mrs. Duncan had destroyed the very first letter Nick sent to Bobby nearly two months earlier, before he had the chance to read it. She knew the closeness her oldest and youngest sons shared; she resented that, too. Bobby recalled the day he saw her pitch the letter addressed to him into the kitchen wood stove, and as the flames had consumed it, he vowed to never let that happen again. Religiously, every morning, he ran to the Red Wing Post Office, hoping there would be another. And about once a week, there was another, but his mother would never see them;

he kept them well hidden in a box out in the woodshed where she wouldn't find them. Bobby cherished those letters, just as he cherished the relationship with his brother.

"That wouldn't be a letter from your good-fer-nothin' brother, would it?" Dorothy demanded.

"What if it is?" Bobby barked in response. He suspected that the postmaster had probably tipped her off to the letters he was picking up; denial would only add to the problem he faced now. Before his mother could say any more, he thought he would take his stand, once and for all. "There's a riverboat goin' down to Lake City next Sunday... and I'm goin' to see Nicholas."

Mrs. Duncan's eyes widened with anger. "You'll do no such thing, young man."

"But, Ma! I want to see Nick. Why can't I go see him?"

"Because he ran off and left us, just to get himself killed in the Army!"

Ran off? Bobby thought. He had admired Nicholas for wanting to serve his country; joining the Guard was an honorable thing to do, so everyone in town was saying in those days of 1890.

"Now, get to your chores and forget about such nonsense."

Bobby lowered his head and started for the woodshed to gather up an armload of kindling to be carried into the kitchen wood box. Perhaps, if he didn't mention it again, his mother would forget about the excursion by Sunday. One way or another, he would be on that riverboat.

With chores finished and his lunch eaten, Bobby retreated to the privacy behind the woodshed. His mother had retired to her bedroom for a mid-day nap, as she usually did, and brother Bradley had departed with friends for an afternoon that would probably result in mischief. They had invited Bobby to join them, but Bobby wasn't too fond of Bradley's choice of ruffian friends, and he declined the invitation.

He pulled his brother's letter from the breast pocket of his bib overalls and read it again, as he had done at least a dozen times or more. Unlike the other letters Nick had sent during the past weeks that told of his great experiences as a Minnesota National Guardsman, this one whispered a twinge of mystery, and warned Bobby to keep its contents a secret. But the letter heralded an invitation to adventure, and lured

Bobby to pursue one of his fondest desires – to ride a riverboat down the Mississippi.

At thirteen, Bobby was too young for the ruggedness of the true river men who laughed in the face of danger. He wasn't quite big enough or strong enough, yet, for any steamboat captain to give him a second glance as a deck hand. He had some growing to do, but he knew some day the river would be his life, and a riverboat would be his home.

At thirteen, Bobby Duncan *wasn't* too young to dream; he would climb to the top of Barn Bluff with his best friend Seth Miller, and there, overlooking the magnificent river and Red Wing, the town they knew as home, they could gaze for miles. Lake Pepin, to the south, seemed their gateway to the world. They would watch a tiny speck on the distant lake horizon grow to the grandness of a familiar shape as it came nearer – that of the gallant riverboats, depositing their brown and black smoke into the air. Whether the boat had come from a far-away port – St. Louis, Memphis, Natchez – or from a nearer town – La Crosse, Winona, Wabasha – it made no difference; all those places seemed a world away. And one day, Bobby would see that world.

Nothing in Red Wing quite matched the excitement whenever a riverboat was tied up at the levee. It was as if the circus had arrived. Children ran to the riverfront to gaze in wonderment of the huge vessels; ladies strolled down to gaze discreetly at the passengers coming and going; the men were usually most successful with cunning tactics to gain boarding privileges to look at the engines, chat with friends who worked the boats, and to partake of the latest river gossip and racy stories brought there by the boatmen.

Bobby Duncan was no exception when it came to joining a curious crowd at the landing. The distant drone of a whistle, the thrashing of paddlewheels, and the sight of a steamboat coming around the bend always sent him running to the levee. He loved to watch the activity boiling around the docked boats. Frequently, there would be a stack of furniture, suggesting that a new family was arriving; sacks of grain, barrels of oil, and crates of goods piled high on the levee awaited the teamsters and wagons to haul them off to the expecting merchants in town. Horse-drawn carriages lined up, ready to carry passengers and their baggage to hotels, eateries, the railroad depot, or to private homes around the city. There was nothing more exciting to Bobby Duncan.

He had paid close attention to the boatmen's talk; their conversations suggested the important role riverboats played over the years, while the American frontier was being tamed. Cities were born with the advent of the steamboat; cotton and tobacco plantations in the south, coal, iron, and steel industries in the east, and the thriving lumber industry in the north relied heavily upon river transportation. Nothing could compare to the romantic and colorful stories told by the men who made the rivers their life. But Bobby heard plenty of sorrowful tales, as well; as glamorous as river travel seemed, it held a high risk of danger. Even the best of engineers and captains told of collisions, fires, and boiler explosions, sometimes claiming lives, and almost always, the depths of the river claiming the craft and its cargo. They told of the many boats that had had their hulls ripped open by snags and rocks hiding beneath the river's surface, undetected by the keenest pilot's eye. Hundreds of such wrecked boats littered the river's channels from St. Paul to New Orleans.

Bobby understood the hazards involved. But at the age of thirteen, the hazards were merely a part of the intrigue that lured him. Some day, he wanted to be a part of it all.

Bobby quickly folded the letter and stuffed it back into his pocket when he noticed Seth sauntering up the lane toward him. He planned to share the secret with Seth, but this was not the time; a more secluded environment where there was less chance of other ears listening would be a better choice.

"Hey, Bobby," Seth called out. "Wanna hike up the bluff?"

"Thought you'd never ask," Bobby replied, as if it had been the only thing on his mind.

A cool dip in the river was more what Bobby had considered, but it had been quite a while since they climbed Barn Bluff. Not a cloud in the sky meant perfect viewing and dreaming, and it would be the perfect opportunity to persuade Seth to join him on a great adventure.

Seth Miller favored more the adventures that involved keeping both feet on dry land. He'd climb any hill or explore any forest, but although he didn't like to admit it, he was a little timid when it came to the river. Swimming in shallow water along a sand bar on a hot day summed up his desires for intimacies with it.

There was no need for any more discussion on the subject; Seth had come prepared – his usual canteen on a leather strap slung over his shoulder indicated that he would climb Barn Bluff, with or without Bobby. But they were both in agreement on their afternoon activity.

Barn Bluff presented a long, steep, grueling ascent, but it was well worth the effort, even on a hot day. A breeze always seemed to stir the air on top of the bluffs, and a warm breeze was better than none.

Bobby and Seth plopped onto the edge of the rock cliff facing Lake Pepin as if they were sitting down at the supper table. Inches away, a three-hundred-foot drop-off did little to intimidate them. Dangling their feet over that edge seemed no different to them than sitting on the edge of the back porch at home. The warm breeze pressed against their backs. Lake Pepin stretched out before them like a giant mirror, reflecting a brilliant blue sky. Hundreds of feet below, a trail of brown smoke curled from the stacks of a steamer guiding a log raft at least ten times its own length. Bobby watched and dreamed as the raft and steamer moved steadily down the main channel toward Lake Pepin.

"Can I have a sip from your canteen?" Bobby asked.

Seth unscrewed the cap, took a gulp, and handed the canteen to Bobby. "So, what's this big secret you mentioned on the way up here?"

Bobby sipped the water that was no longer cold, but it was wet, and that's all that mattered. "Got a letter from Nick yesterday."

"Well, you get lots of letters from Nick. What's so special about that?"

"This one's different. You gotta promise not to tell anybody."

Seth knew that Bobby and Nicholas were about as close as two brothers could possibly be. Nicholas was seven years older than Bobby, and even their sixteen-year-old brother, Bradley, couldn't merit the kind of attention that Nicholas gave to his youngest sibling.

"Okay, I promise," Seth replied.

"Next Sunday there's a boat goin' down to Lake City where Nick is at the National Guard camp, and we're gonna be on it."

Seth gasped. "Whatya mean, *we?*"

"You and me."

"I don't know, Bobby."

"They're havin' this big celebration at the camp for the guys in the Guard – a picnic, a band concert, a parade – it'll be great fun."

"If it's for the guys in the Guard, then why—"

"It's for all their families and friends, too."

Seth shook his head slowly. He wasn't fond of riding a boat nearly the full length of Lake Pepin, and back. "So, what's the secret? A picnic and a parade don't sound like no secret."

Bobby pulled the letter out of his pocket. "This is the part you can't tell anybody." He carefully unfolded the paper and held it in front of Seth. "Here... you can read it yourself."

Seth took the letter and began reading. His eyes widened as he scanned the page. When he finished, his hand holding the letter dropped to his knees; a bewildered stare took command. "I don't get it. Why doesn't Nick just keep it there with him?"

"Well, didn't you read the part where he says he's afraid it might get lost, or stolen?"

"Why does he want *you* to come get it?"

"'Cause he doesn't trust anybody else, that's why."

Seth just stared out over the river, worrying more about the long boat ride than thinking of the extraordinary mission that his best friend was inviting him on.

"You're not afraid, are you, Seth?" Bobby asked with a bit of daring in his voice.

"N-no. No. I'm not afraid."

"Then, will you come with me?"

"I-I guess so." Seth peered at the paper and then offered it to Bobby. Just as Bobby reached for it, a wind gust snatched it from his grasp. Bobby grabbed at the air desperately trying to catch the fleeting paper, but within seconds, it was floating on the wind like a dry leaf, tumbling, twisting, zigzagging about, its destination dictated by the hand of fate. Bobby watched it flying away until it was merely a white speck, and then it disappeared out of sight.

"I'm sorry," Seth mumbled.

"It wasn't your fault," Bobby said. "But we have to try to find it." He studied the trees along the backwaters where he thought the letter might have ended its flight.

"Why? It's just a letter," Seth protested.

"'Cause I don't want nobody else to find it. C'mon. Help me look for it."

Bobby ran toward the trail leading down the steep hillside. Seth scrambled to his feet and followed.

All afternoon they tramped through the brush and weeds along the backwater sloughs. A bright white sheet of paper would certainly be easy to spot, Bobby thought, but as the shadows grew longer and daylight faded to dusk, he had lost all hopes of finding the letter that had vanished with the wind.

Chapter 2

Ａll of Red Wing buzzed with excitement; signs tacked up around town announced the arrival of an excursion vessel, the Sea Wing, that next Sunday morning. Its destination was thirty miles downriver, just below Lake City at the widest point of Lake Pepin, where the First Regiment of the National Guard -- many Red Wing boys among its ranks -- were to host a gala event for their families and friends from whom they had been separated since early spring, and would be until Christmas. Sweethearts would be together; families would reunite and be whole; buddies could be buddies again for a few brief hours.

No one was more eager for the day to come than Bobby Duncan. He missed his brother, Nicholas, and now he had the opportunity to ride a riverboat, even though it was an act in defiance of his mother's wishes. Bobby had a plan.

Excitement brewed in another form along the Mississippi bank about a mile south of Red Wing. Gunter Griswold sat by a small campfire, cooking his catch of the day. His fondness of whiskey had kept him from achieving any degree of success in any line of honorable work, and hardly anyone knew him by any name other than Grizzly, or recognized him as anything more than the town drunk. A sour-mash personality hung on him like the dirty shirt he always wore, and not a single storekeeper would let him out of sight when he entered an establishment; they knew he couldn't be trusted any farther than the front door.

Grizzly tipped a whiskey bottle, gulping the last swallow from it, as he stared at a mud-stained sheet of paper he had found caught in a tangled heap of driftwood on the riverbank. It was a letter, dated just a week before, and it spelled temptation. He knew the sender and the recipient

-- Nicholas Duncan and his younger brother, Bobby.

A devious sneer squirmed under Grizzly's disheveled black beard. By Sunday night, his reputation in Red Wing would be confirmed as that of a thief, but that didn't worry him – by then, he would be long gone down river and lost in the hills of Wisconsin, never to be found by anyone in Red Wing.

There was yet another kind of stir in Diamond Bluff, a much smaller river town on the Wisconsin side of the Mississippi, about seven miles upstream from Red Wing. A curious crowd gathered around an itinerant preacher known only as Georgas. A meek-looking, gray-bearded man with a voice like a bullhorn, he had wandered into Diamond Bluff several days earlier; a premonition had drawn him there, and as the days in the little town passed, he realized that the mysterious vision had laid the groundwork for his foothold in the community.

There, resting at the bank of the Mississippi, was the Steamer, Sea Wing, destined to carry excursionists to Lake City on the following Sunday. Georgas knew that if he could persuade the people to believe a pending disaster loomed, and if he could convince them to cancel the excursion, then he would possess the power to lead a newfound flock in any direction of his choosing.

"My eye hath foreseen a calamity," he boomed out to the gathering. "A warning from above hath befallen upon my ears. Brothers and Sisters of this fair town... heed this vision of dire portent from God!"

Absorbed in the missionary's open-air sermon, a few of the listeners gasped in awe, and silently vowed to abstain from entering their names on the Sea Wing's Sunday passenger list. But most shrugged it off and walked away, going about their usual activities. Georgas realized he had not been thoroughly successful; he decided to visit the Sea Wing. Perhaps, he thought, the captain would be a God fearing man, and a bit of heavy persuasion could prevent the Sunday trip.

Captain David Wethern stood on the main deck of the Sea Wing, one foot planted firmly on the gunwale railing, peering down at Georgas on the riverbank. Upon hearing the Padre's plea to cancel the Sunday excursion, Wethern replied, "With all due respect, Preacher, I appreciate your concern. However, a lot of people are looking forward to this outing, and I can't let them down."

Georgas continued his deplorable quest, but to no avail. Captain

Wethern remained committed to the Sunday cruise. The Sea Wing, usually a log rafter, had been idle for weeks during a lean season; this excursion would render a desperately needed handsome profit.

Bobby darted into Berquist's Drugstore. It wasn't one of his planned stops, but it seemed his best escape. He headed for the counter where Emma Nelson greeted him with a smile. "Good morning, Bobby."

"G'mornin' Emma." Bobby glanced nervously over his shoulder toward the front door. "I was wondering if I could sneak out your back door."

"Something wrong?" Emma asked.

"Well, yeah. Grizzly's been followin' me all morning."

"Now, why would that vile creature be following you?"

"Don't know, Emma. I was just on my way to the barbershop to get a haircut, and he started followin' me."

Emma came from behind the counter, stepped closer to the door, and stared at the front windows, only to see the disgusting man's scruffy black beard and dirty shirt vividly poised in the morning sun, staring back at her. When he saw Emma scornfully watching him, Grizzly casually turned away.

"Okay, Bobby. He's not looking. Hurry on out the back door."

"Thanks, Emma. I owe you a favor." Bobby scrambled out into the back alley. The barbershop was just a couple of buildings down the block. He snuck back to the sidewalk and peeked around the corner. Grizzly still waited in front of the drugstore, but he was looking the other way. Taking advantage of the opportunity, Bobby shot around the corner. With a little luck, Grizzly wouldn't see him enter the barbershop.

George Nelson's shop was a popular gathering place for the men folk, and it seemed that George was entertaining the men gathered there more than he was cutting hair or trimming beards. One could learn as much about the local news and gossip there as picking up the daily paper. Although Bobby didn't exactly consider himself *men folk*, being only thirteen, his presence didn't seem to bother the gentlemen sitting in the corner; they continued their chatter.

"Good morning, young Mr. Duncan," George said. "Need a haircut today?"

"Yes, sir," Bobby replied. He climbed into the empty barber chair; George gave the big white cloth a shake and draped it around Bobby.

Bobby always savored his visits to the barbershop; it was almost worth the two bits and sacrificing his hair just to take in the gossip, and to breathe in all the wonderful aromas of shaving lotions and hair tonics. He watched the locks of brown fall onto the cloth as George snipped and the men talked about the hot weather and how the National Guard boys at Lake City must be suffering in the heat. He knew a couple of the gentlemen doing most of the talking: George Hartman ran the hardware store, and Ira Fulton worked at the Red Wing Pottery. Ira was bragging about his steam yacht, and about how he was sailing down to Lake City on Sunday to see the military demonstrations. Mr. Hartman said he was considering the trip, too, on the Sea Wing.

Just then, John Ingebretson, one of Bobby's school friends popped through the front door. A canvas bag filled with newspapers slung over his shoulder, he immediately strutted to the gentlemen in the corner. "Paper?" he announced in the form of a question. George and Ira dug into their pockets and handed the dimes to the paperboy. John gave them each their papers and turned back toward the door. He noticed Bobby in the chair, waved and said, "Hi, Bobby."

Bobby wanted to wave to his friend but he only grinned, fearful of the slightest movement that could ruin his haircut.

"Say, Bobby," the barber said. "You going to Lake City on Sunday to see Nicholas?"

Bobby desperately wanted to tell the world that he was taking a steamboat ride, but then he thought about the trouble it might get him into if his mother learned of his plans. "No. Ma won't let me go."

George Hartman overheard Bobby's statement and threw a curious stare in his direction. Ira commanded George's attention, though, with more bragging about the yacht.

Everyone who knew them knew the closeness Nicholas and Bobby Duncan had shared ever since Bobby was just a tyke. The loss of their father had drawn them even closer, but their mother had suffered a near mental breakdown when her husband died, and she hadn't been the best parent to the boys since. She worked nights as a waitress at the hotel restaurant to sustain a home for them, but not much more. Everyone knew, too, that Nicholas and Bobby had earned their own way for the past few years, picking up odd jobs wherever they could. But Bradley, their sixteen-year-old brother, had only earned the reputation of a lazy, spoiled brat.

Bobby had won the admiration of many people with his ability to cope with the stress that a thirteen-year-old boy shouldn't have to. Nick's absence, now, only magnified the void his father had left. Even a best friend couldn't fill that void completely.

By Friday morning, almost everyone in Red Wing, Minnesota knew about the excursion to Lake City. An advertisement had appeared in Thursday's newspaper announcing the event, and that tickets for passage on the Sea Wing could be purchased at Lillyblad's General Store. In a town with a population of 6000, and with the large number of Guardsmen from Red Wing stationed at Lake City, the Sea Wing would surely be carrying a capacity load. Bobby wasn't taking any chances of being too late to acquire an available ticket. As soon as all his chores were done for the day, he hurried downtown to meet Seth.

A hand-lettered sign in Lillyblad's front window proclaimed "Sea Wing Tickets – 50 cents," and plenty of people were on the same thought train as Bobby – they wanted to be sure they were among the boarding passengers on Sunday. But Bobby was still nervous about his mother discovering his plans, so he and Seth lay back until the crowd had thinned a little. When it appeared that no one was waiting to buy their tickets, Bobby and Seth edged their way to the counter, made the request, and each deposited their fifty cents in the clerk's hand. As they took their tickets and turned to exit the front door, Bobby collided with a man who had been standing behind them, and that they had not noticed his approach. It was George Hartman, the hardware store proprietor.

Bobby gasped. He had been caught. In his cautious attempt to acquire the Sea Wing tickets, so that no one would know that he had done it, Mr. Hartman had witnessed the act.

George just smiled at the boys. "Well, Bobby, I see you're going after all."

Bobby looked around to see if anyone else had heard or seen. Mr. Hartman was alone, and no one in the store appeared to be paying any attention.

Nearly in tears, Bobby glanced at George. "Ma doesn't want me to go... but I really want to see Nick." Then with a pleading frown, he added, "You won't tell her, will you?"

George Hartman had known the Duncan boys since they were babies. He had sold them fishing line and hooks since they were old enough to hold a fishing pole, and he knew and understood their close bond as brothers. George recognized the importance of this trip to Bobby. "Your secret is safe with me," he said quietly and winked. "I'll take it to my grave."

"Thank you, Mr. Hartman," Bobby replied with a worried smile.

George Hartman wasn't the only person to see Bobby and Seth purchase the Sea Wing tickets. As they left through the front door, Grizzly stood on the sidewalk, watching and sneering. Bobby noticed him, and recalled the previous day's encounter. It seemed peculiar, to Bobby, that this social outcast appeared everywhere he went, but he didn't mention it to Seth. He just looked forward to Sunday when he could escape Grizzly's pursuit – at least for the day.

Chapter 3

The Mississippi River, and Lake Pepin to the south, sprawled out in a smooth, glimmering plain of quicksilver under a blazing July sun. Captain David Wethern and his crew of ten had made the final inspection and preparations aboard the Sea Wing, confident of her seaworthiness, and were ready to greet their passengers. It was to be a joyous day filled with fun and relaxation for many, and although the heat and the humidity had been nearly unbearable for a week, a day cruise on the river might ease the weather's stressful burden it had levied on everyone.

The captain leaned against the steering wheel in the pilothouse, high atop the craft, and watched as a few excited picnic basket-toting travelers neared the landing at Diamond Bluff. He had expected more of his homeport neighbors to join in on the festive day, but the walking missionary, Georgas, had evidently discouraged many would-be excursionists. David caught a glimpse of Georgas at the top of the slope where he was making his last-minute efforts to turn people away.

Ed Niles, the ship's clerk, entered the pilothouse. He, too, displayed a mournful stare.

"Why so down-in-the-mouth, Ed?" the captain asked.

The clerk gazed out over the calm river. "Well, David," he paused, hesitant to express his gut feelings. "If I weren't employed on this boat, I might very well stay ashore today."

Captain Wethern knew the answer without asking for Ed's reasoning, but he asked anyway. "Why do you say that?"

"Well, Captain," Mr. Niles began, "you know that preacher came to our house a few days ago looking for a place to stay."

"Yes, Ed, I'm aware of that," the captain answered.

"Well, last night at supper, he sure seemed convinced that the Sea Wing was in for trouble today."

Wethern put his hand on Ed's shoulder. "Ed, take a good look at the river. It's as calm as a sleeping baby. Let's not give in to some crack-pot preacher who--"

"But you have to admit," the clerk interrupted. "There were some pretty bad storms out west on Wednesday, and with this heat, lately, we're probably in for one here, too."

The captain stared at his clerk with concern. "Are you doubting my ability as a master pilot?"

"No, David. Not at all."

"Well, then. You know we can always slip into a safe landing anywhere along the river, in case of bad weather."

"Yes, David, I know that."

"Okay. So put on a happy face, and quit worrying about the weather... or that preacher."

Ed Niles forced an artificial smile.

"There. That's better," the captain grinned. "Now, let's go down and welcome aboard our passengers."

Only eleven Diamond Bluff area passengers boarded. It seemed needless, to some, that a barge had been tied to the Sea Wing's port side bow to accommodate a large number of people, but David Wethern was confident that in Trenton and Red Wing the boat would fill to its permitted capacity with paying customers. A band would entertain them on the trip, and the barge, specially fitted with a canvas canopy to further provide a little more shade, would serve as a makeshift dance floor.

Captain Wethern showed no foreboding signs of worry as he eased the Sea Wing out into the main channel. He seemed supremely happy; his wife and two young sons were aboard, making this a family outing for them, as well, and any time a riverboat master could fill his vessel with passengers for an excursion, he was entitled to wear a smile.

An accomplished steamboat pilot, David Wethern had learned the Upper Mississippi well during a long apprenticeship aboard other boats, and for the past three years he had piloted the Sea Wing, towing rafts of logs from the Wisconsin and Minnesota riverbanks as far south as Illinois, delivering the cargo to lumber mills there. No one knew better than he, that the Mississippi, and especially Lake Pepin, was unpredictable, more like a sleeping giant than a sleeping baby, as he had convinced Ed Niles it was that day. He knew, too, that with the weeklong unrelenting hot weather, anything was possible; he had witnessed plenty of squalls spawned by this kind of weather, but he was confident of his navigational skills, and should bad weather threaten, David Wethern knew how to bring the Sea Wing to safety.

As the Sea Wing churned its way downriver toward Trenton, the pilot had time to reflect on his past. He was saddened with the thought of his father's fate, twenty years earlier: David was but fifteen years old when his father was shot and killed during a holdup while on a business trip to St. Paul. The sorrow subsided, though, as David overpowered his grief with thoughts about his own success, beginning a riverboat career at the age of thirteen, and eventually rising to a general store owner in Diamond Bluff. But he had never given up his passion for the river. In 1888, he and his business partner, Mel Sparks, built the Sea Wing, this 135-foot-long, 109-ton steamer, and continued their commercial river quest.

And on this splendid Sunday morning, Captain David Wethern was exceptionally pleased with the fair skies and placid river that were certain to ensure a prosperous turnout at the next two passenger pickup landings. The log rafting business had been on a steady decline over the past months; at fifty cents per ticket, a full load of passengers would give him good reason to smile.

Just after 9:00, the Sea Wing steamed into the Trenton landing, met by twenty-two eagerly waiting voyagers. David recognized a few faces among several small groups on the levee; there was Frank Way and his fiancée Mattie Flynn and Frank's two sisters, Ednah and Adda -- the captain knew the Way family, as their father, Benjamin Way, was the Trenton postmaster and general store operator. On his last visit to Trenton, David had been cordially invited to Frank's upcoming wedding.

He knew the Adams youngsters, Mamie, Willie, Ella, and their cousin John, too. They were the teen-aged children of the two most successful farm families in the neighboring area. As a general store operator, David Wethern enjoyed strong ties with the farming community, and the Adams were among his best customers.

The Ways and the Adams, and all the rest, mostly youngsters in their teens and twenties, looked as though they might well be attending a formal ball, dressed in pinstriped suits and flowing white dresses. Spirits were high; everyone seemed eager to escape the doldrums of everyday life, if just for a few hours.

With all the passengers on board, the captain sounded the whistle; the Sea Wing paddled away from the Trenton dock, winding its way back to the main channel, with Red Wing, Minnesota only a few minutes away.

Bobby and Seth sat on the levee, patiently waiting to see the first signs of the steamer. They had been there since dawn, and they had expected to encounter a lot of people as the morning hours wore on. It was nearly an hour before the scheduled arrival of the Sea Wing, but already there were fifty anxious excursionists waiting to board the anticipated boat, and the crowd grew by the minute. Bobby quickly scanned the gathered crowd; he recognized a few people by name, and a few by face only, but most were strangers. He didn't want to mingle with the assemblage just yet, fearful of too many people noticing his presence, and word getting back to his mother. Once they were on the boat, Bobby thought he could easily avoid anyone he knew by remaining amidst the strangers.

"Now, Seth," Bobby lectured, "If they ask, don't give your real name."
"Why?"

"'Cause I don't want my Ma to know we got on the boat."
"But what name should I give?"

Bobby looked around. He spotted another young fellow in the crowd he knew, but not very well. "Tell 'em your name is George Seavers. They won't know the difference."

Seth wiped the sweat from his forehead. "Okay, but I don't know why we have to be so..."

"I just don't want Ma to know we're here."

The crowd grew more, and the sun radiated its steadily increasing intensity. The day was already promising to be another scorcher, just like the entire past week had been.

Bobby vigilantly watched the river northward for the Sea Wing to appear. He knew he would hear the whistle, and perhaps, see the smoke, long before the boat came into sight. He wanted to be ready to jump into position at the front of the crowd.

Intrusive pangs of guilt bombarded his visions of a day to be filled with fun and adventure. Betraying his mother's trust tarnished his reputation as an obedient son; he only wished that she could shed the bitterness she held toward Nick. But this trip was important to Bobby, and he was ready to suffer the consequences it might produce.

Black smoke rose over the treetops, and then the whistle sounded. Bobby nudged Seth and jumped to his feet. "C'mon! Let's go!" he told Seth, and together they sprinted to the landing, among the other excited travelers.

By the time David Wethern maneuvered his craft into the Red Wing landing, almost everyone back in Diamond Bluff had returned to their usual Sunday activities. One man, though, Georgas, the traveling missionary, was beside himself with frustration. He had miserably failed to suspend the Sea Wing's departure, and his hopes of gaining control of his followers diminished. His plans to build a church in Diamond Bluff, at the expense of its residents, and to lead a parish that would support him for the remainder of his years, was quickly slithering away. Storms were approaching the area – everyone suspected that. But when, and if, the Sea Wing returned to its homeport, unscathed, Georgas feared that he would become the laughing stock of the community; his reputation as a prophet would be looked upon with little regard, and few, if any, would place their trust and faith in his religious leadership.

He gathered together his few belongings and began yet another walking journey away from the little river town with hopes of finding another opportunity.

"Where are you going?" asked a curious citizen, witnessing Georgas' apparent permanent departure.

"I cannot bear to share the sorrow the people of this town will endure when the sun rises tomorrow," was the preacher's only reply, and he disappeared into the hills.

The gangway lowered to the Red Wing levee; everyone scrambled to it. The ship's clerk stood waiting to begin compiling the boarding passenger list, but the crowd's overwhelming enthusiasm abruptly halted the name taking. Bobby quickly scooted by before the clerk had a chance to change his mind, and Seth followed closely behind.

Seth was still a little leery of boarding the boat. His stomach squirmed at the thought of spending two hours out in the middle of Lake Pepin, but he couldn't let Bobby see his nervousness. He just kept pushing on with the flow of the crowd, following Bobby onto the main deck. The gangway creaked and groaned under the rumbling of footsteps, increasing Seth's uneasiness, but by the time he and Bobby had tunneled their way through a tangle of duck trousers and billowing white skirts, and they were standing on the solid deck of the Sea Wing, Seth had been drawn into the thrill of risk and danger, swept up in the aphrodisiac effect of fear.

Many of the early boarding passengers – the women with small children, mostly – headed for the cabins on the Sea Wing's two lower decks to escape the sun's searing heat. Bobby was too excited about being on board a riverboat to worry about the weather, or about seeking shade. His curiosity drew him to the top deck, the Hurricane Deck, where seven skiffs claimed a good share of standing room, and the pilothouse towered high above all the rest. Bobby and Seth peered in through its windows to see the captain standing at the giant steering wheel, smiling at their awe.

It was a dream-come-true – one that had danced in Bobby's imagination hundreds of times; he went wild with joy, like the river suddenly overflowing its banks. In just a short while, he would be gliding along the Mississippi's silvery surface; a paddlewheel would be pushing him on a journey into tomorrow. For the moment, he gave little thought to his mother's mandate, and the odds that she would learn he was aboard the Sea Wing. The odds were against him, but he didn't think of life in terms of odds and probability right then.

Nor, was he thinking of the letter he had received from Nick, or the secretive mission he was on; in fact, everything in the real world had ceased to exist – everything except the Sea Wing and Bobby's presence there, on the upper deck, gazing out across the sun-sparkled water, and sniffing the smoke from the Sea Wing's stacks, and watching all the people coming aboard.

People! People who knew him; people he wanted to avoid, at least for right then. Reality started settling in again. At the top of the stairway, Bobby saw Joe Carlson strutting across the deck with an expression, one part guilt and two parts half asleep. Wild, reckless, and spoiled, Joe was one of Bradley's friends that Bobby didn't care much for – he had a streak of cockiness that his young followers admired, but rubbed against the grain of most people in Red Wing. Bobby attributed his brother's ruffian lifestyle to Joe Carlson's influence. His father was a wealthy businessman and the city council chairman; yet, Joe had gained a particularly colorful reputation of a different sort. Mr. Carlson had finally been pressured into sending the problem child off to a private school where, perhaps, he would receive some needed discipline, after riding horseback down Seventh Street, shooting at gaslights.

Amidst the increasing number of passengers boarding the Sea Wing, Bobby and Seth found little difficulty in sneaking to the stairway without Joe noticing them. On the second deck, there were even more people crowded along the walkway railings. It was a noisy but good-humored symphony of shouts, howls and squeals as the swarm packed into every available inch of standing room, leaving little space to navigate without trampling on somebody's toes or testing the durability of a picnic basket.

The boys finally found a few vacant inches of space along the railing overlooking the barge that was lashed to the port side bow of the Sea Wing. Most of the late arrivals were being shuffled onto the barge, as little room remained on the Sea Wing's decks. Mass confusion seemed to dominate, and with nearly two hundred people herded into such a small space, it wasn't surprising. Families separated; mothers scolded youngsters far out of earshot, darting about the crowd, too busy investigating and exploring to heed their elders' orders; fathers gathered, here and there, too busy shaking hands and chatting with each other to observe their wives' demands. Teen-aged girls waved their arms, trying desperately to gain the attention of lost boyfriends or companions; many people just wandered about aimlessly, hoping to find a shady spot to sit.

Bobby spotted quite a few familiar faces that were, for the most part, absorbed in a charge of sensationalism. He wanted to wave and call out their names and share in the gaiety among those he knew, but remaining incognito seemed the safer alternative, as he really wasn't supposed to be there. He and Seth were supposed to be fishing – as far as his mother knew.

On the deck below, many of their school friends scurried about, passing from the main deck onto the barge, and back again; Henry Newton and Phoebe Bearson, Del Blaker and Mabel Holton, John Strope, Bertha Winter, John Ingebretson, and Lenus Lillyblad, the grocer's son. They all seemed to be having so much fun. Emil and Henry Gerken were there, too, with their whole family of seven; their father was a saloonkeeper, not far from the St. James Hotel, where Bobby's mother worked.

Several of Bradley's friends milled about; Tom Leeson, Melissa Harrison, Mary Olson, Charlie Peterson, Hattie Scherf – they were all older than Bobby and Seth by three or four years, and because they were Bradley's friends, Bobby didn't associate with any of them much.

Nick's friends, though, who were all much older, Bobby knew well. Fred Hempftling and Eddy Christopherson were Nick's best friends; Bobby had gone fishing with them quite often, and they always treated him like he was one of the gang. Bobby liked Nick's buddies, and they liked him.

Annie Schneider strolled up the gangway with her new fiancé, Fred Hattemer. Nicholas had courted Annie for a while, but when he announced his intentions of joining the National Guard, their relationship ended; Annie decided that she didn't want to be left alone. Bobby wondered if Annie was going to Lake City because she was having second thoughts about Nick, or if she was just showing off her new boyfriend.

It was just a few minutes before the Sea Wing would depart for Lake City; spirits soared as the clamorous crowd settled in. A four-piece band aboard the barge started playing lively tunes and a few couples began dancing. Bobby noticed the Sea Wing's crewmen busily preparing for the start of the journey, hauling in the gangplank and casting off the mooring ropes. The captain had given the engineer's orders for a full head of steam and had returned to the pilothouse, ready to point his vessel downriver.

And then a wave of sensationalism washed over Bobby as the whistle sounded, the paddlewheel started churning, and the boat eased away from the landing. He had been on fishing skiffs and rafts many times with Nick and his friends, but then, they only oared their way around the backwaters, mostly, and rarely ever ventured out into the more dangerous main channel. Only a couple of times had they boldly crossed to the distant other side, and followed the Wisconsin shoreline to Maiden Rock for a few nights of camping. But now, he was about to fulfill a dream.

As Captain Wethern navigated his trim, no-frills little steamer out onto Lake Pepin, he saw nothing but a calm, shimmering, sleeping spirit. He respected this thirty-mile stretch of the Mississippi, as did all the men who made their livings on the river, fully aware that the sleeping spirit's awakening moods could be bizarre and unpredictable. Father Louis Hennepin, the first white man to ply the upper Mississippi in a canoe, had called it the "Lake of Tears," and it had since been notorious for its abruptly changing conditions. But on that Sunday morning, clear skies, not the slightest promise of a cooling breeze, and the inviting, placid blue water wouldn't have struck a note of fear in any river man.

Bobby and Seth nudged their way to the bow end of the deck where they could view both the Wisconsin and Minnesota shorelines as the Sea Wing steadily progressed southward. Gray roofs of farmhouses and cottages, each in their own little fields and suggesting a feeling of isolation, peeped out from amid the brilliant green shades of summer foliage. Towering Maiden Rock on the Wisconsin side, and the limestone bluffs guarding Frontenac on the Minnesota banks slowly passed by. They had seen those sights many times, but from the middle of the lake the panorama seemed more dramatic than they had ever witnessed before.

Captivated by the spectacle, Seth appeared to be a little more at ease. He questioned himself, now, why he had been so apprehensive of the river in the past. There, aboard the Sea Wing, he felt a new surge of exhilaration, of freedom, of adventure; now he understood Bobby's intense passion, and he was beginning to feel it, too.

Bobby was nothing short of spellbound. Absorbed in the experience, he had all but ignored the crowd of people around him, and he was no longer concerned about boarding the Sea Wing against his mother's wishes. He was there and his actions were committed; it was too late for he or his mother to do anything to change them.

He let his eyes wander from the breath-taking scenery to scan the crowd aboard the boat. The aroma of freshly brewed coffee hinted a touch of hospitality; many of the excursionists searched the depths of their picnic baskets for the deviled eggs, ham sandwiches and apple pies they had so carefully packed.

Pete Gerken and George, the barber, chatted on the bow while Pete's wife rounded up the children for lunch. Fred Seavers, the blacksmith, and George Hartman, the hardware store owner, were talking about tools and sipping coffee. White lace dresses twirled as young couples kicked up their heels to the lively music on the dance floor. Everyone seemed so happy, so relaxed, yet enthused by the excitement of the day.

Bobby didn't recognize, at first, the man who seemed to be keeping close watch on him and Seth from down on the bow of the barge. Bobby's eyes narrowed and gazed away, as if hunting cobwebs in the rafters. But he could almost feel the hot stare on the back of his neck from the suspicious stranger. Unwilling, yet unable to resist, he returned his stare to the man below, like a field mouse transfixed by the stare of a timber rattler. His heart jumped up a notch in rhythm; the man was no stranger – Bobby had never seen Grizzly with trimmed beard, combed hair, and clean shirt, but he was still an evil-looking cuss, like a man in a boiling passion, and even with clean clothes, no one seemed to want to include his presence at this social gathering.

"C'mon, Seth," Bobby mumbled. "Let's go to the back of the boat."

Seth was quite content with the prime spot they had secured to view the passing landscapes on either shore, but reluctantly he followed Bobby along the starboard walkway past the cabin, dodging the other passengers and obviously disrupting a few conversations, and interrupting a ham sandwich or two. When they reached the open deck to the rear that was roofed by the deck above, a friendly, familiar face met them as they searched for a vacant spot at the outer railing.

"Hello, Bobby," Emma Nelson said, smiling warmly. "I saw you earlier and I was just about to go find you."

"Oh! Hi, Emma." Her abrupt appearance startled Bobby.

"Would you and Seth care to join me for some lunch? I have plenty." Emma was traveling alone, and when she first noticed Bobby aboard the Sea Wing, she suspected he was there without his mother, and without food.

"Well, thank you, Emma," Bobby replied. "That's mighty kind of you." He had not given any thought to packing a lunch before the trip, and now Emma's offer seemed quite appealing; his stomach was growling just a little. Seth was equally appreciative, as Emma dug into her picnic basket and handed each of them a roast beef sandwich.

"Reckon I owe you another favor," Bobby said. A sheepish grin crawled onto his face.

"Nonsense... you don't owe me a thing."

Bobby had always admired pretty, young Emma Nelson, and for a boy well into puberty, she was an eyeful. His knees would weaken every time she slipped an extra piece of candy into the bag at the drug store. If he had been a few years older, or she, a few years younger, Bobby would have proposed marriage on the spot. But he knew that she viewed him as just a little boy, and that was painful to Bobby. He knew, too, that Emma had eyes for Nicholas – he had caught her flirting with Nick at the drug store soda fountain more than once, and for a boy of thirteen, his emotions were confused with feelings of joy for Nick, and jealousy of him. He was almost certain, too, that Emma was only using him as a pawn to charm her way into Nick's heart, and if it ever came to a competition, he would let Big Brother win. After all – he was only thirteen.

"So," Bobby blurted out between gulps of the sandwich, "Are you going to see Nick?"

"Oh... the thought did cross my mind to look him up today," Emma replied in a syrupy tone.

Bobby sensed that Emma's words shadowed a near lie; seeing Nick was probably her sole purpose for making the trip to Lake City.

Bobby noticed that the paddlewheel had slowed a bit; the Sea Wing had passed Central Point quite some time earlier, and now the whistle was singing it's cheerful arrival notice as the craft made its approach to the landing at the foot of Washington Street of Lake City. Commotion and clamor among the passengers steadily rose as they bustled about, preparing to disembark the boat, escape the sweltering heat of the mid-day sun, and perhaps, seek the comfort of a shade tree and a cool drink. Spirits soared in anticipation of a fun-filled afternoon. With picnic baskets repacked, parasols furled, and children in tow, everyone seemed eager to set foot on Lake City soil. Soon they would join with sons, brothers, boyfriends and buddies at the National Guard camp.

Seth studied the excitement in Bobby's eyes; he could only imagine the thrill his best friend was experiencing. It had been months since Nick and Bobby shared time together, and he knew how Bobby idolized his older brother. Their reunion would be best left to privacy. Seth only hoped that some day his younger brothers of seven and nine would look up to him the same way Bobby did to Nicholas.

Emma had urged them to hurry along with her toward the gangway, and then she had disappeared into the mass movement. But Bobby suggested that they lay back, near the stern on the second deck. From there, he could watch for Nicholas, and risk less chance of broken ribs among the pushing crowd. And most of all, he wanted to be certain that Grizzly was well off the boat and lost in the throng before he and Seth made their way to the levee.

Not far from where the Sea Wing tied up, Bobby saw Ira Fulton, alone on his private yacht. He seemed to be having some sort of difficulty with his machinery.

"Captain Wethern," he called out toward the Sea Wing.

"Aye," the boys heard the skipper respond from the pilothouse.

"I seem to have developed some engine trouble," Ira yelled. "I may have to leave 'er here till repairs can be made. Have you room for a few more passengers back to Red Wing?"

"I'm sure that can be arranged," Captain Wethern's voice boomed. "We will depart at six o'clock."

Ira gave the captain a gratifying wave and returned to his tinkering that would render no useful results.

Chapter 4

Grizzly had, indeed, vanished among the excursionists making their pilgrimage toward the festive welcome awaiting them in Lake City and Camp Lakeview. Bobby desperately hoped that he had seen the last of him for the day.

There seemed to be a bottleneck at the gangplank; Captain Wethern's business partner, Mel Sparks, was there reassuring the curious voyagers that the Sea Wing would not leave port until the day's activities concluded, and everyone had returned to the boat, even though the captain had announced six o'clock as the departure time. A dress parade was scheduled for seven o'clock, and many passengers had expressed their dismay, thinking they would miss that final event. But Mr. Sparks put them at ease, and the joyous crusaders scattered in all directions.

Bobby scanned the area trying to catch a glimpse of his brother, but he only saw popcorn, lemonade and ice cream stands, and lots of unfamiliar faces.

At the entrance to the camp, Bobby and Seth realized that finding Nick might not be an easy task. Hundreds of soldiers stirred about, many acting as guides for the visitors, showing off the artillery, the mess tents, and the stables of fine steeds used by the mounted corps. Some of the soldiers mingled with the crowd, greeting family and friends. And many were strolling arm-in-arm with pretty girls among the rows of tents, their ill-fitting khaki uniforms contrasting with white lace skirts, silky blouses and parasols. To the guardsmen, this day meant a brief release from the regular camp routines that would have been rather depressing in that boiling, humid weather.

After about twenty minutes of ambling along the pebble stone path through the tent city, briefly scrutinizing every strange face in a soldier uniform, Seth poked Bobby's ribs and pointed to a small gathering near the corner of a tent. "There he is," he said with excitement. "There's Nick!"

Fred Hempftling and Eddy Christopherson had already found Nicholas, and so had Emma Nelson and Katie Daily. It appeared to be quite a joyous reunion of friends. Nicholas had his back to the pathway and didn't notice Bobby's approach. Eddy saw him coming, though, and motioned to Nick. "Look who's here." Nick turned, and instantly broke away from the group without saying a word. The two brothers collided in a wrestling sort of hug and with smiles as wide as the Mississippi; Nick's friends didn't have to be reminded that Bobby would receive top priority.

Nick ruffled Seth's blonde hair, too, to make him feel welcomed; he had always accepted Seth, and admired Bobby for his choice of best friend.

"Hi, Squirt," Eddy and Fred teased when Bobby, Seth and Nick rejoined the group. They had affectionately given Bobby the nickname during a fishing excursion in the backwaters aboard a log raft when Bobby was only eight years old; it had stayed with him all this time, and coming from Eddy and Fred, Bobby didn't mind.

"Hi," Bobby returned, acknowledging Nick's buddies, but his attention was drawn more to Nick.

Small talk resumed among the older members of the group. Bobby noticed Emma studying Nick in a kindly, almost loving manner. When Nick turned to look at her, she glanced away, and the spell was broken. Nick seemed to possess some secretive admiration for Emma, too, that he was trying to hide from his other friends, but it was clear to Bobby that he shouldn't expect Emma to wait for him to grow up, although he wasn't ready to give in to defeat just yet, either; Nicholas had not yet *won* the competition.

Eventually, Eddy read Nick's expressions and suggested to the others that they should probably move on to see the shows and demonstrations, and to let Nick and Bobby have some time together. He invited Seth to join them, too.

Bobby and Nick watched the others strolling away toward the parade grounds. They had so much to say to each other, but neither of them knew where to begin.

"So, how's Ma? Why didn't she come?" Nick started.

Bobby shook his head. "She's still down-in-the-mouth somethin' awful. Reckon she's powerful riled up at you for leavin' and joinin' the Army."

"Thought she might've gotten over that by now."

"Naw, she ain't. She threw a conniption fit when I told her I wanted to come on the boat to see you."

"But she let you come, though."

"Well, not exactly. I hornswoggled her into thinkin' me and Seth went fishin' today. I left a note on the kitchen table."

"Dang it, Squirt! I oughta take a cowhide to ya. You shouldn't lie to her like that."

"Aw, shucks, Nick. I ain't seen you in a coon's age. I had a real hankerin' to come here, and Ma woulda hogtied me sure if I'd fessed up."

Nicholas gazed at his little brother and reminded himself that Bobby had lived most of his life substituting an older brother for a father. It had not been easy for either of them, but Bobby was showing his steadfast loyalty to their kinship.

"And b'sides," Bobby whined. "That last letter you sent express... you said that you wanted me to come."

There was a sudden uproar of cheers, whistles and applause from the distant crowd. Nick knew it must be one o'clock, as that was when the first demonstrations on the parade grounds were to begin. The mounted troupes pranced their saddled sorrel thoroughbreds and bay stallions and Appaloosas in perfect formation, and the teamsters at the reins of the huskier Morgans darted about the field aboard caissons, wagons and the big-wheeled cannons, gallantly signifying the battalion's mobility at a moment's notice. The visitors seemed quite impressed.

"Oh, yeah," Nicholas mumbled, remembering the letter. "You didn't tell anybody about that, did you?"

"No... well... Seth, but he keeps secrets real good."

Nick looked around. Hardly anyone was wandering through the tented encampment except a few lean, tanned guardsmen who squired the bodacious young girls in their Sunday dresses, and trying to look oh-so-important. The dwindled activity made it easy to spot one man, standing alone, five tents away. Nick studied the man, who seemed to be concentrating his attention on Bobby and Nick.

"Now, what's that critter doin' here?" Nicholas asked no one in particular.

Bobby craned his neck to get a glimpse of the man, and quickly cowered down when he saw Grizzly staring and sipping from a flask. It appeared suspiciously obvious to Bobby that Grizzly might be stalking him, but he couldn't think of any logical reason.

"That scalawag still hangin' around the gin mills in town?" Nicholas asked.

"Yeah," Bobby replied. "And I think he's been followin' me. I see him everywhere I go."

"Well, if he's been botherin' you, I think I'll just go fix his flint right quick."

"No, Nick," Bobby begged. "I know you can whip your weight in wild cats, but don't go gettin' yourself in no trouble... not today. Let's just skedaddle."

Nicholas just stared at Grizzly, as if daring him to come another step closer. Bobby, though, didn't wish for any confrontation. He wanted this day to be joyous. Nick had been gone for months, and he would be gone for several more; this was one day for Bobby to spend some quality time with his brother, and fighting wasn't on his list of fun things to do.

"C'mon, Nick," Bobby whispered. "I know how we can get away from him. Do these tents have back doors?" He was remembering the day at the drug store; sneaking out the back while Grizzly watched and waited at the front had kept him there most of the day. It would probably work here, too.

Nick ducked into the tent and Bobby followed. From inside they peeked out through a narrow slit between the door flaps. Grizzly had taken the bait and was eyeing the front of the tent. Bobby and Nick stepped gingerly past the rows of cots toward the rear, slipped out the door and circled around several other tents to where they could spy on Grizzly, only to find him keeping a vigil on the empty tent.

"There," Bobby whispered. "That'll keep him busy for a while."

"Why is he following you?"

Bobby shook his head. "Don't know. Figured when I got on the boat I'd be rid of him for the day, at least, but there he was, starin' at me and Seth, 'til we scooted to the stern where he couldn't see us."

Nicholas was as eager to find some seclusion to carry out the planned transaction with his brother as Bobby was curious about it. There was plenty of time before the dress parade, and with Grizzly well occupied, nothing restricted the Duncan brothers from scurrying off into obscurity. Nicholas grabbed Bobby's arm, urging him to follow. "C'mon, Squirt. I got somethin' to show you."

Bobby's eyes sparkled with excitement; this would be the high point of the day, second only to the riverboat ride.

While Nicholas and Bobby trekked off into the hills, unnoticed, and while the afternoon continued to produce more entertainment provided by the guardsmen, Captain Wethern paced nervously among the crowd; his attention was drawn toward the sky more than the rifle-twirling drill team on the parade field. Ugly clouds had banked up in the northwest, and heavy, humid air bathed Camp Lakeview. Sporadic puffs of wind ruffled the treetop leaves and sent shimmering little ripples racing across placid Lake Pepin. The sleeping baby, Captain David Wethern thought, was apt to awaken as a howling, rampaging devil's child by nightfall. With the long mid-summer days, Red Wing was reachable before darkness swallowed the lake, and the Sea Wing could deposit its precious cargo safely in the shadows of Barn Bluff before Mother Nature unleashed her wicked brew -- if the return journey commenced soon.

Captain Wethern circulated casually throughout the throng of spectators who were delighted and awed by one particularly talented rifleman. "That's Charlie Betcher... from Red Wing," he heard someone say, and he noticed that the performer *did* handle a rifle quite smartly, but the captain had his sights trained more keenly on Ed Niles and the Sea Wing's co-owner, Mel Sparks.

"I think we should get the passengers boarding, and prepare to shove off," the captain said to his officers, loud enough to be heard by several bystanders.

"But it's early," Mel Sparks replied. "This crowd isn't ready to leave just yet."

Ed Niles glanced at the captain. "There's the band concert in a few minutes, and the dress parade after that. I'm sure these folks don't want to miss either."

Captain Wethern discretely nodded toward the darkening, ominous sky to the northwest. He could tell that not many people had noticed the threatening weather looming in the distance, but he didn't want to cause any alarm.

A sudden solemn frown wrinkled Mr. Niles' forehead. "Maybe David is right," he whispered to Sparks, and then lifted his eyebrows as a gesture for Sparks to take notice that the sun had prematurely retired for the day behind approaching dark clouds.

"Just a little shower... it'll pass," Sparks grunted. "I told the passengers the Sea Wing would stay until they are ready to leave after all the activities are ended."

Even though Ed Niles seemed to be in agreement with an earlier departure, the captain knew he wouldn't collect Sparks' sympathy; he turned away and began mingling with some of the other spectators that he recognized as Sea Wing passengers, hinting that he would like to get under way on the return journey as soon as possible. The older excursionists nodded affirmatively, but David soon realized that the young couples strolling about with little concern of time or weather conditions distinctly outnumbered them, and the younger children scattered around the camp investigating tents, cannons, and thoroughbreds had no concerns at all. Picnic baskets produced more ham sandwiches and deviled eggs, as even the older members of the crowd settled in on a patchwork of blankets and tablecloths spread on the ground, enjoying the opening musical numbers played by an energetic band. Captain Wethern's hopes for a daylight arrival at Red Wing rapidly vanished. He had been young once too, and he appreciated everyone's unwillingness to cut the festivities short, even if it meant coping with a little rain.

Hot as it was, the band played on fiercely, intent on giving the visitors their very best performance. The booming bass drums echoed across the river valley and handily disguised the distant rumble of thunder. To almost everyone, the cooling temperature seemed more a relief than cause for alarm. David Wethern, though, kept a watchful eye on the northwestern heavens; he could almost feel the freakish, eerie pulse of a storm, but he was much too tactful to call anyone's attention to it.

Bobby hung on to the last good-bye hug as long as Nicholas allowed. He was fighting off the tears, knowing that these were the final minutes he would spend with Nick for several months. Their time together had passed too quickly.

"Okay, Squirt," Nick said. "I have to get into formation for the dress parade. Sounds like the band concert is just about over." He pried loose from his brother's grappling hug and held Bobby at arm's length.

"I wish I could stay here with you," Bobby whimpered. He knew that wasn't possible, but it seemed like the right thing to say.

"You and Seth, go back to the boat now. You gotta go home and take care of Ma."

"Promise you'll be home for Christmas?"

"Promise."

Bobby dropped his hands to his sides, bowed his head and stared at Nick's shiny boots. "You sure you can't come down to the boat with me?"

"No, Squirt. It'll be easier this way. And besides... I promised Eddy and Fred I'd say good-bye to them, too."

Bobby nodded and tried to smile. He couldn't deny Nick the opportunity to bid his best friends a farewell. "Okay," he said, and raised his hand in a pathetic little wave. "Bye. See ya at Christmas."

Nicholas returned the wave. "See ya." He could feel his brother's pain as he watched Bobby walking slowly away toward the parade field crowd; he felt his own pain, too. Saying good-bye, this time, was just temporary; Nicholas knew that. But to a thirteen-year-old, a few months would seem a lifetime. Bobby faced a difficult time ahead without big brother to protect him from their mother's state of depression that had gone on far too long, and especially now, that Bobby had lied to her about where he was that day. If she found out, there would probably be hell to pay.

But Bobby carried in his pocket, back home for safekeeping, a treasure that would certainly brighten their mother's spirits, come Christmastime. And perhaps it would bring Nicholas and Bobby back into her good graces again.

Nicholas peered into the northwestern sky and realized that it was not only the bass drums in the band that he had been hearing. Faint lightning bolts lit up the tops of distant clouds and a nearly constant rumble of thunder rolled over the hills. Another storm front was creeping in from the west over the hilltops behind the camp, and that one, much closer, appeared to promise a damp interruption of the parade. But even with the imminent threat of rain, the camp's visitors remained staunch with a desire to finish the day's celebration as planned.

Light rain started to fall as the First Regiment marched onto the field. Bobby hastened his pace among the spectators, but now, small groups of people huddled together with their blankets tented over them because of the rain, making his search for Seth a bit more challenging. Grizzly had once again honed in on him and had resumed the irritating surveillance, but there were no front door-back door escapes available nearby, and Bobby suspected that Grizzly probably wouldn't fall for that maneuver again, anyway. But, he thought, if he could locate Seth quickly, they were capable of running faster than the big man who had been sipping whiskey all day.

Driven by a gusty wind, the increasing rainfall abruptly halted the parade. A strong voice boomed out from among the formation on the field announcing that the exhibition would be postponed until the rain let up, and then commanded the troops to "fall out."

Most of the visitors scurried for shelter as well. Bobby caught a glimpse of Eddy and Fred sprinting toward the tents, but Seth wasn't there. He ran to intercept them. "Where's Seth?" he shouted to Nick's friends.

Eddy stopped momentarily, long enough to say, "Last I saw him, he was headed toward that clump of trees over by the entrance gate," and then Eddy continued his pursuit of shelter in Nick's tent.

Bobby leaned into the wind and made a dash for the trees. Several others were doing the same, seeking refuge under the spreading oaks. Seth, having made the wiser decision much sooner than the rest, had procured a spot opposite the wind behind a huge tree trunk; he waved, attempting to snare Bobby's attention. "Bobby," he yelled. "Over here!"

His vision blurred by the rainwater in his eyes, Bobby stopped just under the sprawling branches when he heard Seth's voice, swiped the water from his eyes, scanned the many strange faces huddled there, and waited for another directive from Seth.

"Over here," Seth called out again, and this time he stepped out from behind the tree so Bobby could see him better. Bobby homed in on the call, and within seconds he stood behind the big oak tree with Seth.

"Well? Did ya get it?" Seth beamed with curiosity and a grin that could only come from a youngster who didn't care that he'd been caught in the rain.

"Yeah," Bobby said. As if the rain were a playful prank, he grinned too; tiny rivulets trickled down his cheeks from his rain-soaked hair and dribbled off his chin. But then a sudden grimace replaced the smile as he spotted Grizzly again.

"What's wrong, Bobby?"

"How fast can you run, Seth?"

Chapter 5

The rain had diminished to just a sprinkle; at a fast-paced stride, Bobby and Seth led Grizzly on a wild goose chase through the streets of Lake City. When they were certain that he might be tiring, Bobby gave a backward glance to see nearly a block-long advantage. He and Seth scooted down the alleyway between the freight office and the meat market, emerged from the far end in a dead run, circled around the block and headed for the boat landing.

What had been a picturesque lake vista earlier that day was now a blurry mass of gray. Dusk was lowering its curtain sooner than usual because of overcast skies, and a few of the excursionists were returning to the Sea Wing, seeking a dry retreat and ready to finalize a busy day.

Even before the delayed dress parade concluded, Captain Wethern had gathered up his wife and their two young boys and were already aboard the boat. Mrs. Wethern persuaded the youngsters to settle into the captain's stateroom for a much needed nap, and then busied herself brewing more coffee while the captain, Ed Niles, and several other experienced river men debated on the Sea Wing's departure from Lake City. The wind had kicked up again; choppy waves broke against the shoreline rocks and sloshed about the Sea Wing's hull. Deteriorating weather conditions throughout the late afternoon hours, and steadily increasing lightning in the northwest had convinced the old river men that a severe storm was sweeping down the Mississippi.

Bobby and Seth hustled to the stern of the middle deck where they had been that morning, and where they could watch all the others filing aboard. The hardier men and young couples, once again, filled the space under the barge canopy; Captain Wethern directed the women and small children into the comfort of the cabins where they would be protected from the harsh weather, and from the captain's conversation with other crewmen, Bobby figured there might be a delay in the Sea Wing's departure.

Gaiety and wise laughter was gone from the party now; instead, there seemed to be a kind of dim terror among the passengers as they peered out onto the windswept, choppy lake. Sitting quietly, solemnly, like birds in a cage, the women cradled their young and assured each other that everything would be alright, while the undaunted young men joined in with their older counterparts displaying gestures that men make to pretend they aren't frightened.

Seth nudged Bobby's elbow and pointed toward the levee where a few stragglers meandered about, making their indecisive way to the landing. Some had tried to acquire railroad passage back to Red Wing when they noticed the approaching bad weather, but now they were forced to board the Sea Wing, as the northbound train had already departed.

Bobby clenched his fists and gritted his teeth; he saw Grizzly strolling among those stragglers. He stepped back from the railing, hoping to avoid being seen, but it was too late. Grizzly stared right at him and sneered.

Seth nudged Bobby's elbow and pointed again. "Ain't that Nick... over there?"

Bobby turned his attention away from Grizzly; there was nothing he could do, now, to rid himself of that disgusting man for the remainder of the trip, other than trying to stay out of his sight. He looked to where Seth was pointing. Nick *was* there, but he had not come to see his brother; in dusk's dimness, Emma Nelson's white dress stood close at Nick's side. Nick was waving good-bye to Eddy and Fred, and when they turned their backs to him to return to the Sea Wing, Nicholas stole a kiss from Emma's lips.

Bobby's heart sank. He thought of the many times he had caught them flirting at the drug store, and the many times that he, himself, had been the recipient of her sweet, loving ways. She had even kissed him on the cheek once, as she slipped an extra piece of candy into his shopping bag. Surely she could not have made such a hasty decision between two brothers! Nicholas would be gone for several months; perhaps, that would be his chance to sway Emma to wait another four or five years.

Word circulated swiftly among the passengers that Captain Wethern had decided to delay the Sea Wing's departure until the weather calmed and he could be somewhat certain that the worst of the storm had passed. It came as a relief to many; by then a stiff, gusty wind drove heavier rainfall and higher waves, creating certain discomfort, especially to those on the barge and the open decks. Being youngsters, Bobby and

Seth were offered the protection of the cabin with the women and children, but they declined honorably. "We're not children," they proclaimed. "We'll be just fine out here," and then they wedged their way through the mass of people to the wall at the stern that prevented spray onto the deck from the paddlewheel. Bobby didn't want to enter the cabin, anyway; he had seen Emma go in there shortly after she had boarded, and he wasn't ready to confront her, yet, after witnessing her good-bye kiss with Nicholas.

He hadn't seen anything of Grizzly, though, since he stumbled up the gangway. It was just as well that he and Seth were hunkered down along that wall; even though the Sea Wing's decks were brightly lighted, there seemed little chance that Grizzly would notice them there, even if he did come looking.

Seth seemed a bit skittish again, and Bobby thought talking, rather than just watching all the other worried faces, might help to ease his tension. "Me and Nick had a real good time this afternoon," he started.

"Yeah? What'd ya do?"

"Hiked up in the hills behind the camp. You shoulda seen the view from up there... almost gooder'n Barn Bluff."

"You're plum crazy as a loon. Ain't noplace gooder'n Barn Bluff."

"Well, I'm tellin' ya... I could see all the way past Maiden Rock--"

Just then a loud creaking noise sounded as a hard gust of wind pushed against the Sea Wing. Seth gasped. He jerked his head back and his eyes widened as big as wagon wheels.

"Don't worry," Bobby said in a loud whisper, attempting to sooth Seth's restored tension. "It's only the wind."

Seth settled back. "So, what else did you and Nick do?"

"We talked a considerable lot... 'bout all the things we'll do when he comes home... and 'bout Ma... and, 'course, he gave me this." Bobby looked around at all the strange faces that stared out into the weather. No one seemed to be paying much attention to the two boys squatted down at the back wall. He straightened his right leg and dug deep into his pocket.

Seth's face beamed with a different kind of excitement; anticipation overwhelmed him; he was finally about to see the *secret* that had led him on this incredible adventure.

Bobby pulled a clenched fist from his pocket and held it tightly against his belly.

Seth leaned closer. "Lemme see it," he said eagerly, and then he noticed Bobby's rigid, frightful stare. He turned and looked up to see what had suddenly startled Bobby into muteness. There, not more than three feet away stood Grizzly, towering over them and watching their every move, sneering, as if he were waiting for the opportunity to snatch what Bobby held in his hand.

Seth jumped up to his feet and confronted the despicable character that smelled of corn whiskey. "Go away," he blurted out bravely. He knew he was no match for a man three times his size, but there were others near that would surely come to his aid if he put up enough of a fuss. Several other men did take notice of the confrontation and stepped in, suspecting Grizzly of some dishonorable act. They said nothing, just glaring at Grizzly as if they were aware of his reputation as a no account, urging him to take his trouble elsewhere. A blank stare replaced Grizzly's sneer; he turned and walked away, as if nothing had happened.

"You boys okay?" one of the strangers asked.

"Yes sir. Thank you," Bobby replied. He shoved his hand back in his pocket.

Seth kneeled down again beside his friend. "Why is that bastard hawkin' you like this?"

"Don't know, Seth. Reckon it's 'cause of this." Bobby patted his pocket.

"But how could he know about that? D'ya reckon he found Nick's letter out in the woods?"

Bobby's face flushed red as a tree-ripened apple. That suggestion made perfect sense to him; Grizzly had begun preying on Bobby just a couple of days after the wind carried Nick's letter away, never to be seen again. Grizzly *must* have found it. There was no other reason for his behavior, and discovering the lost letter was the only way he could possibly know.

Until that day, Bobby had considered Grizzly as nothing more than the town drunk, ever present and as useless as flies at a picnic. For the past few days, he had been an annoying pest. But now Grizzly had emerged as a threat.

Almost two hours had passed since Captain Wethern's originally planned departure time. He stood in the pilothouse with Ed Niles, scrutinizing the atmospheric developments and was patiently waiting for some improvement in conditions. He didn't question his ability as an accomplished pilot to navigate on the rough water; he had proven himself worthy of that many times.   Nor did he question the seaworthiness of his vessel; he, himself, had supervised its construction. The Sea Wing was strong, rugged and agile, and had survived nearly three years readily handling all the perilous iniquities that the mighty Mississippi could bestow upon any vessel.   But it wasn't his own comfort level that concerned him.   Two hundred passengers were aboard, among them, his wife and two sons, and several family members of crew.   Their safety and comfort was important too, and already they had been exposed to the displeasures, that of which he had no control.

Early darkness had all but consumed Lake Pepin and its shorelines. Had there been clear skies overhead, David Wethern, as well as his passengers, may well have taken pleasure in a moonlight cruise back to Red Wing.   But this was an eerie sort of darkness teeming with uncertainty.   David had always been rightly impressed by adverse weather conditions, and was always willing and eager to observe the advice of veteran river pilots to hug close to the Minnesota shoreline, being ever ready to make a run for it in the event of an unsuspected squall. But now he was obeying his own better judgment, avoiding the risk altogether, by remaining in port instead of attempting the return voyage in the face of a storm.

Ed Niles was no novice at river boating; during his years aboard the Sea Wing, he had been witness to the countless hazards that plagued river vessels, and unsettled conditions such as these painted indelible images in his memory. He wasn't a pilot, but he valued David Wethern's competence; he wouldn't question the Captain's decision, although he wasn't much in favor of beginning the journey, regardless of a break in the weather.

Restlessness among the voyagers fostered their anxiety. It had been a long, tiring day; the mid-day, relentless heat and humidity had tapped out a good share of energy from many, and the late afternoon rain, sending everyone scurrying for shelter, had finished the job.   Too exhausted to complain, most sat or stood quietly, anxiously awaiting a nod or a nay; they desired to be homeward bound, but to many, a soft bed in a Lake City hotel would be an acceptable alternative.

Shortly before eight o'clock, Captain Wethern had nearly decided to postpone the return voyage until morning, and to allow the passengers, if they wished, to seek lodging in town. But then, he noticed the wind had drastically diminished and within minutes it seemed to stop entirely. No rain was falling, and the lightning that had been illuminating the northwestern sky faded. The roll of thunder became more distant. He studied the sky and the lake, and leaned an ear toward the window that he had opened. The calmness came as relief, and as an invitation.

"Seems like the worst is over," David said. "I don't think that storm to the north is going to hit Lake Pepin at all." Searching for encouragement, he looked at his clerk. "What d'ya think, Ed?"

Mr. Niles stared out into the night. "I don't know, David. It's your call. You're the captain."

David peered at the distant, faint, less frequent lightning flashes for a couple of minutes, and then turned toward the door. He had made his decision. "I'm going below to tell the engineer to get up steam. Let the passengers know we'll shove off in ten minutes and that we'll land in Red Wing in about two hours."

Grizzly had disappeared for the time being, but Bobby and Seth suspected that he still lingered somewhere on the deck, and that the threat of a thief lurked nearby; the minutes passed slowly.

Low-toned murmurs among the passengers began to take on the sounds of enthusiasm as the passing storm calmed its grip on the Sea Wing. Mr. Niles' announcement that the boat would soon be northbound to Red Wing, though, didn't carry much gusto.

Proclaiming a victory over nature's tempestuous outburst, the explosive, sibilant whistle trill sliced through the night air, signifying the Sea Wing's departure. Bobby watched the stirring passengers, shaking the rain from blankets that had provided them with minimal protection from the wind and precipitation. A few worried faces remained and an occasional protest was mumbled amidst the chatter as the paddlewheel started churning and the Sea Wing and its barge eased away from the levee.

Chapter 6

Seth began showing signs of uneasiness again, too; Bobby didn't know if it was because of Grizzly, or the weather, but he knew he had to lift Seth's spirit. He stood upright, making himself as tall as his tiptoes allowed, and searched the crowded deck for Grizzly's presence. Everyone there seemed to be directing their attention to the lake and the weather, and if Grizzly was among them, Bobby couldn't see him. This was his chance to show Seth the treasure buried in his pocket. He nudged Seth's shoulder with his knee and slid his hand into his pocket. Seth stood up beside him and gave a puzzled stare. Once again, Bobby pulled a clenched fist from his pocket, guarding it with utmost caution. He looked around again to make certain that no one was watching, especially Grizzly. When it appeared that there were no curious eyes pointed in his direction, Bobby slowly relaxed his fist to an open palm.

Seth's eyes widened and his jaw dropped as he stared at the lustrous sphere of blue glow in Bobby's hand.

"Dang! I ain't never seen a real pearl up close before."

"Me, neither." Bobby urged Seth to keep his voice at a whisper to avoid attracting attention. "Nick has, though, and when he dug it out of that clam he fished out of the lake, he knew right off that it was worth a lot."

"How much?"

"A jeweler in Lake City told him it could bring two thousand dollars... maybe more."

"Dang! Why so much?"

"'Cause it's blue... they're the rarest of all, and 'cause this one's so big and perfectly round."

"So, what are ya gonna do with it?"

"We're gonna give it to Ma at Christmas... she can decide. Nick says it's our lucky charm."

Luck was what they needed most, just then. As if it were a magnet, the pearl had drawn Grizzly's interest; he couldn't see it, but by watching the boys as they scrutinized the object in Bobby's hand, he knew for sure that Bobby Duncan had in his possession the valuable pearl that Nicholas wrote about in his letter. Before the boat docked at Red Wing, he would hover on the possibilities and weasel his way into Bobby's weakest moment.

Bobby peered across the open space on the deck and Grizzly's ever-present, devious sneer. He quickly closed his fist again and jerked his hand down to his side. Now there was little doubt of Grizzly's intensions.

The Sea Wing had been under way only a short time, steaming out onto Lake Pepin far enough to safely clear Central Point that jutted out from the shore north of Lake City. Many of the passengers who had taken refuge in the cabins earlier were once again braving the tamer elements on the open decks. There was no clear view of land anymore – only a dim, dark outline of the Minnesota shore – as Captain Wethern set a course due north at full speed. One more jutting peninsula to clear, Point Au Sable, less than three miles upstream at Frontenac, and then he could turn the Sea Wing back toward the distant Minnesota shore.

Once past Central Point, David Wethern noticed that his steamer struggled considerably across the rough open water of Lake Pepin. With the Wisconsin and Minnesota shorelines both at least a mile or more away, an alarming wind, once again, combed up hearty waves with ever-increasing force. The vessel pitched side-to-side, forward and aft, pressured by converging winds from two different directions. David had navigated through worse; he was confident that the Sea Wing could handle the rough weather facing him now, too. Twisting and turning the searchlight, he could barely make out the bluff at Maiden Rock on the Wisconsin side; it was still fairly distant, but he decided to set his course for that shore and continue upstream under the protection of the lofty Wisconsin cliffs.

Bobby noticed, as did the other passengers, the steadily increasing wind. Everyone seemed to be scurrying toward the cabins again, anticipating more of the same unpleasantness they had experienced in the early evening hours. But of the two hundred people on board, less than half could squeeze into the limited cabin space, and the women and small children already occupied most of it.

It was mostly men on the barge deck now, as the young women who had been there earlier abandoned the boisterous atmosphere generated by a few bottles of good cheer being passed around. Bobby and Seth kept expecting Grizzly to join them, as he would certainly fit in with that group. But instead, he and his disgusting sneer lingered on the second deck. Now that the boat was encountering some rougher water, Grizzly was encountering a little difficulty in maintaining an even stance, and his fixation on the boys was distracted by the need to find something to hold onto.

Bobby saw his opportunity to practice a little deception of his own. He leaned toward Seth and whispered, "When Grizzly's not looking, I'm gonna give you the pearl. Put it in your pocket. Then he won't know where it is."

Seth felt a sudden sense of importance, that Bobby was about to entrust him with the highly treasured pearl. He glanced toward Grizzly clumsily dancing about the swaying deck like a mule on glare ice, and then he looked down at Bobby's hand slipping into his pocket.

Captain Wethern maintained his course toward the Wisconsin shore the best he could. Pressing ferociously against the port bow, the howling wind listed the Sea Wing to starboard, and then it would shift weirdly and come charging up behind the vessel from the southwest. Each time the bow climbed a mountainous, foamy wave, a wall of lake water bombarded the deck, and the flat-bottomed hull slapped down with a thunderous boom. With every jolt, the Sea Wing shuddered and groaned, punctuated by muffled screams of terror from within the cabins. Although the captain, alone in the pilothouse, remained optimistic, levels of anxiety mounted among the terrified passengers again.

David persistently fought the wheel. At times, it seemed useless, as the boat tossed on taller waves, lifting the rudder completely out of the water, and the wind sending the craft careening beyond his control. At every possible opportunity he swept the searchlight across the vicious lake's surface, keeping his sights set on the shoreline at the foot of Maiden Rock. The minutes ticked by, but his destination didn't seem to get any closer, as the gale-force wind allowed little forward progress.

As the vessel bounced and swayed, Bobby waited patiently for the right moment to slip the pearl into Seth's ready hand. But Grizzly had resumed some stability, wrapping his arm around a beam that supported the deck above. Not too eager to join the stumbling, falling men and women attempting to move about in search of protection from the wind, Bobby assessed his and Seth's position at the back wall next to the railing as good as any, although it left them in Grizzly's view.

Not far from where they stood, another man pulled several life belts and vests from under a wooden bench, and was distributing them to whoever was within reach. He leaned toward Bobby and held out a cork preserver; Bobby grabbed it and passed it to Seth, and then reached to the man for another. It really didn't seem necessary to him, but a few other passengers were donning the belts, Fred Hempftling and Lizzie, his sister, among them.

Bobby looked around for Nick's other friend, Eddy Christopherson, but he only saw hysteria and confusion among many faces he didn't know. Eddy was nowhere to be seen in the mounting chaos.

Seth had already strapped on his life preserver, and he urged Bobby to do the same. It was clear that Seth was scared, and Bobby realized a little fear creeping in, too, but he tried to ease Seth's tension once again. "It'll be okay... It's only the wind," he said calmly as he tied the preserver around his torso.

Amid all the confusion, Bobby noticed that Grizzly no longer clung to the post. Now there were too many people crowding under the roof for him to distinguish anyone in particular. Bobby turned his back to the mob and faced Seth. He reached into his pocket, quickly pulled it out again and held the shimmering pearl in front of Seth at waist level. "Here. Take it. He's not looking."

Just as Seth opened his palm under Bobby's hand, the Sea Wing jarred violently against a mammoth wave without warning. Everyone lurched with the sudden movement, including the boys. The pearl jumped from Bobby's hand and bounced uncontrollably across the deck. In the swiftest of judgment, Seth made a bold and daring dive toward the escaping gem.

Bobby had been standing freely, not holding on to anything to steady himself, and as he stumbled about trying to regain his balance, he realized what a foolhardy risk he had just taken. Before he could get complete control of his motions and join Seth on the pearl's rescue attempt, he felt a pair of strong hands gripping at his neck. He twisted around, only to see the big man's sneer just inches away. Grizzly had taken advantage of the chaos, too, and he had taken command of Bobby's weak moment.

Flashes of lightning illuminated the sky again, and David Wethern kept battling the ever-increasing wind, trying desperately to keep the Sea Wing pointed toward the Wisconsin bluffs. It seemed his best option. But as the lightning flashes grew brighter, he caught a glimpse of the dark, concentrated low cloud off the port side toward the Minnesota shoreline. At first, it appeared to him as a heavy cloudburst of rain – a squall that would intercept the Sea Wing's path. David knew he had to turn the steamer into that wind to avoid a broadside attack by the gale. As he attempted to maneuver his craft to meet the oncoming tempest head on, another bright lightning flash identified the horror that was about to strike. David stared for a long moment into the ugly face of a tornado, and he knew there was no escaping the twister that danced swiftly across Lake Pepin from the Minnesota side, headed directly toward the Sea Wing.

Whitecaps battered the ship and the violent turbulence vibrated the twin smokestacks like bass fiddle strings. The twenty-two-foot-high superstructure rocked to the starboard side, tugging viciously, again and again, at the ropes holding the barge, until they could no longer withstand the brutal punishment.

Grizzly did not see the failed transfer of the pearl from Bobby's hand to the intended recipient, or see it bouncing across the deck, or see Seth's diving attempt to recover it. He assumed that it was still in Bobby's pocket. Nor, did he notice the deadly tornado at his backside. Fiendish greed had overtaken his senses; his commanding grip on Bobby Duncan would go unnoticed, now, with everyone engaged in mass confusion over the weather conditions. Just a snippet of a boy, Bobby's size would be no challenge to overpower, and maybe even fling him – and his equally small sidekick – overboard, once the pearl was commandeered.

Bobby knew there was no one to come to his aid now. Fred was nowhere in sight, and now Seth had disappeared, too, among the tangled mess. His yells for help went unnoticed, camouflaged by the roaring wind, the crashing waves, a multitude of frightened yelps, and a creaking, groaning vessel.

Two hundred horrified faces gaped in shock into the inky black night, their eyes widened at the sight of the ominous dark funnel cloud as the lightning revealed its hostile advance. Women in the cabins, some of them bundled in life preservers, held their youngsters tightly and prayed for deliverance from this unbelievable nightmare. Out on the open decks, some envisioned the barge as a safer retreat and jumped; some managed to light on the barge's canopy and tumbled onto its deck; some slid over the edge and clung to the outer railing; and some were unfortunate, missing the barge altogether, and plunged into the raging black water. Those remaining on the boat, unable to escape the onslaught, were jostled and tossed about like a handful of beans in a rolling barrel.

Just as Bobby thought he had met his doom, choking and gasping, struggling at Grizzly's hold, the strongest yet blast of wind slammed against the Sea Wing, heaving it violently to the side. Knocked completely off balance by the gyration, Grizzly released his stronghold on Bobby and went reeling across the deck. Bobby gripped the railing tightly, barely saving himself from sliding down the deck's surface that was now at a forty-five degree angle. The boat settled back down to level; Bobby pulled himself up to his feet and looked down at the barge that had broken loose from the Sea Wing, its canopy torn to shreds by the fierce wind. Then another blast hit, and the steamer once again tipped to a precarious angle, but this time it didn't seem as though it would return. Bobby's eyes raced across the deck hoping to see Seth among the many people sprawled out, desperately grasping at anything that was fastened down. Hoping to reach out a helping hand to his best friend, whom he knew had been frightened with the very first puff of wind, Bobby soon realized that he was in no position to be of any assistance to Seth, or to anyone else. He struggled over the rail as the Sea Wing continued to tip, and then hurtled himself out into the darkness, hoping to reach the barge while it was still close. He was a strong swimmer, and he was confident that he could make it.

For a while, it looked as though the Sea Wing would weather the storm, courageously cutting through the breakers. David was too busy manhandling the wheel to think about what the passengers were experiencing on the lower decks. He had instructed his crew to ensure the women and children the protection in the cabins, and he knew his wife and sons were safely in the captain's stateroom; his main concern, now, was turning the Sea Wing on a course straight into the wind, even though it would not take him any closer to the Wisconsin shoreline.

But as the lightning bolts illuminated the rapidly approaching ominous funnel, Captain Wethern knew his ship faced monumental danger; there was no outrunning a tornado. And now it slashed across Lake Pepin, about to seize the Sea Wing and her passengers as likely prey.

Waves grew higher and more violent, and were pounding even the upper decks. When the second forceful wind gust hit the Sea Wing, David could do nothing more than hang on. The boat tipped to a sharp angle toward the starboard and hesitated for a few seconds, resisting the wind's murderous attack. The engine room and lower cabins flooded, and then as if a giant pair of hands pressed against her side, the Sea Wing capsized completely; only the shiny underside of the hull remained on the surface, bobbing on the waves like a lazy whale.

Chapter 7

Thirty silent, dark seconds under water seemed like eternity to Bobby. The strong winds had kept him aloft over the angry waves, and then sent him plunging into the black depths. The last bit of light he remembered had revealed other passengers leaping – or falling – from the Sea Wing's decks, but in those final moments – in that fraction of a second when he made such a crucial decision, he had not tried to identify any of them.

The life preserver's buoyancy floated Bobby to the surface. Time after time, he filled his lungs with air, only to be buried under one breaking wave after another. His sense of direction was one big void, and nowhere did he see any signs of other people, or the barge, or even the lights of the Sea Wing. Frequent lightning flashes showed him merely black silhouettes of the bluffs on the distant Minnesota and Wisconsin shores, but he didn't know which one was which. Acres of water surrounded him; never before had he felt so alone, or so helpless, or so lost.

His sense of time had escaped. Ten minutes, maybe fifteen, he thought, had passed when the waves settled to a chop again. The windstorm had moved on, and in its wake, a torrent of rain and hail poured from the wicked sky.

Bobby felt a sudden, sharp prod at his shoulder. He turned in the water to investigate the object that had nudged him; lightning illuminated a ten-foot-long, heavy wood plank drifting on the waves, and Bobby grabbed at it in desperation, holding onto the only solid thing in sight. He pulled himself partially onto the timber, hoping it would help keep him afloat.

More pieces of debris floated nearby, and then a prolonged lightning flash revealed, off in the distance, the ugly truth that Bobby had feared, but didn't want to accept. The Sea Wing lay upside down in the middle of Lake Pepin, and he could just barely distinguish a few dark figures of people trying to climb onto the overturned hull, but he could not hear their voices over the roar of wind and rain. Another lightning flash allowed him to see the barge that had drifted even farther; it was still afloat, upright, with many people aboard, but it was too far away for anyone to hear his cry for help. He knew that he was just a tiny speck among the rest of the floating debris; no one aboard the barge would see him, and even if they did, there was little chance that any of them could help him.

And then the worst horror of all this madness came into Bobby's view. In the darkness, it was hard to distinguish, at first, what the white objects were, floating nearby. He had seen one in the lightning, and now there were two. As they drew nearer, he could see the faces of the lifeless bodies – two young girls in their long, pretty summer dresses – just before they vanished beneath the dark waves. He wanted to scream, but his voice seemed paralyzed. Another body – this one a young man – rose to the surface, and then soon disappeared again. And the barge floated farther away.

It seemed to Bobby that he was drifting too, at an angle away from the barge, toward the shore, and he could only assume that it was the Minnesota shore, if the barge was drifting downstream with the current. He had already seen three dead bodies, and he just wanted to close his eyes so he wouldn't see any more, but he had to keep focused on the shore that appeared to be getting closer. With his left arm wrapped around the plank, he paddled with his right, trying to make more headway.

His thoughts were getting clearer, and the reality of the situation haunted him. He tried to imagine Seth as being among those attempting to climb aboard the capsized Sea Wing hull; he hadn't spotted Seth again after Grizzly had grabbed him. He thought about Emma, and all the others, trapped inside the Sea Wing's cabin; how could they have possibly escaped the watery doom? And what fate did of all his other friends meet? And Eddy and Fred?

After at least an hour of struggling toward the shore, the mental anguish persisted. The rain had stopped, and the wind had calmed a little. The lightning flashes were less frequent and not so bright, and Bobby's eyes began to adjust to the darkness. As he paddled on, he heard a rumbling noise – sort of a creaking groan, and a muffled rushing of water. Faint voices shrieked yells of despair. Bobby paused and turned to look out into the flood of darkness, mysterious and holding menace. It was only a shadow of an image, but Bobby could see that the boat had partially righted itself again, laying on its side, and a portion of the cabin decks were, once again, just barely visible above the water's surface. The survivors who had struggled onto the boat's hull, had once again been tossed unmercifully back into the water.

David Wethern, trapped inside the pilothouse by the pressure of the water against the door and windows, took one last gulp of air before the tiny cubicle filled with water. Unable to see the task, he knew what it was: he groped at his surroundings, pressed his back to a window and braced his feet against the steering wheel. With all the strength he could muster, he gave a mighty shove; the window frame collapsed under his weight, allowing his exit from a would-be tomb, and David swiftly started swimming away from the wreck. When he thought he was clear of the sunken structure, he turned upward toward the surface.

Gasping for air, he dogpaddled on the surface for a few seconds, trying to gain some perspective. He heard no voices – only the wind and the crashing waves, and then pellets of hail hitting the Sea Wing's hull. Still in disbelief of this terrible tragedy, he saw the capsized hull in the lightning flashes; fighting the breakers, he swam toward it. Several other men were clinging to the hull, but he couldn't tell who they were in the inky darkness.

By the time he could pull himself up out of the water and onto the overturned craft with the aid of another crewman, Warren Sparks, he could sense that there were others there too, but numbers were nearly impossible to determine. The lightning revealed twenty-five or thirty, he thought, spread out over the 135 feet of slippery boat hull, but all the while the weather pounded them with its brutal punishment, no one spoke or even uttered a sound. Gripped by fear, their identities remained unknown.

David knew there were casualties – perhaps as many as half of the total number aboard was trapped in the cabins, now submerged. His wife and two sons were among them, and it seemed impossible – useless – to attempt any sort of rescue now. Weakened by the shock of reality, David Wethern sat helpless, forlorn and nearly insignificant, wishing he could turn back the clock and make a wiser decision. Agony gnawed at his soul. Nearly certain that his family, among scores of others, had perished only because he had made the wrong choice to start the return journey back to Red Wing, he could do nothing to help those trapped, dying inside the cabins.

At the far stern end of the bottom-up boat, another passenger, Andrew Scriber, who had been tossed into the lake when the Sea Wing rolled, clung to the keel and managed to pull himself, and David Wethern's 10-year old son, Roy, onto the flat surface. But father and son were separated by the harsh, noisy weather and blinding darkness, and neither was aware of the other's safety.

Passengers aboard the barge had taken cover the best they could as the smaller craft careened about the waves, while chairs, band instruments and decorations were swept overboard. They could only watch in horror as the Sea Wing's upper structure, pushed by the unmerciful crosswind, crashed into the raging water and disappeared, leaving nothing but the flat-bottomed hull exposed above the surface. There was nothing they could do to help the many other passengers and crew floundering in the water, desperately fighting for their lives.

David sat solemnly, hoping and praying for the turbulent weather to subside, and that help would eventually come, while there were still survivors left to save. He had caught glimpses of several people – one of them he thought to be his engineer and partner, Mel Sparks – holding onto pieces of the wreckage, trying to ride the splintered debris to shore. But now they had disappeared into the darkness, and he had no way of knowing if their attempts had been successful. And he saw the undeniable, horrible truth – lifeless bodies of the young women, unable to swim in their long white dresses, and young men stunned and injured and drowned.

The Sea Wing drifted southward toward Central Point; the top of the superstructure drug on the lake bottom, and the current's force caused the craft to shift to one side. As if being lifted with a crane, the boat rolled again, partially righting it, turning the bottom of the hull sideways. Screams of terror sliced though the night as all those who had found refuge there were thrown back into the water, their only defense being the minimally renewed strength they had gained during the brief rest. Once again, they were forced to struggle for survival.

Instead of attempting to return to his crippled boat, Captain Wethern thought his best option was to swim to shore. Too many lives had already been lost, and perhaps, if he could find a fishing skiff along the bank, he could row out to the wrecked Sea Wing and rescue those still alive. He knew his chances were slim; the shoreline was distant in terms of swimming in rough water, but he was a proficient swimmer, and it seemed his only hope. He had nothing more to lose.

Bobby was beginning to tire. His arms felt as if they were weighted with concrete, and his whole body ached. Although the shore seemed closer now, he began to lose hope. No one had seen him, and he knew no one was coming to his rescue. He couldn't paddle anymore, and it was becoming difficult to keep a firm grip on the plank. His certainty of joining the other drowned victims in the depths of Lake Pepin was near.

He said a little prayer for Seth, and then for Emma, Eddie and Fred, and all the others that he feared had perished by now. And then he said one final little prayer for himself.

Chapter 8

More than a mile downstream, a couple of strapping young fellows, Harry Mabey and Theo Minder, were aboard the barge that had been battered by torrential rain and hail and was tossed about like a bottle cork. But its wide, flat configuration kept it upright and afloat; although it had taken on a lot of water, the high winds did nothing more than send it staggering aimlessly, and making the experience quite miserable and discouraging for those aboard. Of the sixty people marooned on the powerless craft, most of them were men; only a handful of women and young girls had remained there with boyfriends and fiancés in defiance of the orders from the crew to take cover in the Sea Wing's cabins when the storm had not yet delivered its full force.

Harry and Theo, Lake City teenagers, had booked passage on the Sea Wing with several of their buddies for a visit to Red Wing friends. By the time the barge drifted near Central Point, they realized that they had been separated from their traveling companions when attempts to reach the barge had failed for some. Taking advantage of the lightning flashes as the only source of light, they searched the frightened faces; their best friend, 17-year-old Boze Adams, a Lake City doctor's son was not among them. They had all donned life preservers well in advance, and in those last few horrible seconds before the Sea Wing capsized, they had all made the death-defying leaps to reach the safety of the barge. Boze Adams had apparently been unsuccessful; Harry knew that Boze was a good swimmer, but he didn't know how well he could handle the rough water. With a life preserver, he stood a strong chance, and Harry could only hope that Boze had been among the survivors clinging to the overturned vessel.

Lake Pepin is an integral part of the Mississippi River, and although the wind pushed against the barge from the west and southwest, twisting and turning it uncontrollably, the river's strong current tugged it nearer to Central Point. Harry studied the shadowy surroundings with every lightning flash; he had lived his entire life on the banks of Lake Pepin; swimming, fishing, and oaring a skiff around the lake were among his usual, everyday diversions. He knew Lake Pepin and its shores well, and as he focused on the barge's position, he was certain that it had drifted into the shallow water surrounding the Point. Vivid images of Boze Adams and all the others, struggling to survive in the hostile, wind-swept lake, and the gruesome images of the drowned victims he had witnessed kept flashing before him. A rescue mission for those left out in the middle of the lake was crucial, and Harry knew there was little time to waste if he ever wanted to see Boze alive again. He and Theo, both strong swimmers, could easily make it to shore. In desperation, Harry convinced Theo to join him in attempting to swim to the very near shoreline just as the barge lurched, its hull digging into the sandy bottom.

Harry saw several other men jump overboard after he and Theo were in the water, but most of the other passengers remained on the barge, timid, fearful to brave the elements, even in the shallows. Theo, as well as the others who had abandoned the barge, was especially relieved to feel his feet touch the bottom, but the brief attempts to coax more to follow fell on deaf ears.

Those who remained on the barge were now relatively safe, considering the harsh conditions the small craft had already endured and survived. Harry saw little purpose in lingering, trying to lure more followers, and quickly started making his way to the nearest solid ground.

Young, agile, and of strong physical character, Harry didn't tire as readily as some of the older men following him to the shore. He noticed some collapsing from exhaustion on the beach, while others, seemingly disoriented and fatigued, wandered into the adjacent woodlands seeking any help they might find. But Harry was quite familiar with the area; even in darkness, his thoughts remained focused and clear, and he knew the exact route that would lead him into Lake City, over two miles away. With Theo right on his heels, they began running the distance.

Harry could see in the lightning flashes as he ran that the barge had worked its way free from the shallow water along the point. Once again, it was adrift, propelled by the wind, out into the lake. Now, the rescue mission had taken on a multiple task; the urgency had increased.

The same twister that claimed the Sea Wing, too, had swept Lake City into a scattered mass of devastation. As Harry and Theo made their way into town, an eerie darkness blanketed the entire city; fallen trees and limbs, broken glass, tangled telegraph wires, mangled roof tin, and all sorts of debris littered the streets. Most of the business district lay in ruins; nearly every building was severely damaged, and in some cases, entire city blocks were demolished. Harry only hoped that the fire station still existed; ringing the bell there would surely attract some attention, if there were anyone left to hear it.

Harry knew that if he and Theo split up, they had a better chance to locate assistance for the Sea Wing victims. "Go to the hotel," Harry told Theo. "There's bound to be people there. Tell them what has happened."

The hotel seemed to be one of the few structures that had resisted the storm's fury, and many people had found refuge there. Harry continued on to the fire station and frantically rang the bell. Theo, nearly out of breath, burst into the hotel. "The Sea Wing has been hit by the tornado!" he yelled, without waiting for anyone to acknowledge his presence. "It's sinking, and they need help!"

The response was immediate. A crowd of men rushed to the door, pushed Theo aside, and swiftly stampeded toward the Washington Street landing. Exhausted, Theo sat down on the nearest chair with his elbows on his knees and buried his face in open palms. He listened to the sobs and cries of terror from the women left in the room, and then he heard one young girl tell the others that she had missed the Sea Wing's departure while waiting in a tent at Camp Lakeview for the rain to stop.

A few blocks away, Harry sounded the bell alarm at the fire hall; winds had calmed, and the sharp, resonant clanging split the deadly stillness. He wondered if Theo had found anyone at all, and he prayed the bell would arouse someone – anyone – who was still able to come to the aid of the unfortunate souls stranded on the lake.

Harry's spirits lifted when he heard thunderous footfalls, and in the dark night shadows he could just barely see what appeared to be several men running toward the boatyard. Theo *had* been successful, he thought, and he frantically rang the bell louder and faster. Then several more men appeared, stumbling through the debris-cluttered streets, rushing as best they could toward the fire station, answering the alarm peeling from out of the darkness.

Nearly every Lake City resident had been affected by the storm; their homes and places of business lay in shambles; they'd had little warning before the tornado blasted its way through. But they had been granted a few minutes in the aftermath to assess the situation and to account for their family members and neighbors. Those responding to this call quickly abandoned their worries of property damage when they learned the fate of the Sea Wing and its 200 passengers. Lives were at stake. With little regard for their own losses, now, the band of concerned citizens that Harry had rousted out joined forces with the group, already gathered at the boatyard. Harry collapsed to his knees and leaned a shoulder against the brick wall. His strength was all spent and he could do no more.

Camp Lakeview had not been spared from the storm's wrath, either; dozens of tents had been ripped from their stakes and sent flying through the air; equipment was tipped; pots and pans from the fallen mess tents were strewn about; soldiers' personal belongings and clothing was scattered everywhere. Word of casualties filtered throughout the encampment, although none sounded serious – a few broken bones, cuts and bruises – but no one spoke of lost lives. Nonetheless, Camp Lakeview had suffered its share of the calamity. As the guardsmen scurried about in near chaotic fashion trying to reclaim the camp's integrity, fear of a worse tragedy out on the lake bore a heavy burden; tensions rose as the news of the Sea Wing's disastrous fate spread quickly. Details were sketchy, at best, but it seemed clear that the safety of the guardsmen's families and friends aboard the steamer was at risk, or worse yet, they could be in mortal danger.

The commanding officers recognized the lake disaster's magnitude as being far more urgent than even the camp's most severe wounds and damages. Minor injuries could be tended to; a few downed tents could wait, but 200 lives in jeopardy could not. Their troops were in training to serve and protect, and what little information they had received about the Sea Wing, so far, appeared reason enough to prove their obligation to a public in need.

With every new arrival into Lake City of those who had abandoned the barge or were fortunate enough to swim to land and had eventually found their way to the town came more of the gruesome eyewitness details. Each one had seen the disaster from a different perspective:

some had been tossed overboard when the steamer first tipped and had managed to swim to the barge or to shore; some had crossed over to the barge long before the Sea Wing capsized and had viewed the entire nightmarish event; and some had barely made their escape just as the barge broke loose from the mother ship. But all concurred – many lives had been lost, and many more were in grave danger. Women and children, trapped inside the cabins, had no chance of escape. Some who fell into the water were stunned or injured, incapable of saving themselves. But many had survived, too, and it was they who were pelted with hailstones, battered by the waves, and desperately clung to the capsized hull, their lives in the hands of luck alone. One man who swam from the sinking vessel to shore told of the boat's master, Captain Wethern, collapsing on the beach, his physical condition rendering him unable to continue any rescue efforts and requiring help to walk to a nearby farmhouse.

As the accounts trickled into Camp Lakeview, the First Regiment Commander combed his storm-stricken base, organizing a platoon of men; all those who were able and uninjured were asked to assemble quickly; Guardsmen gathered lanterns, ropes and blankets, and headed for the disaster site.

Nicholas Duncan's tent was on slightly higher ground and had not been flooded or totally destroyed like many others; it had sustained only moderate damage. When the alarming news of the Sea Wing's unfortunate encounter reached Nicholas, he was retying a rope from an anchor stake to the edge of the tent roof.

"The Sea Wing was hit by the tornado," he heard someone say. Nicholas froze in position.

"She capsized and sank," the voice continued. Nicholas felt his entire body go numb.

"They say a lot of people drowned."

Nick's legs went limp and he dropped to his knees.

"What's wrong with you?" the voice behind him said.

Nicholas couldn't move; he couldn't speak.

"Are you alright? What's wrong?"

Nicholas felt the tears welling up in his eyes.

Chapter 9

Weak, forlorn cries for help from the distressed victims, desperately clinging to life out in the middle of Lake Pepin, were lost in the distance between them and the rescue party organizing at the Lake City boatyard. They had no way of knowing, for sure, that help was on the way; to them, the outlook seemed bleak, as the storm had wiped from their sight any signs of lights on either shore, and the current weather conditions certainly diminished the possibility of other boats passing by. Their number had steadily decreased since the boat rolled to its side again; those still remaining knew that the wind-driven hail and the punishing waves, relentlessly pounding against the wreck, had consumed more lives, and they could only hope that some of the survivors who had bravely attempted to get to shore were successful, and that aid would soon come.

Bobby's optimism had steadily diminished, too, as he floated along the waves midway between the sinking boat and the shore, at least a half-mile away. He hoped that his prayers would be answered. He was scared, but he had resigned to accepting this as the end; his strength was nearly gone.

He could hear the mournful cries calling out from the Sea Wing, and he wanted to call out, too, but he didn't have even enough energy left to utter an audible sound. There were no answers coming from shore, and trying seemed futile.

Bobby closed his eyes, imagining the clear blue skies overhead, and the magnificent view from atop Barn Bluff, and Seth standing beside him, sharing the beauty of it all. He wanted this to be his last conscious vision. Though he was only thirteen, he thought his life had been quite complete; he had been granted the God given right to live his life in the grandeur of the most splendid place on earth; he had enjoyed the companionship of a wonderful brother and a terrific best friend; and he had finally been allowed to satisfy his most sincere desire – to ride a riverboat down the Mississippi.

Black smoke billowed from the stacks of the *Ethel Howard*, tied up at the Lake City landing. Its owner and pilot, Captain J. S. Howard, had ferried passengers and freight across Lake Pepin to Stockholm and Maiden Rock on the Wisconsin side with the new steamer for only two months. Now, Howard and his craft were being called upon for a most urgent mission. He agreed, and quickly assembled his crew to make preparations.

A full head of steam was up; his crew was ready; members of the rescue party waited anxiously to board. But Howard was showing signs of hesitation. The wind was picking up again, indicating another probable storm. He stepped out onto the deck from the pilothouse and scanned the many eager, worried faces. "We have to wait for this next storm to blow over," he called out.

"But there are people dying out there," one man from the crowd said. "We have to get out there... now!"

A low rumble of voices erupted into an unorganized volley of shouting. Howard knew he had infuriated the townspeople, but he would stand firmly with his decision. "This boat is not designed to withstand a powerful storm," he urged. "And it appears there may be another on the way."

Although Captain Howard had made a wise choice to wait for calmer weather conditions, the men on the landing did not see eye-to-eye with his reasoning. "Those people can't wait much longer," a spokesman yelled.

Another voice, that of Lake City's mayor, George Stout, beckoned for Howard's attention. "Captain Howard!" he said, demanding silence among the crowd. "My councilmen and I will guarantee the price of your boat."

"That's all well and good... an honorable offer, Mr. Mayor," Howard replied. "But it's not the price of the boat that concerns me."

A hush fell on the landing; everyone listened for Howard's counter offer.

"Take a good look at the weather," Howard continued. "There's another storm coming. This boat will not survive any more than the Sea Wing did. We have all suffered losses tonight, and I'm quite sure that none of you desire to add another catastrophe to this chain of events.

We don't need *another* sinking vessel or any more people to save out on Lake Pepin."

The stillness was broken by a persistent, irritated reply; "We can take your boat by force! There's more of us than there is of you!"

Captain Howard strongly suspected that he had a fight on his hands as he saw a group of men gradually inching toward the gangway with the intent of mutiny in their eyes. His four crewmen stood on the deck below, and they had little chance to resist the overpowering number. Howard reached into his coat and pulled out his Colt .44, raised it above his head and squeezed off a deafening shot into the air. It echoed briefly, and then was lost in the wind. Startled by the blast, all the men stopped in their tracks and abruptly stepped back from the gangway.

"The first one of you setting foot aboard this boat without my permission is a dead man," Howard announced with a stern voice. Though he was just as anxious to save lives as the rest, he knew, better than they, the consequences he faced, should the weather turn for the worse. He would not jeopardize his boat and more lives with a foolish decision, even if it meant making his point clear with a little violent action. "Now," he said in a calmer voice, once he knew he had gained their attention. "We will proceed to the Sea Wing when the conditions are safe... is that understood?"

No one in the crowd stepped forward, and no one voiced a disagreement.

Another throng of curious citizens had already gathered on the beach at the tip of Central Point, but none were bold enough to venture out into the nasty conditions. Intimidated by the weather and the furious lake, their best efforts were restricted to only assisting a few exhausted swimmers onto land. Sorrowfully, they stood in awe, listening to the pitiful calls from the darkness.

Marching in a relaxed formation along the shore toward Central Point, the First Regiment platoon hastened its pace as the faint whimpers for help were heard more clearly, the closer they came. Obviously, this *was* a mission of rescue, and not just an exercise in recovery.

Platoon leader, Captain Charley Betcher, and other officers assessed the situation as the rest of the detachment mingled with the shocked citizens. For the time being, it was decided that offering assistance to those who had miraculously made it to shore was their best course of action, considering the definitely treacherous conditions. They would escort those who were able to walk to the Hotel Lyon in Lake City, and carry those who were not. More troops would be arriving later; by then, perhaps, the weather and lake conditions would improve, and a plan for rescue could be formulated.

Corporal Perry didn't mingle with the crowd or volunteer to escort anyone to the hotel. He stood near the officers, listening to their solemn chatter as he gazed out into the unknown. Time, to the people stranded on a sinking ship, he thought, was a precious commodity. Unable to see the precarious setting out on the lake, Perry speculated that there was, perhaps, less time for them than the officers were intending to take.

Perry had been with Nicholas Duncan back at the camp when the crushing news of the Sea Wing disaster was delivered. Every soldier in the immediate area had rushed off to help others in need, or to join the ranks departing for Central Point while he stayed by Nicholas, knowing that something was dreadfully wrong. He learned about Bobby and Seth during those few private minutes, and he made a vow that he would bring Nick's little brother and his friend back to safety.

He continued to stare into the darkness hiding the lake; hearing the calls for help, he grew more impatient with every critical tick of the clock. Beyond the growing crowd of people lay a dozen or more fishing skiffs. Perry considered himself an expert swimmer, and he had proven himself quite capable with oars on several recreational outings with other soldiers throughout the summer. Without any more hesitation, he ran to the beached rowboats, picked out the largest, most durable-looking craft, and drug it to the edge of the lake. "Who will go with me?" he asked, eyeing the rest of his comrades. He knew he would need help rowing the distance out to the Sea Wing.

Four Guardsmen stepped forward, indicating their willingness to accompany Perry. The corporal eyed each of them and then pointed to the one he thought seemed most capable. They were just about to push the boat into the water when voices in the crowd behind them yelled, "Don't go! You're committing suicide! You'll never make it!"

To Perry's dismay, his volunteer backed away and rejoined the crowd, and the three others disappeared with him. "Okay," he mumbled. "I'll go it alone."

Another young man stepped out of the crowd and ran to the boat as Perry pushed it into the water.

"You're crazy, Wesley!" Perry heard someone yell.

"I can't swim," Wesley Hills said to Perry, "But I'm good with oars."

Perry grinned at Wesley and nodded; together, with a mighty shove, they plowed the craft into the waves and hopped aboard. Within minutes, they were gone from the view of those on shore.

Theo Minder gathered his wits and strength. He had dozed off for a while sitting in the chair, and the increased noise created by more people crowded all around him in the hotel lobby jolted him awake. The clock on the far side of the room struck ten; it had been an hour since he and Harry had sprinted into town and alerted the people there of the Sea Wing's mishap. Not too eager to begin discussing the issue with mostly strangers, Theo rose from the chair and quietly headed for the exit. He remembered hearing the firehouse bell ringing repeatedly; now, only silence rode the wind, and he wondered where he should begin to look for Harry.

Harry Mabey hadn't made it any farther than his resting spot at the fire station; Theo found him sound asleep, his legs outstretched on the ground and this back leaned against the firehouse wall.

"Harry. You okay?"

Harry came to with a startling burst of energy. "Theo! Where were you?"

"I think I must've fallen asleep over at the hotel for a bit."

"Heard anything more about the Sea Wing?" Harry asked.

"No. But Mayor Stout and a bunch of other men ran out of the hotel when I told 'em what happened."

"Yeah, I know. I saw 'em head to the landing."

An hour-long nap had revived the boys' energy level, and still vividly etched on their souls was the vision of the sinking Sea Wing and the people left marooned there, and the uncertainty of Boze Adam's fate. They had, without a doubt, performed a vital task in alerting the townspeople, and now they had a driving desire to do more, if they could.

Only a handful of men remained at the landing waiting for Captain Howard to launch his vessel. Impatience and anxiety had motivated many to walk to Central Point to join the rescuers there. When Harry noticed that Howard was not too eager, yet, to set out in the less-than-favorable weather, it seemed necessary for him and Theo to return to the Point, too. He stared toward Central Point for a few moments; he could see the lights of many lanterns flickering on the distant beach, and he and Theo had noticed at least two or three groups of National Guardsmen marching off in that direction; they knew that some sort of rescue operation must be under way.

At a brisk pace, Harry and Theo set out. As they rounded the bend where the Central Point peninsula started, they were gaining on the last unit of guardsmen; they noticed one soldier straggling behind, all alone, and when they soon caught up to him, he seemed hesitant to continue any farther. They slowed their pace and fell in step with the lone guardsman.

"You okay, soldier?" Harry asked.

Nicholas Duncan stopped abruptly and stared at the ground. "Not exactly," he said.

"What's wrong?" Theo asked. "Are you hurt?"

Nicholas had committed to keeping the knowledge of Bobby's presence on the boat to himself, and he had convinced Corporal Perry to do the same, until he knew if Bobby was among the survivors. But the agony he had suffered for the past hour, not knowing, was finally overpowering him; he had to talk about it... to someone.

"It's... it's... that I'm afraid of what I'll find out there."

Harry studied Nick's face; it seemed familiar to him. A sudden recollection came to mind – he and Nick had sat on the beach below Camp Lakeview together, talking for an hour or more, just a couple of weeks earlier. He felt as though he knew Nick as a friend, although he couldn't remember his name. Not seeming strange at all, Harry speculated about the troubled soldier's worry. "Somebody you know on the Sea Wing?"

Nicholas gazed out into the eerie darkness, nodded and said, "My... brother," and then he began to sob.

More details of their previous meeting filtered into Harry's thoughts. "Didn't you tell me a couple weeks ago on the beach that your brother is eleven years old?"

Nicholas, taken a bit by surprise, turned to Harry and stared at a compassionate face. He too, now recalled that day at the beach. "Thirteen... Bobby's thirteen."

Harry put a caring hand on Nick's shoulder. "Me and Theo, here, were on the Sea Wing, too." He hesitated, thoughtful not to mention anything about the bodies he had seen floating lifelessly in the water. "There's a lot of people still on the barge, and they're okay. Me and Theo jumped overboard and swam to shore... and a lot of others did too. Bobby's probably one of 'em."

Nick's thoughts were still clear enough to realize that it was only an attempt to cheer him up, but he appreciated the hope that Harry was trying to deliver. Nick nodded and tried to force a smile, but staring once more into the malicious night, he knew the odds were also high that Bobby was still out there.

Weakened by fear, Nicholas struggled to keep pace with Harry and Theo the rest of the distance to the Point. By the time they arrived, Perry and Hills had already paddled out into the lake. Nicholas heard some of the other guardsmen talking about Corporal Perry's courageous act as he scanned the many swimmers who had been helped ashore, now organized for escort to the Hotel Lyon. His hopes were high to see Bobby... or Seth, or Eddie, or Fred... or Emma. None were there.

Harry's fishing skiff lay tied to a tree just a few yards down the beach. He and Theo heard the reports of the corporal's brave deed, and although they knew it was a dangerous undertaking, rowing Harry's boat out to the Sea Wing wasn't beyond their abilities. They had already been exposed to worse hazards that night, and now, not only were they determined to find their friend, Boze Adams, but they had been touched by Nicholas Duncan's emotion as well. A thirteen-year-old boy named Bobby had been added to their list of priorities.

Ignoring the shouts of disapproval from bystanders, Harry and Theo thrust the small boat into the waves and rowed out of sight.

Chapter 10

Ⓘt had been twenty minutes since Corporal Perry and Wesley Hills were last seen rowing into the night; Harry and Theo had been gone ten. Fears ran high as onlookers at Central Point became more curious when the shouts and cries from the lake diminished to silence. They speculated the worst.

The mournful calls stopped as the remaining survivors realized that help had arrived. Few of them could see Perry and Hills, but word passed quickly among them. All knew that only a small number could be taken aboard the little fishing boat at one time, but just knowing that their rescue was in progress seemed gloriously satisfying.

Perry could tell the toll must have been heaviest among the women, as he detected very few. It was mostly men clinging to the hull, and some had managed to climb out of the water and onto the floating wreck. As he and Hills pulled three women into the small craft, they assured the others nearby that they would return for the rest, even if it took all night. They didn't know, yet, that another rescue boat was close behind them.

Nicholas ran to the water's edge when he noticed the commotion as Perry and Hills appeared out of the darkness with the three women; although he was glad for those who had been saved, he was still disappointed that Emma Nelson didn't climb out of the boat. His eyes met Perry's, but Perry's silent frown expressed a clear message to Nicholas: he had not seen two thirteen-year-old boys.

Bittersweet cheers filled the air; attitudes changed and feelings of optimism rose; the daring young corporal and the courageous volunteer had been successful, and now only words of encouragement and praise followed them as they set out again.

The waiting crowd clamored once more as Harry and Theo returned two girls and a young man to the beach; Nicholas was right there to assist the rescued victims from the skiff, and once again, nearly the same expression on Harry's face told the same story: he had not spotted Bobby.

But that didn't mean that Bobby wasn't there; neither of the two rescue teams knew Bobby by sight, and out there in the darkness, he could have easily been missed. Nicholas would wait, and he would hope.

Nick's anxiety feverishly tore him apart; his brother's safety was his most favored concern, but how could he not grieve for Seth as well; and Eddy Christopherson and Fred Hempftling, his two life-long best buddies who had helped him through so many difficult times; and Emma Nelson, the one girl in whom he had found true love. His heart was breaking for all of them, and he wanted to just walk away from this nightmare, but he knew he couldn't.

The doomed Sea Wing drifted nearer to the Point and the treacherous conditions weakened, making the rescuers' trips easier and more frequent. Perry and Hills were returning for the third time; Nicholas could just barely make out the form of two young boys and a couple of older men in the boat. His heart raced in anticipation. But as the boat came closer to shore, Nick's spirit sank again. Neither of the two boys were Bobby or Seth, and Corporal Perry still wore the same frown.

The calming water had lured several more pairs of men in rowboats heading for the Sea Wing. By 11:30, all the survivors were off the wreck and on their way to the Hotel Lyon for dry clothing, food, medical attention, and rest. Nicholas had assisted nearly all of them from the rescue vessels, and now his hopes were shattered. Only bodies of the dead were coming back with each landing of a rowboat. There had been no Bobby or Seth. There had been no Eddy or Fred. And there had been no Emma.

Some good news came swiftly through the night to the Central Point rescue party from a half-mile down the beach. The barge, not totally forgotten but out of sight until then, had drifted too far away from the Sea Wing to be spotted by the rescuers in the small boats; it had finally drifted back to shore with some 80 people aboard.

During the past hour, the mission had turned from the joys of rescue to the solemn task of recovering the dead; fifteen bodies had been pulled from the water and brought to shore. A fog of grief hung in the air, and everyone knew there was little hope of finding any more survivors after all this time. But the report of the barge and its occupants, alive and safe, uplifted the spirits on Central Point. Many of those waiting in agony rushed down the beach, hopeful of finding their missing friends and loved ones.

By the time Nicholas arrived, a squad of National Guardsmen, their pants legs rolled to their knees, were already wading into the shallow water assisting the shaken people from the barge and preparing to take them to the hotel for immediate care. Nicholas rolled up his pants legs too, and pitched in, desperately searching the weary faces coming off the vessel. He was feeling almost a bit of jealousy for those who were making some joyous reunions. There was no Bobby or Seth, Fred or Eddy... and no Emma.

Then there came another encouraging bit of news: one of the Sea Wing's crew members had washed up onto the shore, nearly three miles downstream. He had been thrown into the air as the boat rolled over and rendered unconscious; he was battered and bruised, but he was alive. This gave further hope to some, that there was still a chance that more had survived, and the current had carried them beyond the scope of the searchers. And there were others; one by one, stories of someone making it to shore, far from the disaster site, came trickling in. Every time the news arrived, Nicholas rushed to the messenger, asking who it had been. But every time, the identity was that of someone other than Nick's lost brother and friends.

Just before midnight, the lake had calmed; Captain Howard piloted his steamer out onto the lake to provide a base for the workers where the devastated Sea Wing lay, barely moving now, as the turbulence had subsided. Rescuers now faced the most difficult, ghastly job yet to be performed, that of boarding the Sea Wing to remove the bodies of those trapped inside the cabins. From the information reported by the survivors on shore, there were bound to be many. The Sea Wing was still on its side, largely under water; most of the men who had rowed out to the wreck were the soldiers of the National Guard, and they were determined to make their best effort.

Meanwhile, the citizens of Lake City continued to row their fishing boats around Central Point and the area where the ship had capsized, searching the water for more bodies. Lake City's Dr. Adams, his son still missing, worked by lantern light on the beach trying to breathe life into the recovered drowning victims. But it had been too long; his efforts were in vain.

The National Guardsmen cordoned off an area on the beach where the victims were laid to keep them undisturbed by the curious spectators. Torches lit up the shoreline and soldier sentries posted along the beach kept a vigilant watch on the water for drifting bodies. Nicholas stood nervously by, hoping and praying that the next body he helped carry to the makeshift morgue would not be his brother's. He had hardened himself to the sight of the rising number of corpses lined up on the beach, but when Fred Hempftling's swollen, lifeless body lay before him, he could not fight back the tears, nor could he combat the weakness draining his emotional and physical energy. He kneeled down at Fred's side and bawled.

Another guardsman stepped near, waited a few moments, giving Nicholas his time to grieve, and then said, "A friend of yours?"

Nicholas couldn't speak. He just nodded slowly. The other soldier helped Nicholas to his feet and gently guided him away to a clump of nearby trees. "Sit down here and rest a while," the soldier said. He understood the emotional trauma that Nick had just experienced.

Nicholas looked up to his fellow guardsman. "He was my best friend," he whimpered. He couldn't get out in spoken words about Bobby or the others.

Pity oozed from the soldier. "My name is Frank. I'll check back with you later. You just stay here and rest." Frank squeezed out a mournful smile and walked away.

After a few minutes, Nicholas thought he should return to his duty at the shoreline. He tried to stand, but dizziness overwhelmed him and he sat down again, leaning against a tree. He closed his eyes. The pain was just too great to bear.

Chapter 11

Something brushed against Bobby's leg, and then his foot struck something solid. He had struggled nearly four hours, fighting the wind and waves, trying to reach the closest shore until exhaustion prevented any further effort. Now his grip on the plank was lost, and the waterlogged life preserver barely kept his face in breathable air. The lake's surface had settled some but the storm's turbulence had put the large body of water into motion; although the giant swirl pushed the Sea Wing closer to Central Point, the pulsing, rolling waves had drifted

Bobby some distance northward, as it had with some other parts of the wreckage.

Again, Bobby's feet struck against what seemed to be rocks, and what he thought must be weeds brushed his legs. With every rise and fall of the waves, he felt his feet dragging on the rocky surface beneath him. He opened his eyes to the shadowy tree line looming above; the shore was merely a few yards away. Now that he had allowed himself to relax, the short rest had rejuvenated some energy, and the sight of the near shoreline gave his spirit a new outlook on survival. At least one of his prayers had been answered.

Bobby gave a push with his feet and propelled himself into a prone torpedo-like swim. The heaving waves worked in his favor, now; one breaker after another thrust him forward and finally deposited him on the beach. On hands and knees he crawled across the narrow strip of sand and stones, perched in the wet grass and weeds up on the bank, and watched as his tracks in the sand were quickly erased by the next crashing waves.

Almost choked by the life preserver that had worked its way up around his throat, he grabbed and pulled at the lanyards. Shedding the vest, he hurled it with all his strength out into the water. Cursed by the wind and challenged by death, his battle with the Mississippi and Lake Pepin's worst hazards was over; Bobby had emerged the victor.

He had lost all sense of time, and he wasn't sure of his location. There was no more lightning and the cloudy sky offered no moonlight; he could see only twenty feet in any direction. The last few hours seemed a blur, but he recalled thinking, while still afloat in the lake, that he was drifting toward the Minnesota side, and concluded that that's where he was. His only clear memory of the entire event now, was his last few moments aboard the Sea Wing and plunging into the raging waves. Everything else was as hazy as an early morning fog.

Bewildered, a thirteen-year-old boy sat on the bank, but inside was the ruggedness of a strong soul – one that had advanced far beyond his years. No more than an hour earlier, he had accepted death, and he had not been frightened by it; he had carried a burden far greater than he had ever imagined; he had made a decision out of solid judgment. And now, even as insignificant as the mighty lake had caused him to feel, wherever he was, whenever this was, his new lease on life that he earned with his faith would carry him on with the strength of a giant.

Little by little, subconscious thoughts resurfaced one by one, and he started reconstructing the day in his mind. He remembered it beginning with the grand excursion aboard the Sea Wing, and the satisfaction he had felt. He remembered his meeting with Nicholas and the joy that reunion had given. And he recalled the moment that Nick had handed him the pearl and how important it made him feel.

The pearl. Nick's prize. Their mother's Christmas present. The Duncan family's ticket from a life of poverty. And now it was gone – lost in the depths of Lake Pepin, all because he had tried to keep it from the hands of an evil man by giving it to Seth at the wrong moment.

Seth. His best friend. A companion whom he trusted with his most valued secrets. One who was always there and understanding of his troubles. An innocent boy who didn't deserve to die. But now, in all reality, he was probably gone. It seemed unlikely that Seth could have survived as the Sea Wing toppled into the water, crashing down on all those who fell from that side of the boat.

Tears rolled down Bobby's cheeks as he thought of Seth's pleasant smile, and all the good times they had shared, and how Seth had helped him on this mission to retrieve the pearl; how he had been on the lookout, and pointed to Grizzly when he approached the boat at the Lake City landing; and how he had alerted Bobby when he spotted Nick and Emma stealing a good-bye kiss.

Emma. His secret love. His brother's secret love. Beautiful, affectionate Emma. Somehow, he knew she had perished; he had seen her enter the cabin on the Sea Wing just before the storm hit, and like all the others in there, she was trapped with no time to escape.

And Grizzly. The evil Grizzly. The disgusting man who had tried to steal. The man who caused him to lose the pearl. The man who had cost Seth his life. Even though Bobby felt no remorse for Grizzly's loss, he uttered a prayer for his soul.

With so many thoughts tumbling in his head, and recalling all that he had been through, and reviewing the losses he had suffered, mental exhaustion set in again. He could see some bright lights off to his right that appeared to be at least a mile away, but his sense of direction escaped him; the lights seemed to be across the water, and it just added to his confusion. Unable to withstand the punishment of stumbling through the darkness, his body told him to stay put until daylight, when he would be rested again, and when he could see well enough to choose a logical direction.

By 3:00 a.m. the rescue and recovery crew had decided to call off any further action until morning. They had recovered the bodies that were accessible in the Sea Wing's cabins, but they knew that many more were still there. Until the boat was towed closer to shore and righted, it seemed impossible to reach those remaining.

The small boats patrolling the nearby water had retrieved several more bodies, and some had drifted near the shore. The total count had reached 52.

Dr. Adams had identified many of the drowned victims by examining wallets and engraved jewelry; with the aid of several National Guard officers and a few coherent survivors, he compiled three lists of names. The first list contained the names of the known dead; the second was the known survivors; the third, and the most difficult to complete – the suspected missing. Since there was no official passenger list, they could only question the survivors for their knowledge of who might have been aboard the Sea Wing when it left the Lake City landing. The lists were left for all to see, in case someone could identify a person not yet accounted for.

Loaded with fifty-two bodies – thirty-four women, nine men, and nine identified as children, all from Red Wing, Trenton, and Diamond Bluff – the Ethel Howard steamed toward Red Wing to deliver them closer to their final resting places. Among them were Captain Wethern's wife and youngest son.

Nicholas studied the three lists. He had been away from the front line for a while, passed out from psychological fatigue. The sharp whistle from the Ethel Howard signaling its departure had jogged him into consciousness, and Frank had led him to the lists.

He knew many of the people on the deceased list as he scanned down the column – most were from his hometown. Like a hard blow to the gut, he shuddered with pain when he read Eddy Christopherson's name. Just as he had cried for Fred, he knew he was about to do the same for

Eddy. Now he had lost *both* of his best friends. His only consolation was that Bobby's name didn't appear.

Trying his best to regain his composure, Nicholas moved on to the missing persons list. A few more familiar names were there, and among them was Emma Nelson. Everyone including Nicholas was quite certain, now, that the people on that list were there only because their bodies had not yet been found, and there was little chance that any of them would be found alive.

He continued down the list and let out a deep sigh of relief; Bobby's name wasn't there. That meant that he would surely find it on the list of known survivors; somehow, Bobby – and Seth, too – had slipped by, and they were probably at the hotel in Lake City with the others. But there was no Bobby Duncan or Seth Miller on that list, either; they weren't on *any* list.

With higher hopes, now, Nicholas thought that perhaps they had not even boarded the Sea Wing at all. Even though he had instructed Bobby to do so just before the rain came, maybe they hadn't made it to the boat. Once again, Nick's optimism rose. Now that the search had stopped for the night at Central Point, *his* search would begin in Lake City.

Dawn's first hint of gray, dreary light crept onto Lake Pepin, calm, peaceful, smooth – hardly a ripple to be seen. Only the squawks of gulls coming awake and the occasional rhythmic taps of an ax blade chopping into a fallen tree limb punctuated the stillness. Relief from the sweltering, weeklong heat wave bathed the countryside, but the smell of a deadly storm lingered. The people of Lake City were getting their first daylight glimpses of a town ravaged by the twister that had made its unwanted, bludgeoning visit the night before. Some had not slept at all, but worked through the dark hours, clearing paths across debris-cluttered yards for access into their homes. Some boarded up smashed windows, and others merely sifted through heaps of total destruction, searching for any salvageable personal belongings.

Daylight revealed the shocking reality of what had happened on the lake, too. Torches still burned and sentries still guarded a beach strewn with deck chairs, boards, clothing, empty life preservers, and bits of wreckage washed ashore from the Sea Wing. The desolate steamer laid just a quarter-mile off Central Point, still laden with unreachable bodies – the victims of an indiscriminate wind.

Dr. Adams slumped on one of the Sea Wing's wooden chairs that had washed ashore. His eyes burned from lack of sleep, and his knees ached from kneeling on stones beside the victims he could not revive, but he couldn't allow himself to be tired; he was loyal to his profession and to the people he served, and he remained on the beach in the event that someone needed his skillful attention. But his motivation for staying didn't end with that; his teen-aged son, Boze Adams, was still among the missing. Harry Mabey told the doctor that he, Theo and Boze, all wearing life preservers, dove into the water just before the Sea Wing rolled. Harry and Theo had managed to pull themselves onto the barge, but when they looked for Boze, he was nowhere in sight.

Even with a life vest, Boze had been in the water too long. It was 5:00 a.m. and hours since any survivors reaching shore had been reported. Although Dr. Adams didn't want to accept his son's death, Boze was probably gone.

For the first time since the Sea Wing's lights had disappeared, Bobby could actually see his surroundings. He rubbed his eyes that stung from an abrupt awakening and discovered that he had rolled back into the weeds during his sleep. Rising up on one elbow, he peered out over the serene lake. It would have been difficult for anyone not there the night before to imagine the fierceness that had so quickly turned to a peaceful silence. But Bobby *had* been there, and as he focused his thoughts, he was fully aware that it had not been just a bad dream, but rather, a living nightmare. Vivid recollections of the entire event started rolling around in his head again, and then voices interrupted the visions.

"That's Central Point," he heard a young man's voice declare. "Lake City is about three miles."

Bobby looked through the weeds to see two teen-aged boys walking briskly along the shore. Their clothes were wet and they appeared quite bedraggled. One of them was George Seavers from Red Wing, but he didn't recognize the other one who had spoken. They continued walking, not noticing Bobby partially hidden by the tall grass. Bobby didn't make a sound; he knew George had been aboard the Sea Wing, and as pale as they both looked, Bobby was certain that he had just seen ghosts.

A few minutes passed. The sky brightened some, but a solid mass of gray wasn't about to let the sun shine through. Bobby watched the two ghostly figures until they were out of sight around the bend; he sat up and scooted down closer to the shore. He gazed out across the water again, toward the strip of land that jutted out into the lake. That's where he had seen the lights shining, and now he understood why it had appeared so confusing to him in the darkness. If that really was Central Point, then Lake City lay just beyond it.

His eyes focused on a long, low, dark mass on the water's surface some distance off the tip of Central Point. It was too far away to determine what it was, exactly, but it didn't appear to be a steamboat; he had seen too many of them, even at a distance. Bobby squinted and strained, trying to identify the strange object in the dim morning light.

"I think it's the Sea Wing," a voice, so familiar, said.

Bobby froze. Chills raced down his spine. He held his breath and he could hear his heart pounding.

"Wanna take a walk down there and get a look?"

Bobby jerked his head around toward the voice. Tears of joy streamed down his cheeks that smiled wider than Lake Pepin. "Seth!" he blurted. "You're alive!"

Seth brushed back the wet hair matted on his forehead. "Well... yeah... shouldn't I be?"

"No! I mean... yeah! But I was afraid you had drowned!" Bobby sprang to his feet, threw his arms around Seth and hugged the best friend that he thought he had lost.

They sat down on the bank, both thankful and glad to know that the other was safe. Not speaking for a while, they just stared off into the distance toward Central Point, and the dark object they thought might be the Sea Wing.

"Were you scared?" Bobby finally asked.

"It all happened so fast," Seth replied. "I didn't have time to be scared. I hit the water, and the next thing I knew, the current pulled me away. And then I saw the boat tip over and all the lights just disappeared!"

"What did you do?"

"There was this big log that came along, and I grabbed a hold of it. I tried gettin' up on it, but the waves kept knockin' me off. After the wind died down a little, and the waves weren't so bad, I managed to climb on."

"Yeah," Bobby said. "I did just about the same thing with a big plank."

Just as Bobby's experience, the current and the wind and the turbulent waves had carried Seth several hours in many different directions, and in the dead of darkness, he didn't know where the terrifying journey had ended. He too, had crawled onto the bank, huddled under some bushes, and waited for daylight.

"I was real worried about you," Bobby said after a short period of silence. "I saw dead bodies floating in the water."

"Yeah, me too. Lots of 'em."

That thought drug them both into solemn silence again. They both were aware that many people they knew – their friends – had certainly died.

Seth wasn't aware, though, of the scuffle that Bobby had had with Grizzly. "Wonder what happened to Grizzly," he mumbled.

"Don't know... don't care," Bobby returned. He proceeded to tell Seth about his experience, and when he finished, he lowered his head, crying.

"What's wrong, Bobby?"

Bobby whimpered, "The pearl. I lost Nick's pearl."

Seth laid a comforting hand on Bobby's shoulder, trying to console his friend. "No, you didn't," he whispered, and dug his other hand into the pocket of his wet blue jeans. He opened his clenched fist just inches in front of Bobby's bowed head. "Look," he urged Bobby to open his eyes. "It really *was* a lucky charm."

The radiant blue pearl shimmered in Seth's palm. Bobby couldn't believe what he was seeing; it seemed totally impossible, yet, there it was. He took the pearl from Seth's hand. "But... I thought..."

"When you dropped it, I jumped after it... remember?"

Bobby just nodded, still in awe.

Seth gave a warm smile. "Well, I landed right on top of it. I scooped it up, and I managed to get it in my pocket just before I fell overboard."

With the pearl clenched tightly in his fist, Bobby threw his arms around Seth again. "You're just the very best friend a guy could ever want."

A little embarrassed, but relishing the praise and Bobby's joy, Seth pushed his friend away at arm's length, gazed toward Central Point and said, "Okay... let's go now."

Corporal Perry had been out in a rowboat all night searching for possible survivors; he had only recovered two more drowned bodies. When the water calmed, he rowed farther out onto the lake, hoping to find Nicholas Duncan's brother. But as the dawn came, so did his exhaustion. He returned to Central Point and strolled to its northern side beach, away from the crowd. He wondered what he would say to Nicholas.

Circling far beyond the area that the other searchers had covered, Harry and Theo rowed their fishing boat over the quieted lake surface, logically, they thought, downstream from the wreckage. It made sense to them that Boze – and a boy named Bobby – would have been carried in that direction by the current. But in the early stages of dawn, they too returned to the Point, discouraged, tired, and with no other passengers.

As they beached the skiff, Harry scanned the few sad faces still lingering from the night, and others that had returned after a couple of hours rest. A National Guard squadron was returning to continue the search and to make preparations for getting the Sea Wing closer to shore; a grim task still loomed before them.

Harry didn't see the soldier who had diligently manned the landing all night, assisting the survivors and carrying the dead from the boats as they were delivered to shore. He knew Nicholas must be hurting, just as Dr. Adams was hurting, and he deeply regretted that there was nothing he could do to relieve them of their pain.

Just then, Harry caught a glimpse of two pale, ghostly-looking forms walking toward him from the far side of the Point. He studied their slow, laborious movement and their clothes that looked a mess. As they came closer, he began to make out the facial features, and when he was absolutely sure of his identification, Harry ran to where Dr. Adams sat on the chair, updating the lists. He grabbed the doctor's arm and pointed up the beach.

The reunion was heartwarming; father and son embraced; Boze Adams had returned – alive – and the elder Adams was spared the continuing agony.

But not so for the young companion, George Seavers, with whom his son had teamed for survival. When Dr. Adams learned the boy's name, he had the unpleasant task of informing George that his sister and father were dead.

Nicholas gave up his search for Bobby and Seth. Only one man at the hotel seemed to remember seeing a couple of kids that could have been them on board the Sea Wing; when a drunken passenger – a big man – appeared to be bothering them, he had stepped in to prevent some suspected wrong doing. But he had been pre-occupied with the threatening weather, and he couldn't be certain that they were the same boys Nicholas was seeking.

Nicholas knew. The drunken big man to whom the informant referred had to be Grizzly. Bobby had mentioned that Grizzly had been following him, and Grizzly *had* showed up at the camp, watching Bobby's every move. Nicholas couldn't recall seeing Griswold's name on any of the lists, either, probably because no one *wanted* to remember him. And now it seemed that Bobby had been quite successful in keeping his identity aboard the Sea Wing hidden, too, to prevent repercussions at home.

With his spark of optimism snuffed out, Nicholas returned to Central Point. An eerie sense of loneliness surrounded him as he slowly walked the distance; he wouldn't accept the possibility that his brother was gone, but his fears continued to mount. His life would seem so incomplete without Bobby.

He checked the three lists once more. A train departing Red Wing just after the Ethel Howard had arrived there brought several Red Wing residents to Lake City and Central Point looking for lost loved ones and friends. They carried with them the news of several more victims who had been identified, and the lists had grown. Several names had been transferred from the missing to the known dead, and among them, Nicholas found Emma Nelson's name. Tears flowed again; now, three important people had suddenly vanished from his life.

He brushed away the tears, trying to be brave, and continued to read the names on the lists. Bobby Duncan or Seth Miller didn't appear. Now, all he could do was wait.

Chapter 12

Uncontrollable cries rode on the still air as more perished victims were lifted from the Sea Wing's cabins, brought to shore and laid on the beach. Nicholas watched the people waiting in hopes that their family members and friends wouldn't be among the bodies, and he listened to moans of anguish when some were. He knew many of the residents from Red Wing who had gathered there – and he knew many of the Red Wing victims, as well. Surely, the merchants, craftsmen, and citizens would be significantly missed by their hometown, as would the number of people from Trenton and Diamond Bluff.

George Hartman's smiling face would no longer greet customers at the hardware store; George Nelson would never cut another head of hair or trim another beard; Ira Fulton wouldn't go to the pottery factory or sail his yacht on weekends; Joe Carlson would never shoot out another streetlight; Peter Gerken wouldn't be pouring drinks at his saloon, nor would his wife or five children be there to grieve his loss, for they were all lost too. Thirteen-year-old John Ingebretson would never be seen peddling his newspapers on the streets of Red Wing again, and Fred Seavers would never strike another hot iron on his blacksmith's anvil. And Emma Nelson would never slip another extra piece of candy into a kid's shopping bag. All these people, and so many more, would be deeply missed.

For Nicholas, the worst was yet to come; he had heard the remarks made that the women and children were urged to occupy the Sea Wing's cabin during the storm, and Bobby and Seth, being only thirteen, were probably considered *children*, and were probably ushered into the cabin that became an inescapable death chamber. Now, it was mostly the bodies of women and children coming ashore in the boats, and unclear thinking had delivered Nicholas into believing that there were no other options left. His hopes of ever again seeing his little brother alive, evaporated.

Corporal Perry sat leaning against a tree on the northern shoreline of Central Point, away from the commotion. Only a few people scavenged bits of wreckage along the beach, and two men in a rowboat, about fifty yards out, hunted the glassy lake surface.

Perry felt good about his accomplishment; he had summoned up his courage and initiated the rescue that everyone else feared, and thirty more souls lived to see the dawn. He hadn't slept in more than twenty-four hours; he and Wesley Hills had battled miles of waves, and now, every muscle in his body ached, but the satisfaction far outweighed the physical pain.

But he had *not* found Bobby Duncan. Perry didn't have any family or close friends aboard the Sea Wing; his friendship with Nicholas, though, qualified his concern for Bobby as the nearest thing to it, although he didn't even know Bobby. Perhaps, being somewhat removed from more direct personal ties is what had driven his ability to respond the way he did, at the time he did, and certainly, no one could fault him for his actions. Yet, his heart poured out for Nicholas.

Under a gray, dismal sky the search for the missing continued without Corporal Perry. He wanted to close his eyes and just go to sleep, but the adrenalin had been pumping all night, and he had gone beyond that point of being sleepy, so he sat watching the scavengers pile junk from the water onto the beach.

After all this time, no one was paying much attention to newcomers, as there had been so many coming and going. Some had serious interests in the rescue attempts, and some were just curious gawkers, and by then, it was difficult to tell the difference. Little heed was given to the probability of survivors from the Sea Wing strolling in from a distant shore.

Perry fixed his attention on a couple of young barefoot boys, carrying their shoes, walking along the beach. As they neared, he zeroed in, first on the light skinned, blonde boy, and then on the dark-haired one. The closer he came the resemblance seemed more remarkable. Perry rose to his feet. "Bobby?" he called out. "Bobby Duncan?"

The boys abruptly stopped their steady pace and turned toward the sound of Perry's voice. Taken quite by surprise that anyone there would know his name, especially a complete stranger, Bobby stared at the young man in a shabby-looking uniform rushing toward him.

"Are you Bobby Duncan?" the soldier asked again.

Bobby didn't know whether to be scared by the stranger or to be glad that someone recognized him. With eyes as big as clamshells, and still curious about how this man knew his name, Bobby silently nodded.

"And you must be Seth," Perry said, glancing at the other boy.

Seth just nodded.

"How do you know our names?" Bobby asked.

"Because you look so much like your brother."

Bobby made the connection. "You know Nick?"

"Yeah... we share a bunk tent. Name's Perry."

"Oh, yeah. Nick mentioned you in his letters." Bobby felt relief, now that he knew the man wasn't exactly a stranger, but instead, Nick's Army buddy.

Perry stepped between Bobby and Seth and put his arms around their shoulders. He could easily see that they seemed healthy and in good spirits. Doc Adams' attention probably wasn't necessary. "C'mon... I'll take you to Nick. He's powerful worried about you two."

A crowd had gathered next to the roped-off morgue area as guardsmen carried two more bodies from a small boat. Nicholas stood back a ways with his arms folded across his chest. He was less interested this time; the victims were women, and he had already learned of Emma Nelson's fate. And he was growing weary from the sight of death.

"Duncan," Perry called out.

Nicholas looked to his right and left.

Corporal Perry called out again, "Duncan... over here."

Nicholas realized it had come from behind, turned and stood at attention as if an officer had caught him lollygagging. The sound of Perry's familiar voice finally registered; Nick relaxed his stance, but teary eyes and fatigue blurred his vision. At first, it was as if he were seeing a mirage – he knew it was Perry, just because of the voice – but the image was nothing more than a vague, hazy shape.

"Look who I found," Perry said. He could see that Nicholas was in a daze.

Nicholas rubbed his eyes and adjusted his focus, staring a long moment at the three figures standing only twenty feet away. His eyes widened. Almost in disbelief, he stepped closer, hoping that his mind wasn't playing cruel tricks.

"Hi, Nick," Bobby beamed, and broke away from Perry.

Nicholas wrapped his arms around his little brother; for the moment, he was speechless. But to Bobby, though, his actions said a thousand words.

Nicholas reached for Seth and pulled him close, hugging him too, and then he looked at Corporal Perry and silently mouthed the words, "Thank you."

The four of them retreated to a remote spot away from the crowd where they could talk privately. Bobby and Seth understood more clearly, now, the impact of their disappearance. Reluctantly, they told of their harrowing separate experiences, afloat in the darkness, and of eventually landing on a beach to the north in the wee hours of the morning.

"Can we just keep this between us?" Bobby said with a sheepish grin. He still didn't want the story getting back to his mother.

"I reckon we can," Nicholas scolded, "But if Ma finds out... you're on your own."

Perry had been thirteen once; he understood the situation the youngsters faced. "I won't say a word to anybody," he assured. He gave the boys each a friendly little hug, winked at Nicholas and wandered off in search of a quiet place to get some needed rest. Now his mission was satisfyingly complete.

"What are all those people looking at?" Seth asked.

Nick's forehead wrinkled with a sorrowful frown. Telling Bobby and Seth of all their friends' disastrous ends, now seemed his most difficult task. "That's a list of all the people who..." He hesitated.

"Who are dead?" Seth finished the statement.

Nicholas just nodded.

With a worried, hesitant, slow pace, Bobby asked, "Who all is on the list?"

Nicholas paused, trying to keep his composure; two solemn faces stared out at the wrecked Sea Wing as Nicholas slowly began reciting the names as he remembered them: George, the barber; Mr. Hartman, from the hardware store; Peter Gerken and his whole family...

Tears formed in the boys' eyes when Nick spoke the names, more significant to them: John Ingebretson, Lenus Lillyblad... Eddy Christopherson, Fred Hempftling...

Bobby buried his crying face into his hands when he heard Emma Nelson's name. He had suspected her fate from the start, but hearing it seemed so final.

"There's another list, too," Nicholas said. "The people still missing. I didn't see your names on it."

"They didn't take anybody's name when we got on the boat," Bobby replied.

Bobby Duncan and Seth Miller's names never would appear on the lists; there was no official ship's manifest, and now, all those who knew of their presence on the Sea Wing were forever silent.

After a few minutes of mourning, Seth finally nudged Bobby. "Ain't ya gonna tell Nick the *good* news?"

Bobby wrinkled his brow and stared curiously at his friend.

Seth leaned closer and whispered, "The pearl."

Nicholas had all but forgotten; his worries for Bobby and Seth had overshadowed any thoughts about a much lesser concern. Bobby slipped his hand into his pocket and produced the blue gem for Nick to see, but he decided not to tell the story of how it was nearly lost.

Nicholas smiled. "You know what to do with it," he said, and urged Bobby to put it back in his pocket.

It was almost 11:00. There was still plenty of time to get Bobby and Seth on the train leaving for Red Wing.

Chapter 13

Lake City was not the only town to be plundered by the devastating July 13th twister. Bobby and Seth gazed in awe through the windows of the Pullman car as the train labored its way along the path of destruction. Toppled trees, flattened cornfields, and the rubble of demolished barns scattered across the countryside had been left behind as a reminder that nature was in command of immeasurable power.

When they disembarked at the Red Wing depot and walked up Plum Street toward Main, evidence showed clearly that the storm had not bypassed their town. The citizens of Red Wing had suffered the brunt of a widespread storm system about fifteen minutes before its mounting intensity struck Lake City. Roof shingles, tree branches and all sorts of trash littered the streets; canvas awnings were ripped from storefronts and hung haphazardly in shreds, and sections of wooden sidewalks resembled splintered firewood piled against the buildings.

The boys turned the corner by Music Hall on Main. A sudden chill tingled the back of Bobby's neck as they passed by the "Closed" sign in the front window of Mr. Hartman's hardware store. Several gentlemen stood waiting in front of George Nelson's barbershop, obviously unaware, yet, that George would never return. And the spot on the corner where John Ingebretson usually took his stand with a bag of newspapers, now, was vacant, lonely and cold.

A large crowd was gathered in front of H. A. Allen's funeral parlor. Bobby and Seth knew why, and they were thankful that they were standing *outside* with all the glum faces instead of lying *inside* among all the Sea Wing victims. They heard people talking about funeral arrangements, burial plots and gravestones, and about some funerals already in progress. But no one there took notice of Bobby Duncan or Seth Miller, of whom no one was even aware, had been aboard the doomed Sea Wing.

Fondling the precious blue pearl in his pocket reminded Bobby that among all the people he knew aboard the boat, all but one had been accounted for – Gunter *Grizzly* Griswold had not been mentioned by anyone, neither on the beach at Central Point, nor here at Red Wing. It didn't seem strange to him, as Grizzly wasn't a very popular or well-liked character midst the townspeople. If he *had* drowned, and if his body *were* still missing, it seemed unlikely that anyone would raise the question as to the whereabouts of the man that almost everyone avoided and ignored, anyway. And Bobby wasn't about to become the first to bring up that question. Grizzly was nowhere around, and Bobby felt a new sense of security with his absence.

The pearl reminded him, too, of the most important entry on his agenda. "C'mon, Seth," Bobby whispered. "We gotta get home now." Viewing all the downtown damage from the storm, the more vulnerable Westside houses had probably suffered the effects, too, but at the moment, he was more concerned about setting his mother's anger at ease; he had been gone since the previous morning, and although he and Seth often disappeared on *fishing* excursions, she was apt to be on a rampage this time, considering the circumstances.

Hardly a street had escaped the storm's ruthless havoc. Huge trees lay uprooted, or broken like matchsticks; woodsheds and livery barns were destroyed; house roofs were stripped of their shingles, and some houses had no roof at all. Chimneys had been pushed over, their bricks scattered across lawns. Lost, frightened dogs strayed through the disruption, and distraught home dwellers shooed them away.

Bobby heard several church bells peeling – funeral bells, he thought – that would echo in the hills for many days to come, for Red Wing now faced the gloomy burden of burying its dead.

The boys reached Seth's family home. It appeared the Millers had been lucky – only a few missing roof shingles and a couple of broken windows. Bobby and Seth said their good-byes, and Seth rushed to the house, met at the front door by his mother, who immediately converged on him with a smothering hug. Bobby felt a little jealousy; he was quite certain that his return home would not render such a warm reception. He hung his head and slowly continued on his way.

As he walked, he silently rehearsed the explanation that he and Seth had worked out on the train. They would both tell the same story, without lying, and it would justify their going to Lake City that morning to find Nicholas, and returning on the train.

The scene awaiting Bobby at the Duncan home was nothing short of shocking; he stood at the gate, staring at their house, partially concealed by one of the giant oak trees that had once graced their lawn, but was now resting in what had once been Bobby's upstairs bedroom. It had smashed through the roof, and the cyclone-force wind had ripped apart nearly half of the upper level of the house.

In an attempt to find material to nail over a broken window, Bradley pulled a loose board from a heap of wreckage in the yard, under which a part of Bobby's broken bed was buried. He stared at Bobby a few moments, and then just nodded toward the front porch, where their mother sat on a kitchen chair, head bowed and hands clenched together on her lap.

Bobby cautiously dodged some debris walking to the porch stoop. It appeared that Mrs. Duncan wasn't aware of his presence, even as he climbed the steps.

"Ma?" Bobby spoke tenderly. "Are you okay?"

Dorothy Duncan looked up suddenly at the sound of her son's voice. Her reddened puffy eyes took on a joyous glow; she sprang from the chair and threw her arms around Bobby. "Oh, Bobby," she sobbed. Tears streamed down her cheeks. "I'm so glad you're home safe. I've been so worried about you."

"I'm okay, Ma... just got a little wet... that's all."

Dorothy released the long, affectionate hug. "Well, it's a good thing you weren't at home in bed last night."

"Yeah, I see." Bobby breathed easier.

"Where were you, anyway?"

"Me 'n Seth were down below Frontenac. After the storm hit, we just waited 'til daylight. This morning, I started to get real worried about Nick, and we walked to Lake City to find him."

"You walked all the way to Lake City?"

"Yeah. The storm hit even harder, there."

"And did you find Nicholas?"

"Yeah, and he's okay, too."

"And if you were in Lake City this morning, how did you get home this soon?"

"Nick put us on the train."

So far, Bobby hadn't lied to his mother, and he hoped she wouldn't ask too many more questions; he wanted to be old and gray before he ever revealed the truth about his first riverboat ride. He was glad that she apparently hadn't heard the news about the Sea Wing yet, but he was a little disappointed that his mother didn't seem concerned about Nicholas.

"I don't know what we will do," Dorothy said, sorrowfully gazing up at their storm-wrecked home. "The neighbor next door said it'll cost hundreds of dollars to fix the house, and I don't have the money." Tears started streaming again.

Bobby saw the despair in his mother's eyes. A widow with three children, she had worked hard over the past years to barely feed her family; Bobby thought her depression had risen to an all-time high when Nicholas left to join the National Guard, but now, that depression was about to magnify ten-fold.

He put his hands in his pockets and wrapped his fingers around the pearl, wondering what Nick would do right now. In the last hours, Bobby had learned to make decisions, and he knew in his heart the decision he was about to announce was the right one.

"This was s'posed to be your Christmas present from me and Nick."

ABOUT THE AUTHOR

J.L. Fredrick lived his youth in rural Western Wisconsin, a modest but comfortable life not far from the Mississippi River. His father was a farmer, and his mother, an elementary school teacher. He attended a one-room country school for his first seven years of education.

Wisconsin has been home all his life, with exception of a few years in Minnesota and Florida. After college in La Crosse, Wisconsin and a stint with Uncle Sam during the Viet Nam era, the next few years were unsettled as he explored and experimented with life's options. He entered into the transportation industry in 1975 where he remained until retirement in 2012. He is a long-time member of the Wisconsin State Historical Society.

Since 2001 he has fourteen published novels to his credit, and three non-fiction history volumes. He was a featured author during Grand Excursion 2004.

J.L. Fredrick is currently exploring the U.S. in an RV.

Made in the USA
Monee, IL
20 August 2023

41299682R00128